ARE YOU SARA?

ARE YOU SARA?

A NOVEL

S. C. LALLI

WILLIAM MORROW
An Imprint of HarperCollinsPublishers

ARE YOU SARA? Copyright © 2022 by Sonya Lalli. All rights reserved. Printed in the United States of America. No part of this book may be used or reproduced in any manner whatsoever without written permission except in the case of brief quotations embodied in critical articles and reviews. For information, address HarperCollins Publishers, 195 Broadway, New York, NY 10007.

HarperCollins books may be purchased for educational, business, or sales promotional use. For information, please email the Special Markets Department at SPsales@harpercollins.com.

Originally published as *Are You Sara?* in Canada in 2022 by Harper Avenue, an imprint of HarperCollins Publishers Ltd.

FIRST U.S. EDITION

Library of Congress Cataloging-in-Publication Data has been applied for.

ISBN 978-0-06-322627-2

22 23 24 25 26   LSC   10 9 8 7 6 5 4 3 2 1

For Saraswati

ARE YOU SARA?

PART I

1.

Thursday, September 29

There's a dead girl in the bathroom."

I look up. Gavin is staring at me, a tray of empties balanced on his left hand.

"Dead?" I ask.

"She's a corpse. Who the fuck was serving her?"

I shrug. Although the place was packed earlier tonight, only Gavin and I were behind the bar. One of us had served her.

"Deal with her, would you?" he says.

"I was just about to leave."

He gestures behind him. "Get her out of here, and then you can go."

"But—"

"Just fucking handle it, Sara."

Gavin takes off before I have a chance to protest. He's

chivalrous like that. Annoyed, I make my way through the bar toward the bathrooms. It's just past 2 a.m. and last call was half an hour ago, but there are still a few dozen stragglers finishing their drinks or falling asleep at the tables.

I push open the door to the women's restroom and find two denim legs sticking out of the far stall. I sigh.

"Hey," I say. "You."

I let the door click shut behind me. The girl doesn't respond and I take another step forward.

"I need you to get up."

Literally, I need her to get up. I'm five foot three and sure as hell can't carry her.

The girl groans and I soften. I wonder how young she is. Gavin tells us not to check IDs on weekdays. It's the reason he's still afloat.

"Are you OK?" I drop to hands and knees and peer under the stall. The girl is flat on her back, her head resting against the base of the toilet. She's sporting a dark-wash jean jacket much like the one I'm wearing, and her long, chocolate-brown hair is all over her face.

I reach my hand out and brush it away, and when she still doesn't move, I crawl under the stall. She's petite, too, and there's just enough room for both of us on the ground.

"Hey," I say, more gently now. I shake her arms. "Let's get you out of here, huh?"

She lets me peel her off the ground, my arms supporting some of her weight. I flip the lid down and manage to get her on the toilet seat. Her Marc Jacobs bag knocks against my hip.

"Who are you?" she asks groggily.

I smile, thankful she's waking up. "Sara."

"Really? *My* name is Sarah! With an H?"

"No H for me." I pause. "Where are your friends? Can I get them?"

"I don't have any friends."

I open my mouth to speak, but then she continues.

"My friend went home with my *other* friend," she says, her voice singsong. "If you catch my drift."

"So you're here by yourself?"

Sarah giggles, as if I'm ridiculous. "I'm here with *you*."

With my arm wrapped around her waist, I help the other Sarah out through the kitchen exit that backs onto a quiet residential street. It's a chilly autumn night, and when she starts to shiver, I button up her jacket.

"You're a fox," she slurs. We're eye to eye, and I laugh.

"So are you."

She leans forward and kisses my cheek, softly. "Do you want to smoke?"

"I've got class in the morning."

"We've all got class in the morning," she says.

"Do you want me to call you a Ride?"

Sarah doesn't answer me as she fetches a joint from her back pocket. I'm tempted to ask her if she's sure that's a good idea in her state, but I'm not her mother, so I stay quiet. Instead, I watch her lean against the brick wall of the building, one foot tucked up beneath her as she lights up the joint and rests it on her bottom lip. She looks impossibly cool. I haven't smoked in ages, and I don't even like pot, but when she gestures for me to take a hit, I do.

Within minutes, I'm high. Sarah is an open book and I'm laughing at something I don't remember her saying. A cloud is enveloping me, pleasant and hot, and I am only vaguely aware when the street lights seem to start flickering to "Hey Jude" by the Beatles. When a black car stops down the road and its lights go off. Then, when Sarah takes my hand.

She seems to think we're friends. She is speaking in earnest, and I can hear her but I'm not listening. My head lolls back, the night air on my face. There are stars winking at me through the trees.

"Shit," she says suddenly. "I'm going to go."

I realize I'm sitting on the curb, and I stand up to join her. She's fumbling with her phone, ordering a Ride. I'm a twenty-five-minute walk from home, but I'm way too out of it to make the trek, and so I do the same.

Our phones ping at the same time. Our Rides are close.

"Do you ever wish you could be somebody else?" I hear her ask. I look up and find her gazing down the street.

"Yes," I say. "All the time."

"Who would you be?"

I don't have an answer for her. Words are hard to come by; they feel lodged deep in my throat.

"I'd be Lady Macbeth."

I'm about to tell her Lady Macbeth is a fictional character when a car inches around the corner and pulls up in front of us.

Sarah wraps me in a hug. "This must be me." My reflexes are all off, and before I manage to lift up my arms in response, she's gone.

I vaguely consider going back inside to tell Gavin I'm leaving, but then another car approaches. I stumble in, my eyes closing as soon as my ass hits the seat.

"Are you Sara?" a voice asks from the front.

"Yes," I say, and a beat later, I'm asleep.

• • •

The driver wakes me up, grumbling at me to get out. I attempt to sit up straight, but my head spins. The driver yells at me again.

"I said get out!"

"All right, all right." I fling open the car door. "Thanks a lot, man."

It's dark and I'm cold. I pull my jacket tighter around my body as I try to figure out on which side of Hillmont Road the driver has dropped me. The street is tree-lined, but nothing feels familiar. The trees are taller, leafier. And the houses . . .

I blink at the one in front of me. It's three stories high with a cherry-red door and window shutters to match. It's what rich people might call colonial. I swivel around, as if my small, shitty house will magically appear across the street. My heart sinks. It's another mansion.

"Fuck!" I squat on the curb, more awake now. The cold is clearing my head. Was the driver screwing with me, or did I get into the wrong Ride? I open the app, and sure enough, my Ride is on its way to Hillmont Road, probably with the other Sarah in tow. I scroll outward on the map. The little blue dot tells me I've been dropped off in a rich suburb on the other side of Windermere.

I try to order another Ride, but the app locks me out and tells me my credit card has been declined. Just my luck to max out when it's after three in the morning and I'm miles away from home.

Suddenly, a light turns on in the house and there's a buttery glow from behind one of the shutters. When I think I see a shadow move past the window, I admit defeat and start walking. I wind my way through the suburb, the first of autumn's leaves crunching beneath my sneakers, and finally, I find Main Street.

At this end of town, the stores are all selling baby onesies made out of organic fibers and kitchen gadgets that zest lemons and other fruits I didn't know could be zested. I rarely come out this way, and I find myself staring through the windows at all the things nobody needs but everybody wants. At a women's clothing shop, there's a cardamom-green gown on display. I wonder who in this sleepy university town would need to buy a cardamom-green gown.

Slowly but surely, the streets change. There still isn't a single car on the road, but now Main Street is lined with a mix of coffee shops and restaurants, used book stores, gyms, grocers and other businesses, like the movie theater, that rely on students. I cut through the intersection that would lead toward campus or back to Gavin's bar, but I keep heading north. It's quarter to four in the morning, and I still have a way to go.

I walk block after block, and finally I'm getting close. Not much has survived in this part of Windermere. Besides the occasional nail salon or convenience store, most storefronts are shuttered. When I get to Hillmont, I head east. I'm only two blocks away now. I pass a block of rundown apartment complexes, then a daycare, and then I stop. Something feels off.

I look up. There's an odd hum coming from up ahead. Lights, too. Are they flashing? I squint, trying to make it out. I can't tell if one of my neighbors has left their headlights on or if I'm still high.

I cross the final intersection before my house, slowly. I'm only fifty feet away now, and the flashing lights come into focus. It's a police cruiser.

"Hello?"

The word comes out as a croak, so I clear my throat and keep walking forward.

"*Hello?*" I try again.

My house is tucked away beneath a broken streetlight, and it's dark as hell. A shadowy figure emerges from my front walkway, and I tense as it draws closer.

"Who are you?"

"Ma'am, I'm going to need you to stay back."

"Why?"

"Ma'am, my name is Officer Reynolds, and I'm going to need you to stay where you are."

"But that's my house. I live there."

The officer comes into full view. He's blocking the walkway with his large frame.

"You live here?"

"Seventy-two Hillmont Road." I pause. "Why?"

Just then, somewhere in the distance, a police siren wails. And then another one. And another after that.

My heart pounds as I realize they're getting closer, and I step off the pavement and push past the officer.

"Ma'am, no—"

He grabs my arm, but it's too late. I see her.

The familiar denim jacket. The mess of chocolate-brown hair dripping down the stoop.

I buckle. I feel two arms catch me as I slide down to the pavement.

"Do you know her?" Officer Reynolds ask.

"Yes," I say, right before I black out. "Her name is Sarah."

2.

SARAH ELLIS
Three years earlier

Everyone is pissing me off today.

I just got home from Journey's house. She, Felix and I were studying for this math test I'm pretty stressed about, and my mother called to check if I'd be home for dinner, and I don't really remember what I said, but after I hung up the phone, Journey told me I should be nicer to her. Then I told Journey she should wax her eyebrows once in a while, even though she has perfect eyebrows, and, well, she kicked me out.

We'll be fine by tomorrow, or maybe Thursday. She's been my best friend for eleven years, since the first grade, and I swear we're fighting half the time, but neither of us has sisters, so there's that. It's nice to have Felix around when Journey and I really get going, because even though he can be the most immature and annoying of the three of us, at least he's a good buffer.

To be honest, I'm feeling a little guilty about the fight, so I just texted Journey an apology. I can be a tad bitchy when I'm stressed, but I'm not that strong at algebra and I *really* want an A. They don't fuck around at Bishop Bailey Hall, because they know the parents' biggest fear in life is that their children won't be as successful as they are. That's why *I* have to be a doctor one day, and why my brother, Adam, just left for Stanford, and why my mother goes through my shit to make sure I'm not on drugs, and why I have to type this diary entry into a password-protected notes app in my phone, rather than writing in one of those tacky Anthropologie notebooks she buys me every Christmas.

It's not just the notebooks. It's the floral dresses she keeps buying me to wear to church, even though we never go, and the mother-daughter spa appointments she makes for us and almost always has to cancel because of work. It's the freaking room I'm in right now, which she decorated for me like it's some kind of dollhouse. We moved into this house when I was too old to want a playroom, but she wanted her little New England Barbie to have one anyway. She decorated it with baby-pink wallpaper, fluffy cushions, a vanity mirror. I swear, the armchair I'm curled up in right now costs as much as some people's cars.

My bedroom is much more my style, but I came down here to make my mother happy, I guess. Sometimes she looks at me like she doesn't know who I am, and I feel angry and sad that I always seem to disappoint her, that whatever I do never seems to be good enough. So I run my mouth and make her cry, and then come down here and wiggle my ass into this fucking armchair and play Adele loudly from the Bluetooth speaker, and this is my way of apologizing to her. Of telling her that I am still her little, darling girl.

Even though I'm not. I haven't been in a long time.

Ugh, this is so stupid. What am I even doing?

Journey's the one who put this diary thing in my head. Last week she bragged to me and Felix that her parents were concerned about her anxiety over college applications and had started sending her to therapy. We were in the lunch hall and she totally wanted everyone to overhear, because she got so many sympathetic looks and sighs and now she'll tell anyone who will listen all about her therapy sessions, that she's been advised to "write things down" for the sake of her mental health.

My parents are both doctors, but they only believe in physical ailments. Daddy once told me that basically all cases of depression could be fixed "if those lazy asses went to the gym once in a while," and when Grandma died a few years ago, no one could understand why I was sad all summer. They got over it *so* quickly. They delayed the church funeral so they didn't have to cancel their couples' trip to Palm Springs, and whenever I cried, or reminisced, or even so much as mentioned Grandma, like total jerks, all they did was remind me that I barely even visited her.

My parents named me and Adam to make Grandma happy, you know, back before she got dementia and forgot how much she loved Jesus and her grandchildren. But my parents *had* to pick the most common biblical names, didn't they? How about Lydia? Miriam? I'd even have taken Delilah. Anyway, I only let Grandma call me Sarah. Everyone else just calls me Ellis.

Daddy is home from the hospital. I can hear them talking in the kitchen, and pretty soon they'll call me down to dinner and grill me about my homework while they half-listen and read the news on their iPads, so I better get to my point:

Not that I'll *ever* admit it to Journey, but I'm going to try writing things down, too. I'm also going to work a bit harder at not making my mother cry, and actually caring about things the way Adam does, rather than just pretending to all the time.

I also wonder if I should start going to the gym. Ugh. I freaking hate the gym.

3.

I'm in the back of a police cruiser, numb. The other Sarah's body is still on the pavement, covered in a white tarp, and there are at least a dozen officers, paramedics and firemen crowding the sidewalk. It's still dark outside, but I can see the first touches of light hanging like fog over the east side of town. I don't know how long I've been here. I wonder if I fell asleep.

A brisk knock on the glass snaps me upright. It's a man, mid-thirties, with black hair and sharp features. Even though he's in plain clothes, I can tell he's police.

I push open the door just a crack, and the guy sticks his head into the opening.

"I'm Detective Kelly. I understand you know the victim."

"Sort of," I say. "I only met her tonight."

He nods, stiffly. "Officer Reynolds mentioned you said her

name was Sarah. Do you happen to know her last name, or anything at all that would help us identify her?"

"Yes," I say, remembering. "I think she lives on the south side. Where all the rich people live."

"The Orchards?"

"That's it. And her house—it's white, the biggest one on the street. The door was red."

Detective Kelly gives me a look, crouches down so we're eye to eye. He seems excited, and I can't help but wonder when was the last time someone was murdered in this town.

"You've been to her house?"

"It's a long story," I say, and Detective Kelly tells me to save it for the station.

A different officer drives me over. I've never been to a police station before, but it's largely what I expect from what I've seen on television. Very few windows and fluorescent lighting. A sad, empty waiting room full of furniture that looks like it hasn't been replaced since the 1980s. I sit there until Detective Kelly appears and waves me through a secured door. I follow him down a hall. The carpet is brown, dark. I wince. It's the exact same color as Sarah's hair.

Detective Kelly stops in front of another door. "Coffee?"

"Sure."

"Black?"

"With milk," I say. "Please."

I go into the room and wait for him. There's an old table and four chairs, and nothing on the walls except chipped blue paint. No one-way mirror. I wonder if that sort of room is saved for the suspect.

Detective Kelly returns with two paper cups, and I remember how tired I am when he presses one of them into my hand, the scent of bitter coffee hitting my nostrils. I thank him and guzzle half of it down in one go.

"So," he says, taking the chair opposite me. He has a pen and legal pad with him now, and I watch him scratch *September 29* on the right-hand corner of the top sheet. "I'm going to need to take a statement from you. What's your full name?"

"Saraswati Bhaduri. But I go by Sara." I shiver, thinking of the other Sarah. "With no H."

"You a local?"

I shake my head. "I'm from Boston, but I've lived here for two years. I'm a law student."

I can tell he's impressed, even though he shouldn't be. Not with my current academic record.

"And you met the victim—"

"Do we have to call her that?"

"No, we don't." He pauses. "You said you met the other Sarah last night. Is that right?"

"I work four nights a week at Gavin's, that bar over by campus. She was there."

"What time did she arrive?"

"I don't know." I rack my brain, trying to remember when I first saw her. "I started at six thirty. Wednesdays are Wings Night, so it was packed. And I remember seeing her around a bit. I might have served her a few times, but I'm not sure."

I watch Detective Kelly scribble furiously on his notepad.

"And then around two-ish, maybe, I was packing up my things, getting ready to leave, and Gavin tells me there's a girl passed out in the bathroom."

"Sarah?"

I nod. "He told me to go deal with her."

"Did she have a purse or backpack with her at that time?"

I press my eyelids tight, picture her down there on the floor. "Yes." I flick my eyes open. "It was a black cross-body bag. Marc Jacobs."

Detective Kelly looks confused by my description, and so I describe the bag and then tell him how I took Sarah outside. That we smoked a joint and talked for a while about nothing in particular, nothing I could really remember. I say that we both ordered Rides and must have mistakenly taken one another's, because the next thing I know, I'm in the Orchards.

Detective Kelly nods as I speak, occasionally jotting down notes. When I'm done, he folds his hands together on the table.

"You're claiming that you and Sarah took the wrong Rides home?"

"Yeah. That's exactly what I'm saying."

He furrows his brows.

"I mean, we must have, right? She was at my house," I stammer. I'm tired and suddenly I'm nervous, too. "And why else would I have ended up in the Orchards?"

"You don't think you could have punched in the wrong address?" he asks me, like I'm a toddler.

"No. I don't."

"And as to why she might have been on Hillmont—"

"She looked rich," I tell him, although I don't tell him why I think so. Her clear, bright skin. Perfectly highlighted hair. Brand-name bag and clothes. "There's no way she lived around there."

"There are plenty of reasons why a young woman of means might be on Hillmont Road."

I purse my lips. My neighborhood isn't exactly Park Avenue. Hillmont is the shithole where the worker bees live, and its residents make sure our picturesque New England university town stays the white-bread wonderland that it is. They paint and clean the townies' houses. Pour the students' beers.

Some of them are also known to sell drugs.

"I know," I say, finally. "But I don't think that's why she was there."

"What do you know?"

Detective Kelly is trying to trip me up. I press my feet into the floor, annoyed.

"Two doors down," I say. "Number 68. There are always nice cars parked outside, every night. And they never stay long." I pause. Detective Kelly is eyeing me. "I know they deal. But I don't think Sarah was there to buy drugs. I think she took my Ride by mistake."

The detective scribbles something on the pad, covering the paper with his hand. I wait for him to press me on the subject, but then he veers off course.

"Let's rewind to before you left Gavin's. Was there a bouncer or another member of staff helping you take care of Sarah?"

I grimace.

"No?"

I shake my head. "We don't have bouncers."

"How many people were at Gavin's last night?"

"I don't know about the whole night, but at its peak, I'd say a hundred and fifty people. Give or take."

"Is that over capacity, would you say?"

"I don't know," I lie.

"And how many of you were working?"

I tell him that it was just me and Gavin front of house, plus the three guys in the kitchen who cook, wash the dishes, bring out food orders and clean tables.

"Why are you asking me all of this?" I say. "Talk to Gavin."

"I'm trying to get a mental picture of the evening."

"It'll be busy again tonight." Thursday evenings he discounts shots. Although I'm desperate for the cash, I'm thankful I'm not on the schedule. "Go see for yourself."

Detective Kelly stares at me a beat, and then looks down at his notes. He's moved his hand, but my eyes won't focus, so from where I'm sitting it just looks like scribbles.

"Let's go back to Sarah. You helped her outside after your shift was over. Can you tell me why you took her out through the kitchen exit?"

I purse my lips, trying to remember. But I don't. Fatigue, the weed—the whole night feels groggy.

"No. Honestly, I can't remember," I say finally. "Maybe she was embarrassed by how drunk she was. Maybe I suggested the kitchen exit because it was closer, or she might have. I really don't know."

Detective Kelly doesn't look convinced.

"Do you remember who she was with last night?" he continues. "If she was there with anyone?"

"She mentioned her friends had left without her, but I didn't see her with anyone." I shrug again. "Like I said, it was packed. But you know what—there should be CCTV of all of it."

"Yes, there should," Detective Kelly says. "We'll be heading down to Gavin's as soon as we can get a hold of him. But I'd still like to see things from your perspective a bit first."

My perspective. I try not to snort. What other perspective could there be?

"Did Sarah mention anything else when you were talking outside?" he continues. "Did anyone leave through the kitchen exit while you were back there?"

I rub my eyes, trying to remember. Although the coffee is starting to kick in, everything is hazing together, and it occurs to me that I've been awake for nearly thirty-six hours straight; I have trouble sleeping at the best of times, but the night before last I didn't even try to go to bed. I had an essay due and pulled an all-nighter.

"Sara?" Detective Kelly prompts.

"Yeah," I say. He looks impatient, and so I start thinking out loud.

"The back street is always quiet. It's residential." I close my eyes, trying to picture it. "There may have been a car around."

Detective Kelly sits up straighter.

"It might have been parked. Maybe it drove up while we were there. I don't really know."

"Was it still there when you left?"

"Look, I have no idea. And I don't remember what we talked about, either. OK? I was exhausted. And high."

"Right." He taps his fingers. "Well—"

"Can I ask you a question now?" I interrupt.

"Depends on the question."

I hesitate. "What happened to her? How did she die?"

"I'm sure you know I can't answer that. It's an open investigation—"

"Well, why would someone do this, then? Christ, she's just a kid."

He pauses, his gaze intense as he considers me. Finally, he speaks.

"Statistically—and I'm not saying this is what happened—but the vast majority of female homicide victims are killed by someone they know." Detective Kelly frowns. "Sometimes an acquaintance, but more often a lover. An ex. A jilted ex."

I nod and widen my eyes for him. The detective continues.

"But the victim—sorry, Sarah—wasn't found with that purse you described. Her phone was missing, too. Now, it's possible that she left it in the Ride." He pauses. "It's also possible it was taken from her. That this was a mugging gone wrong. That she was simply in the wrong place at the wrong time."

On Hillmont Road, that wouldn't be hard. The other Sarah could have been attacked by any number of people who frequented the area. Drunkards or hitchhikers from the sleazy bar out by the truck stop. Overly friendly, often unstable residents of the halfway house up the road. Any one of my meth-head neighbors.

My throat closes up as I think of Sarah. She's white and I'm Indian, but from what I remember, our skin tone and hair are nearly the same color. We're the same size. We even wore a similar jacket.

What if Sarah was in the wrong place at the wrong time because she was in *my* place?

What if . . . the victim was supposed to be *me*?

4.

A brisk knock interrupts us. Officer Reynolds barges into the room and whispers something to Detective Kelly, and then leaves just as abruptly. I don't hear what he says.

"Can I go home now?" I ask, as the detective stands up from his chair. I've drained my coffee, but I can feel a headache coming on. I need more caffeine and a Tylenol immediately.

"Soon," he says vaguely. "I might have a few more questions for you. Would you mind hanging around a bit longer? I'll have someone drive you afterward."

I don't respond. The clock on the wall says it's nearly 8 a.m., and my first class starts in less than an hour, but I'm too shaken to go in today anyway.

"And before you leave, we're going to need to take your phone so we can verify your story."

Verify. *Right.*

"If the night played out as you say, we'll need to speak with the driver who took Sarah to your house. I'll leave your phone at the front desk in a day or two. Sound OK?"

"I guess it has to be," I say.

Detective Kelly leaves the room, leaving the door ajar. I sigh, and then tap on one of the few numbers in my call history these days: my parents' work line.

"I called you last night," Mom says, answering. I can tell I'm on speaker by the echo. "I was worried."

"Sorry." They say this to me whenever I forget to call or check in every single day. "I was studying late. And then I fell asleep."

"You work too hard." Dad's talking now. I can hear him stocking shelves in the background. "Are you sleeping enough?"

"Yes," I lie.

"And eating?" Mom asks. "When are you coming home?"

"Soon." I leave it at that, and then I ask them what's going on there.

I don't consider my constant lying to them a bad thing; it's for their own protection. My parents, Rama and Mira Bhaduri, have enough to worry about and work too hard for too little as it is, but I suppose so do most immigrants. When they first moved to America, they took on the low-skill jobs that needed filling, learned English, and embraced the American ways of eating things like ketchup on macaroni, and macaroni with cut-up hot dogs, and hot dogs with ketchup, and mustard, too.

They saved. Pennies and nickels at a time. And in 2007, just months after they invested every penny they had to set up the neighborhood's first Bengali grocery store, the Great Recession crawled into town.

Bhaduri's Delights stayed afloat, but only just, and only because Mom and Dad began catering to everyone in our ethnically diverse neighborhood. Their dream of creating a home away from Kolkata or Dhaka for their fellow Bengalis to gather became a distant dream, and the store is now full of everything from *dosa* mix to plantains, family-size bags of barbecue chips to vermicelli noodles. Vodka, too. And it's the vodka that keeps the lights on.

"You must go get ready for class," I hear Dad say, after they tell me about the new light fixture above our store's frozen food section.

"I'm already at school," I say. "I was here early, studying."

"We're so proud of you, *beti*."

I nod, ready to get off the phone. "Thanks, Mom."

"One more year of studies, and then our daughter will be lawyer!"

"Right," I say. "Anyway, I need to have my phone fixed. So, if I don't call the next few days, don't worry."

"What happened?" Dad asks.

"I dropped it." I pause. "Where's Tina? Can you tell her . . ."

I trail off when I hear something thud out in the hall. I stand up. There's a commotion. Yelling. I can't quite make it out.

I tell my parents I have to go, and I quickly end the call and walk over to the open doorway.

"You incompetent son of a bitch!"

I recoil. The voices aren't that far away.

"You're telling me our daughter was strangled, and you

idiots are sitting around here picking your assholes doing *what* exactly?"

I know it's none of my business, but my curiosity gets the best of me. I lean forward and chance a look. Detective Kelly and Officer Reynolds are down the hall, with a couple who I can only assume are Sarah's parents. They look like they're in their early fifties, and the mom is crying hysterically. The dad looks like he's about to punch someone.

"I need to know," the mother sputters. "Before she died. Was she—"

"No," Detective Kelly says, and she sobs even harder. "There were no signs of rape."

"Thank fucking god." The dad smacks the wall behind him with a clenched fist, and I can feel the reverberations from where I'm standing.

"Sarah was—"

"Detective," the mom interrupts. "She hates being called Sarah. Everyone calls her Ellis. I would appreciate it if you got her name right. Like my husband has said, you haven't gotten a damn thing—"

"Bev," the dad interrupts. "The detective was speaking." Suddenly, he's as cool as a cucumber. "What were you saying?"

"Your daughter, *Ellis*," Detective Kelly continues, "was at Gavin's last night. It's a student bar—"

"I know that place, and she *certainly* was not, Detective. She was at study group. After dinner she . . ." The mom looks to her husband. "Wasn't she?"

"She's twenty years old." The dad glares at Detective Kelly. "What the hell was she doing there? Was she drunk?"

"We believe so."

"And one of your 'theories' is she later went to Hillmont to buy drugs. Are you out of your fucking mind? No. She would *never* go to Hillmont."

I lean my head against the doorframe, so as not to be seen. My knees shake as I try to imagine my parents in their shoes. What it would be like to come down to a police station and find out that their daughter is dead. That their daughter wasn't where she was supposed to be.

If I hadn't gotten into the wrong Ride, would they be here instead?

After Ellis's father has finished his rant, Detective Kelly continues. He sounds less sure of himself than before.

"We'll be canvassing the neighborhood, the campus, the bar. We're going to talk to everyone who knew Ellis, everyone she texted or came into contact with in the past few days."

"Do you have her phone?" the dad asks.

"No, but—"

"Then how the *hell* do you plan on—"

"Ryan, that's enough."

The men glance over at Ellis's mom. Her voice is final and clear, and she's stopped crying completely.

"You know as well as I do, Ellis's messages will be backed up to the cloud." She glares at her husband, and then turns her gaze on the detective. "But there will be no need for any of that. I already know who you should be questioning. I know *exactly* who killed my baby girl."

I hold my breath, waiting.

"Ellis's ex-boyfriend," the mother says coldly. "Tommy Eagle."

5.

SARAH ELLIS
Three years earlier

I had this weird, rumbling feeling in my stomach the night before this school year started. At first, I thought I was sick, and I texted Journey and Felix to see how they were feeling because we ate that huge platter of nachos for dinner, but they were fine. It wasn't food poisoning. In retrospect, I think it was a gut instinct, you know? I just didn't know what it was yet.

It's tradition for the junior class at Bishop Bailey Hall to get saddled with three scholarship students from across the state. Every year on the first day of school, the principal parades the new batch in front of the whole school and talks about racial and socioeconomic diversity and underprivileged youth like they are our collective charity projects.

The speeches, the scholarships, it is never about *them*. It is about us. It's about how our families' tuition makes these *important* scholarships happen, how it looks good that *we* attend a school that is just so gosh darn benevolent.

I've heard from upper years that it's always hit or miss with these scholarship students. You have this tight-knit class for basically your whole life, and then bam! You're stuck with three new kids until graduation you better hope don't suck.

This year was our turn, and I wasn't really sure what to expect from the first two students, Nathan Price, who struck me as totally average in every way, and Andrea Chan, who seemed OK, although it's embarrassing to think about how there's only, like, two other Asian kids in our whole school.

Anyway, the third student—Tommy Eagle—*he* caught my attention, and not just because he's hot. Tommy rolled into assembly late and everyone saw. Apparently, he'd slept through his first-day-of-school alarm in the guest room of the family he'd been billeted to. And even when our principal made a joke at his expense, in front of the whole school said it was nice of him to show up, Tommy didn't seem fazed. He looked like he didn't even care about being here. About this new life the private school had given him, the advantages it would afford him when he applied to colleges, and jobs, and even country clubs.

And why *should* he care? It doesn't matter. Nobody else believes me when I say this whole world our parents are paying for is bullshit, but it is, and honestly, it was pretty sexy to see someone else think that, too.

"I'm Ellis," I announced after assembly. I'd stayed behind, waiting for him by the exit as everyone else shuffled back to class.

"Tommy." He smiled politely and extended his hand. The formality of this made me want to laugh out loud, but I didn't. I shook it.

"Are you a junior, too?"

"Guilty," I replied.

"So we're classmates."

"Friends, too, maybe."

"I already have a lot of friends." Tommy smirked, and I totally blushed, because I couldn't tell if he was flirting or being an ass, and I keep thinking about that moment, and I *still* can't tell. He must have been flirting. Right?

We're three weeks into the school year now and the rumbling feeling is back, comes on in waves. It's not food poisoning, and this time it isn't a gut instinct, either.

I think I'm . . . in *love*.

The way my parents flip out at each other, I didn't think I believed in love, and I definitely didn't know it felt like this. It's sickening, honestly. My stomach hurts all the time, and if I say something stupid in class I can't sleep at night, wondering if Tommy heard, if he thinks I'm just some dumb girl, if he thinks about me *at all*.

I don't want to sound conceited, but I am used to guys fawning over me—the guys at school who grope at me and pretend it's a joke and who I've known since before their voices dropped. The guys I meet at Model UN and fundraisers who say things like "when I get into Yale" to try to impress me and "I bet you like it from behind, don't you, Ellis" to cut me down. Guys who aren't really guys, but middle-aged men, like a few of Daddy's golfing buddies, who have been staring at me ever since I hit puberty.

Tommy's pretty shy and hard to get to know, but you can just tell he would never treat a girl like that. He would never treat *me* like that.

Deep down in my gut, I just know it. I just know one day he's going to love me, too.

6.

Thursday, September 29

I don't feel right without my phone. Like I've skipped a meal, or forgotten to wear a bra. The same officer from this morning drives me home, and I keep reaching into my back pocket expecting to find it. Besides the information from my Ride app, Detective Kelly won't find anything useful. The number and phone itself are only two months old. I bought it secondhand off Facebook Marketplace.

Finally, I get home. There are still a handful of police officers and crime scene investigators lurking around, but thank god they've taken away Ellis's body. It's easier to think of her that way, as Ellis rather than Sarah. Someone different from the girl I met. I duck under the police tape cordoning off the house and keep my head down as I pass them. I live in the basement apartment, and a narrow, overgrown path takes me around back to my entrance.

Once inside, I lock the door behind me, kick off my sneakers and starfish onto the bed. I close my eyes, waiting to be overcome with fatigue. My body is bone tired, but sleep escapes me.

I can't stop thinking about her.

I was one of the last people to see her alive, and the thought of it chills me to my very core. Could I have stopped it? Would Ellis still be alive if I had noticed her getting into the wrong Ride? If I'd taken her outside through the main door, where the street is always full of college kids?

I open my eyes, roll over and stare blankly at the ceiling. Again, I try to play out everything that happened last night. I don't remember Ellis arriving at Gavin's, but I do remember her. She was beautiful, effervescent. I remember seeing her and thinking how nice it would have been to be a young, carefree student—mindlessly running from class to a frat party, the library to the bar, with no responsibilities other than taking care of number one. Pressing your credit card into the bartender's palm and telling your friends, "It's fine—I've got this round" because it is fine; your parents pay the bill.

Ellis was twenty years old, eight years younger than I am. When I was her age, I was living at home and still sharing a bedroom with Tina. I worked in my parents' store evenings and weekends, around the undergrad classes I managed to squeeze in. It took me six years to finish my bachelor's in economics, but I finished. It took me two more to get into law school with a first-year scholarship, but I got here. And now . . .

My toes curl in my socks. They're cold, dried sweat sticking to the skin.

Now I don't know what I'm doing.

My laptop dings, startling me. I roll onto my side and

scrounge around beneath the covers until I find my year-old MacBook Pro buried deep beneath the duvet. I have several notifications. Another pissy email from student administration, which I delete without reading, a few texts from Tina, and a new email from Ajay.

Ajay Shah
9:54 a.m.
Subject: Where r u
Professor Miles doesn't look happy . . .

I groan softly into my pillow. I am in my third and final year of law school, and more than half my classes are seminars. Right now, I am missing Corporate Financing. There are only sixteen students, and Professor Miles notices when we don't show up. She expects us to be there early and come prepared with pointed observations about the readings she assigned, to spend all ninety minutes in feverish debate about the case law and rules that enable rich companies to keep getting richer.

I am going to get a lecture for skipping. At least today I have a reason not to be there.

Long story. Tell you later.

Shivering, I sit up in the bed and close the window. I know I shouldn't leave it open in this neighborhood, but I have a south-facing apartment, and it can get hot down here during summery afternoons.

I hear a thud above me and wonder if I should go upstairs

and check on my landlady. Zo is elderly and quiet as a mouse, so I only ever hear her when she drops things, which is happening more frequently these days. I know I got lucky with Zo. Rent is dirt cheap, even for Hillmont Road, and when I showed up two years ago with a few cardboard boxes full of clothes and a kettle, she let me furnish the apartment with odds and ends from her own house, which she claimed she no longer used. Dishes and crockery, yellow with age. The desk and office chair that her sons used to do their homework in the eighties. A paisley duvet cover she sewed herself.

My basement apartment is 320 square feet, the plumbing groans, and the hardwood leaves splinters in my bare feet, but it's the first place I've ever called my own. It's as at home as I'll ever feel.

I am restless, and I know I won't be able to sleep. I check the time on my alarm clock. If I shower right now, I can probably make it to my next class. I might even have time to do some of the readings beforehand. With a sigh, I take my laptop to the desk. I open my syllabus for Civil Procedure. We're only a few weeks into the semester, and I'm already behind. I pinch my cheeks, hard, and then get to work.

I read rule after case after rule after case. But the information goes in one eye and seemingly out the other, because no matter how much I try to focus, I can't stop thinking about Ellis.

Last night she was alive. Now she's dead.

I bite my lip, and on an impulse, I open up a web browser. I type in "Sarah Ellis" and "Windermere, Massachusetts," and several hits appear. The first is her Instagram profile, which is private. I can't see anything—her photos, her friends, not even a descriptive caption. Nothing but a tiny profile picture. I can only just make out that it's her.

I click on the next few hits and read a handful of articles about her parents, where she's listed next to the rest of their accolades. Her father, Dr. Ryan Ellis, is a cardiologist and professor at Windermere's medical school. Dr. Beverly Ellis is a family doctor, with a bustling practice on the rich side of Main Street. They have a son, too. Ellis's brother, Adam, is a physics major at Stanford. I find a photo of the four of them, arms linked, at a hospital fundraiser two years ago. They look like a picture-perfect family, with their sparkling white teeth and white linen outfits. I would be irritated if I didn't know that one of them was just murdered.

Remembering what Ellis's mother said at the station, hesitantly, I start a new search.

There's no Tommy Eagle on social media, at least none under the age of fifty, and there isn't much of a trace of him on Google, either. The only match I can find is from a press release dated three years earlier from Bishop Bailey Hall, a prestigious prep school just outside of town.

> We are overjoyed to welcome this year's scholarship students to the future graduating class: Nathan Price, Andrea Chan and Tommy Eagle. Bishop Bailey Hall has a rich history of sponsoring three young persons of diverse backgrounds who have shown considerable, demonstrable academic excellence . . .

I click out of the article, my mind racing as I try to fit the pieces together.

Presumably, Ellis went to Bishop Bailey Hall, where she met Tommy. But why does Ellis's mother think he killed her—because he wasn't from their upper-class world? Because Tommy was a scholarship student?

I search Ellis's name one more time, but nothing comes up, and, reluctantly, I return to my studies.

It won't be long now until the newspapers catch wind of this. Until the entire country has been informed that a rich white girl was strangled. They'll demand answers. They'll hound the police until the ugly truth is exposed.

I can't help but wonder if the same thing would have happened for me.

7.

I don't finish my readings, shower or go to class. Still, I'm late for my second job. I need to pick up Benji.

It's a twenty-minute walk to his school. I only have ten to spare, and so I run, and I'm winded by the time I arrive. Benji is standing primly on the sidewalk, next to his teacher. His black hair is styled into tight cornrows that merge at the base of his skull, but today they're covered with a baseball cap. He's in his little uniform, blue pleated pants and a white collared shirt that somehow never gets dirty.

"Sorry," I say, running up to them. I shoot Benji a grin between breaths. "Sorry I'm late."

Benji is seven. It's that age where he still looks like a cute kid but is actually kind of a dick. He walks two steps in front of me the whole way home, ignoring my attempts at small talk in

favor of kicking stones and occasionally stomping on an innocent bug or flower bed. I compliment him on his new hat, and
he responds by taking it off and hurling it into the street.

I don't bother retrieving it, and neither does he. I am one
thousand percent sure I don't want to have children. I have a
feeling I wouldn't be a very nurturing mother.

We arrive at the house. It's at least a hundred years old and
vines lick their way across the old brick, beneath windowsills
and rain gutters. The lawn has been replaced with a low-main-
tenance rock garden, a cobblestone path cutting through to the
front door. The interior of the house is even more beautiful. It's
like walking into the Four Seasons on Dalton Street.

"Are you hungry?" I ask Benji, as I hang up our coats.

He drops his backpack in the foyer and races to the basement without answering me. Benji is allowed exactly thirty minutes of Xbox before I have to call him upstairs and force-feed
him a snack, something healthy like apple and almond butter,
or yogurt, or avocado on toast, which he sometimes hides in my
backpack. After that, he's supposed to practice piano and do his
homework until his mother gets home. One time I asked him if
he wanted to go into the backyard and play soccer with me. He
told me to go fuck myself.

I hover at the top of the stairs until I hear machine guns
and the blood-curdling shrieks of his video game, and then my
shoulders relax. I have precisely twenty-nine minutes to myself,
and a luxurious house to spend them in. I tiptoe over to the
wide, velvety sectional and make myself comfortable.

I wake up with a start. Groggy, I fumble around for my phone,
and then remember it's with Detective Kelly. I sit up. I pad over

to the window and peer through the curtains. It's dark outside. I press my hand over my face.

Fuck. Professor Miles's Tesla is in the driveway.

"Sara," I hear her call. "Are you awake?"

She's in the kitchen, and when I round the corner, I find her and Benji sitting at the picnic-style table that overlooks the patio. There's a spread in front of them—salmon steaks, asparagus, baby potatoes. Usually, I'm the one who starts dinner for her. I still don't know the time, and I wonder how long I've been sleeping.

"Professor Miles," I say, trying not to look at my feet. "I'm so sorry."

"Sara. How many times do I have to tell you? When we're at home, call me Madison."

I nod, crossing my arms.

"Benji," Professor Miles says. "All finished?" When he nods, she continues, "Why don't you go get ready for bed, is that OK, sweet pea? I'll be upstairs in a minute."

Gingerly, he pushes up from the table. I ruffle the top of his head as he brushes past me.

"Good night, Benji," I say. "See you tomorrow." Unsurprisingly, he doesn't respond.

Professor Miles gestures for me to sit down in Benji's empty seat, and as I sit, my stomach growls, loud enough that she must have heard. She doesn't offer me any dinner. She never has.

"Madison," I say, looking her in the eye. "I'm sor—"

"Don't worry about Benji," she interrupts, smiling at me through pursed lips. "He said he came upstairs after thirty minutes of Xbox and started his homework on his own." She sighs. "He's a good kid."

I bite my tongue.

"But finding you asleep on the couch like that"—she palms the wood of the table—"*after* you skipped class this morning. Well, let's put it this way, Sara. It's hard for me to see you struggle."

I bite down on my tongue, hard. I don't want to say something I'll regret.

Two months ago, when my actions caught up with me and I was desperate for money, I emailed every single professor at the law school, asking if they needed a research assistant. I'd gotten a job at Gavin's pretty easily because nobody wants to work for a creep, but a few shifts a week wasn't going to be enough to cover rent and tuition.

She was the only one who responded, and when her name arrived in my inbox, I thought I'd won the lottery. *The* Professor Madison Miles is everyone's favorite professor, especially among us rare Black or brown students, who see her as something of an icon. She is intelligent and tough as nails, and has a reputation for putting mediocre white men in their place. But as luck would have it, she didn't want an assistant; her daughter, Brooklynn, was about to leave for college, and her little "sweet pea" needed a babysitter.

As luck would further have it, our idol Professor Madison Miles turned out to be *something* of a bitch.

"To be honest," she continues, "I was surprised to see you sign up for my advanced seminar this semester, considering . . ."

She trails off. I don't need her to remind me I barely scraped by academically last year. She does it often enough.

"There are a lot of people on the waiting list. If you're not serious about corporate financing—"

"Madison," I interrupt, "something happened last night."

She narrows her eyes, and I can tell she's expecting just another excuse.

"A student was murdered."

Her mouth falls open.

In as few words as possible, I tell her what happened. I tell her how Ellis and I got into the wrong Rides the night before, that she was killed on my doorstep. I tell her I'm still "in shock," a term the paramedics used when checking my vitals and that might help me now.

"How . . . who . . . ?" Professor Miles sputters. I've never seen her at a loss for words before. "Sarah *Ellis*, you say? Oh god. I *know* her. She was a year ahead of Brooklynn at Bishop Bailey. And her father, poor thing. He's faculty at the medical school!"

I nod, consolingly.

"How could such a thing happen?" She doesn't wait for me to answer. "I bet it was the Ride driver. You know, I tell Brooklynn not to use any of the apps." She shakes her head. "And *this* is exactly why. No regulation. No oversight. There could be a serial killer in the front seat, and we'd have no idea . . ."

I make all the right nods and sounds as Professor Miles processes the tragedy that's just happened in her quiet, safe little town.

I'm so glad I can be there for her right now.

Five minutes later, she seems to remember that she's not in front of a lecture theater and that conversations are supposed to be two-way. She grabs my hand across the table, squeezes twice. "I feel like a cunt being hard on you just now. I don't know how you're holding it together."

"I just needed some sleep," I say.

"Indeed you did."

"And I haven't told anybody about what happened. I'm not sure what the police—"

"Understood." She waves me off, and we both stand up from the table. "This is between us. It's not for me to say anything to anyone."

I yawn, catching it with my palm.

"Anyway, you better get going."

Professor Miles has never offered to drive me home, either.

"And stick to Main Street, would you?" She holds my gaze a beat, and a shiver runs down my spine. "Because to think . . . last night, it could have been you."

8.

I cut through campus on my way home. I breathe in the cool night air, trying to leave her words behind me. I can feel my eyelids droop. My body is tired, drained, but still my mind races.

It's hard to believe that less than twenty-four hours ago, I was on my way home, blissfully unaware of what was waiting for me. I wonder if Detective Kelly is done with my phone yet, if he's located the Ride driver. Is Professor Miles right—could it have been him? But what about Tommy Eagle? Or was it really just a "mugging gone wrong"?

The Ride driver. The ex-boyfriend. A random attack. It all sounds too easy, straightforward, but if I've learned anything in law school, it's that criminal motivations usually aren't that complicated. The most obvious answer is usually the right one.

I hang a left on Main Street. The road thins out quickly, and I find myself alone with my thoughts. If only I could remember what Ellis and I talked about outside the bar, something that might help with the investigation. Of all nights to smoke pot. I don't even like pot.

I hear something rustle, and I glance behind me. A few blocks back, a car is turning off the main road into one of the two gas stations in town. There's nobody else on the sidewalk. It's just me.

I quicken my pace and dart through the next intersection. Just a few more blocks until Hillmont. I pull my shoulders straight and the wind catches my denim jacket. It billows out behind me, and I hug it tighter around my body. I wish I'd brought a scarf.

I weave past a garbage bin that's tipped over. Litter has poured out over the pavement and been scattered in the wind. I worm my way through the debris. Plastic and paper crunch beneath my feet.

I'm nearing Hillmont. I can see the sign up ahead when I think I hear footsteps. I slow down, and they stop. I convince myself I just imagined it, but then suddenly, I hear them again. I whip around and charge out into the middle of Main Street. I turn a full 360 degrees, looking for the source. A puff of wind causes the trees to shiver, and a few leaves fall to the ground around me. I take three giant steps forward, scanning every doorway and alley.

"Is someone there?"

The wind barks again. Somewhere up ahead, a branch bangs against a window. I jump.

"Hey," I say, louder this time. "Is someone there?"

I wait, and I wait, but what I am waiting for? *Who* am I waiting for? As I shiver in the cold, Professor Miles's words ring in my ears like church bells.

It could have been you.

Maybe it should have been. Maybe he figured out what I—

I hear another sound, like tin crunching on the pavement. I cast my gaze toward the garbage can. It's wobbling back and forth on its axis.

It wasn't moving before.

Panting, I stand my ground. I force myself to count to ten. And when no one appears, I turn on my heel, and without looking back, I run.

9.

SARAH ELLIS
Two and a half years earlier

My mother is in pieces these days. Adam left for Stanford months ago, but I think it's finally hitting her that she's stuck here with me and Daddy.

I miss Adam a lot, and sometimes I just want to call him and tell him about my day or whatever, but my parents keep going on and on about how busy he is, how many clubs he's joined, how it's so freaking important for him to immerse himself in college life.

My parents wanted Adam to go to Duke and be a doctor, too, but when he was about eight years old, it became very clear that Adam was much too smart for that. His mind is just built differently. And he's not one of those geeks who doesn't have any social skills, because in high school he was actually pretty popular. He's had two girlfriends over the years, and they were slit-your-wrists gorgeous.

Anyway, he's off on the West Coast doing a physics degree and I'm pretty sure he'll be running Stanford in a few years, or have moved to Houston or wherever to build spaceships, but either way he's not coming back here. And I'm happy for him. I wouldn't come back, either.

So, update on the Tommy situation: He came over last weekend, but cool your jets, we're not dating. My mother said I could have my friends over, but then forgot about it and got pissed when she got home from yoga and found us all in the basement. I invited the whole class so it wouldn't seem thirsty to invite Tommy, but unfortunately, almost everyone showed up. Daddy doesn't care if we drink, so we waited to crack open the beer Felix brought until Mom went to bed, which these days is around 8 p.m. Tommy didn't show to the last few parties, so this is the first time we've seen him drunk, and after like two sips, he goes from being aloof to the class clown, acting like he's the coolest guy in school. He asked Journey if the carpet matched her fiery red drapes, and she got so pissed she threw a drink in his face. Then he teased me for wearing dark lipstick, which I was already so anxious about, but I managed to laugh it off and then spent the rest of the evening ignoring him.

Well, I tried to ignore him. We had a lot of beer. I don't remember exactly what I said to him the rest of the night.

My tummy hurts.

It's Sunday afternoon. The weekend is almost over, which means any second now, my mother is going to switch from the silent treatment to pestering mode: Have you done your homework? Why are you sulking up here? Why can't you be more like your genius, MIA, perfect older *brother*?

Did you know I smoked weed for the first time at Felix's

eighth grade birthday party? His brother grows it. I only had one stupid little puff. I didn't even feel anything, and I told my mother about it because I thought she would be happy that I was sharing my life with her, but she freaked out and grounded me for a week. I think she hates that I'm not her clone, that deep down I don't want to be a doctor like her and Daddy, and that I'm fun to be around and people seem to like me. Sometimes, at dinner parties, she gets jealous when her friends laugh at my jokes and so she puts me down in front of them.

I don't get it. If I ever have a daughter, I think I'd be nice to her. I think I'd at least try.

10.

Friday, September 30

In the light of day, I know I imagined the sounds and footsteps. I was hysterical and overly tired. Still "in shock." I have absolutely nothing to be afraid of.

Still, sleep eluded me. Despite going on forty-eight hours with barely any sleep, I tossed and turned the whole night, and by the time I finally felt like I was dozing off, my alarm clock woke me up.

I make myself an instant coffee with milk, shower, and then pick out a nice outfit to wear. Faded denim, ankle boots and a cashmere pullover. I even throw on lipstick and a little Hermès scarf.

The law school building is a fat sandstone rectangle that sits on the edge of campus, overlooking a manicured lawn and the

Commons, which is a cluster of outdoor tables where students eat and study when the weather is nice enough. I'm early, so I grab a free spot and pull my Antitrust textbook out of my backpack.

After a few pages, I become vaguely aware that a group has joined me one table over. Today's readings are on international cartel investigations and multijurisdictional proceedings, but I keep getting distracted by their high-pitched voices and gasps. I look up, irritated.

"That's so fucked up," one girl says.

Another one whispers a response that I don't catch.

"But what was she doing in *Hillmont*?"

My breath catches and I lean in. There's a newspaper spread open between them.

"Hey," I interrupt. They stop whispering and look over. "Is that today's paper?"

"Yeah." The girl closest to me nods. "Have you heard about the girl who got killed?"

"In that ghetto on the northeast end of town," another one says.

My stomach curdles. I was so tired I forgot to check the news this morning, but it looks like it's out. Everyone knows that Ellis is dead. I wonder what else they know.

"That's terrible," I say.

"It's *egregious*, that's what it is." The first girl turns back to her friends. "They should really get the FBI involved. *All* of our safety is at stake here."

The others nod, and so I do, too.

"I bet she was buying drugs," the second girl says. "Why else would anyone be over there?"

"That's victim blaming," another one snaps. "It shouldn't matter why she was there. She could have been lying down on the road with her legs spread and that doesn't give anyone the right to—"

"That's obviously not what I'm saying," the second girl replies. They stare at each other. It's a game of political correctness and wit that I really don't have time for. I wait a minute, and then clear my throat.

"Would you mind if I borrowed—"

"Go ahead," the first one says, handing me the newspaper. "Keep it. It makes me sick just reading about it."

I thank her, and then glance at the open page. It's today's edition of the *Boston Herald*.

Windermere student strangled

Twenty-year-old Sarah Ellis was found dead early Thursday morning in the Hillmont neighborhood of the picturesque university town of Windermere, after police responded to a 911 call they thought was about a domestic disturbance.

Longtime Hillmont Road resident Zo Bautman, 81, said she was woken up at approximately 3:10 a.m. by what sounded like shouting outside her window.

"I don't tolerate men taking a hand to women. It's not right. I always call the police, and I did that night, too. I thought one of my neighbors was getting abused."

Bautman said "the commotion" lasted no more

than thirty seconds and she immediately fell back asleep.

"But the next thing I know, the police sirens are going off right outside my window. Lots of them. And I know. I know something terrible happened."

Massachusetts State Police said that Ms. Ellis had been strangled, but declined to comment further on the investigation . . .

I scan the rest of the article, taking everything in. It says that Ellis was born and raised here in town, graduated from Bishop Bailey Hall just over a year ago. That she was a sophomore, majoring in microbiology at Windermere University, and a medical school hopeful. Both Dr. Ellises refused to speak to the reporter, except to say that the date of the memorial service was forthcoming.

I set down the paper, trembling.

So it was Zo who called 911. The walls are thin. The house is old. What else did she hear that the reporters aren't saying?

What else could she have told the police?

11.

I leave the Commons a few minutes before nine. Ajay is already in the lecture theater, ready for class. He's sitting in his usual spot in the front row.

"Sara!"

I slide into the seat next him. I used to have more friends here, back when I was absorbed in the novelty of being a law student. Classes were only the tip of the iceberg; law school was really about the mixers and fundraisers, talent shows and beer pong tournaments, career fairs and moot courts. Really, any excuse to drink and dress up.

When I stopped showing up, my new friends slowly turned into old acquaintances. Except for Ajay. We are both determined to go down the corporate track, and so most of our classes overlap—antitrust, bankruptcy, corporate financing, mergers and acquisitions. He always saves me a seat, and he's the only reason I haven't failed out of law school so far. His precise, detailed notes, and his willingness to share them. His total mastery of every topic and case we've ever covered. Ajay is in the running to win the academic gold medal. He's also editor-in-chief of the law review, and has already been offered a job at a white-shoe firm in Boston that typically only hires Harvard and Yale grads.

"Hey," I say, pulling out my laptop. "How are you?"

"Where were you yesterday?" he asks, not answering me. "I was worried about you."

"It's a long story."

"You said that." He pauses, sets his hand on my forearm. It's warm and gentle, just like him. I can tell he cares about me, and that he'd listen if I wanted to talk. But what would I even say?

"Are you OK, Sara?"

"Yeah," I say quickly. "Why wouldn't I be?"

"You know you can trust me, right?"

"I do trust you," I say.

But I definitely don't deserve you.

Ajay is looking at me the way he usually does. Pensive. Anxious. I wish I didn't make him feel this way. "Sara, are you feeling OK? You don't look like yourself. You look tir—"

"*Tired?*" I interrupt, forcing a smile. "What a compliment."

"Compliments haven't worked with you," Ajay says. "Thought I'd try candor."

I feel awkward, and so I shrug and pretend to look at my laptop.

My parents would be thrilled if Ajay and I ended up together. They tried to set me up with a guy like him once, the month before I started law school. They were so proud of me—I would have been embarrassed if I didn't know how long they'd been praying for my success. How hard they'd worked so their daughters could achieve something society deemed meaningful.

Our apartment in Boston is too small to have a party, so they rented out the hall beneath our local Hindu temple and spared no expense. Mom bought fresh flowers from her friend's gardening shop, and Dad had the meal catered from the new *dosa* restaurant that had opened up on our block, which we wanted to support. Tina and I begrudgingly wore colorful *salwars* we'd found in a secondhand shop, and we helped, and smiled, and bowed our heads respectfully . . .

And then Mom and Dad introduced me to a random guy named Rohan.

"I'm sorry about my parents," he said to me, about twenty minutes after both of our parents had not-so-subtly shoved us into a corner together. Thus far we'd discussed the weather and his job as a mechanical engineer, and entirely avoided the fact that our families were trying to set us up.

"They've lovely," I answered.

"They're watching us, you know."

We both turned to look. All four parents were huddled by the food line, looking at us. They didn't budge even when we'd caught them staring.

Rohan's eyes were black and piercing, and he had that nondescript handsome Indian boy look to him. You could tell he was smart, but not a genius. He was kind, but no Oprah Winfrey.

He was an obstacle.

"Are you close?" I asked, turning back to him.

"With my mom and dad?" He'd leaned back in his chair. "Sure. I mean, as close as you can be to Indian parents."

"What do you mean by that?"

"Well, *they* think we're close. Right? I go to temple. I'm going to marry an Indian girl, like they want. But how well do our parents ever really know *us*?"

I sipped my water. I agreed with him one hundred percent, but couldn't admit it. "Are you mysterious, Rohan?" I joked. "What are you hiding?"

"Nothing too sinister, I promise." He laughed. "And what about you? Are you an open book with auntie and uncle?"

"Oh, of course," I said breezily. "I'm extremely close to my parents. I still live with them."

"Until you go to Windermere Law?"

I nodded. "Unfortunately, it's a bit too far to commute. I'm going to miss them so much, though," I lied. "I'm not sure how I'm going to cope on my own."

"You're going to love it. Seriously. The independence is amazing. I could never move back in with my parents—"

"Well, I'm going to." I stared innocently into his eyes. "When I'm done law school, I'm going to buy a house and move them in with me."

Afterward, I pretended to be gutted when Rohan didn't call. My parents felt terrible.

And they never tried to set me up again.

"Did you do the readings?" I hear Ajay ask. I've drifted off, and I shift my gaze toward him. He's staring at me, like I'm familiar to him. A way any other woman might find endearing.

"The first three pages," I answer truthfully.

"I'll send you my notes—"

"Thanks, Ajay. But no thanks."

"Sara," he sighs. "Just take them, OK?"

"I don't want you to think I'm using you." He looks taken aback, and so I shrug. "You wanted to try candor."

"I suppose I did."

Ajay is too nice to me. I should have pushed him away long ago, the way I did Rohan, or any other prospect that would have led to a normal life.

Instead, I take the notes, and a few minutes later, class begins. I ignore Ajay's sidelong glances while the professor speaks. I dive headfirst into the world of antitrust law. I keep myself on track.

12.

After class, Ajay invites me to study with him in the library until our next class, but I can't. I have an errand to run.

The local branch of my bank is in downtown Windermere, right on Main Street. There are a few homeless men camped out on the corner, and I feel bad that I don't have any change to spare as I pass them by. If my errand goes well, then maybe I will.

Inside the bank, there's a small lobby area with red plastic stools by the window. I flip through today's *Boston Globe* while I wait. They haven't picked up Ellis's story yet. I make a mental note to check Google News the next time I have a chance.

"Sara-swi-ti Bah-duh-ri?"

I look up. A guy my age has come out of the back room, with

a cheap suit and a yellow smile. He has a pen mark on his chin.

"I'm Kyle."

"Hi, Kyle!" I stand up. "You can call me Sara."

His face goes red at my correction, and he starts babbling about the bank. He sounds flustered and looks intimidated by me. To put him at ease, I drop my purse on the floor.

"Shoot," I say, bending down. "I'm such a klutz. Sorry."

Kyle joins me on the floor, hands me back my Valentino wallet and Mont Blanc pen, which have spilled out. He doesn't even try to hide the fact that he's looking down my cashmere sweater when I catch him staring.

"So, you're helping me with my bank loan?" I say, standing up, forcing myself to hold my tongue.

"That I am."

I shake his hand, weakly.

"Welcome to the bank, Sara."

He leads me behind the tellers to an office. It's a windowless room, and I have to stand flush against the wall and move one of the chairs for Kyle to close the door behind him. As expected, my fumble seems to have been the confidence boost he needed, and I sit patiently in the chair opposite him as he goes on about the coffee shop next door. He tells me his assistant can go grab me one if I'd like.

"I see from your intake form that you're looking for a student loan," Kyle says, after I decline the coffee and grind my teeth through the small talk he attempts. He swivels toward his computer. "Do you have some ID with you?"

I hand him my driver's license and watch him punch out the keys to my name, but only after he looks at my photo a beat too long. A moment later, the computer whines. Kyle leans back in his chair.

"Sometimes it takes a while. You'd think computers would be fast by now."

"You're so right."

"What do you study?"

"I'm in law school," I say.

Kyle's jaw stiffens. I've gone back to intimidating him.

"Impressive."

"Yeah," I falter. "No *idea* how I got in."

"If I had to guess, then I'd say affirmative action."

I offer him a tight smile, although I would have drop-kicked him in the balls if I didn't need the money so badly.

Kyle's lighter now, confident after his put-down. The computer beeps and he looks over at the screen.

"Everything OK?" I ask. I sound nervous, and it isn't an act.

"Well, your credit score is . . ."

"Bad," I say. "I know. I'm still paying off a student loan from undergrad."

"And you took out a joint line of credit in 2020," Kyle says, scrolling with his mouse. "For fifteen thousand dollars."

"It was a tough year for everyone. The loan was for my family's business."

"Right." Kyle drums his fingers on the desk. I know he's pausing for effect, that he takes a sick sort of pleasure in withholding information and being in charge. But then again, I've known this since the moment I laid eyes on him.

I lean in and bite my lip. "What do you think?"

"I think," he says slowly, "that I need a bit more information from you, Sara."

I hate the way he says my name. I hate the way he's smiling at me, and that stupid pen mark on his face. I hate the way he's yet again trying to look down my sweater.

And I hate myself more for pandering to him.

"What year of law school are you in?" Kyle asks me.

"Just started my final year," I answer. "I have financial aid, but it doesn't cover the whole thing."

"Well, how did you cover it before?"

I know this is irrelevant to my application, and that my answer will threaten him even further. I scored in the top percentile on my LSAT entrance exams.

"I got an entrance scholarship for my first year," I say, blandly.

He smirks. "Affirmative action?"

I bare my teeth at him in return. "Must be it."

"And how did you pay for your second year?"

"I . . . uh." I pause, and then decide to lie. "Another merit scholarship."

"Not this year, though, hey?"

My failure pleases Kyle, and I wonder what past girlfriend or crush wronged him to make him this way. I wonder if his mother didn't love him enough. I wonder if I'll get my fucking money.

"Not this year, no." I tremble, doubling down. "Kyle, I don't know what to do. Student administration is on my case. My tuition is due today."

"Today? You should have come in earlier."

I nod, pressing my fingers against my dry eyes.

"Aw, shit. Don't cry, Sara." He pauses. "Tissue?"

I nod, and when he hands me the Kleenex box, I take one. Dab beneath my left eye and then my right.

"Well, lucky for you, there's a special category of student loans for future professionals."

A jolt of electricity shoots down my spine as I sit up straighter, look up over the Kleenex. "Do law students qualify?"

Kyle holds my gaze, licks his dry, disgusting lips. "The special law students do."

"Really?"

"Really, Sara," he says, like he's offering me use of his private jet. "And we can *probably* work around your credit score. But you will have to prove that you have a job lined up after graduation." Kyle sighs. "You *do* have job lined up, don't you, Sara?"

"Yes," I lie. "I do."

"Can I see your offer letter?"

I hesitate. I could easily get Ajay to invite me over and show me his offer letter. When he's out of the room, I could scan it, change the name, concoct a forgery that would get me the money I need to survive the next six months.

It would probably work, but there's a chance that someday Kyle might take a second look at my file, right after he jacks off to the image he has of me on the floor picking up my purse with my sweater gaping. Kyle might discover that I lied, and he'd get a thrill out of reporting me. And then, not only would I be in default of a loan, I'd also be disciplined by the legal regulatory body. Lawyers are supposed to be ethical, you see. Our clients are supposed to trust us. A record for lying can get you disbarred, and then what would have been the point of law school.

What would have been the point of everything I've sacrificed.

"My offer letter is at home." I smile sweetly at Kyle. We both know I'm lying. "How about I come back tomorrow?"

"I could swing by tonight and pick it up."

I wonder if this tactic has ever worked for him.

"I'll bring it in soon," I say firmly. "It's on my way to work."

Kyle leaves the office, but before I follow him out, I grab my intake form and stuff it in my purse. I don't want a man like that to have my personal information.

He walks me back to the lobby, playing with the collar of his shirt. The hall is narrow, so our shoulders touch as he thanks me for coming in.

"I'm sorry I couldn't help you there, Sara." He stops in front of the bank tellers and is speaking loudly, so they can hear us. He likes an audience when he feels he has power. "Can't win them all though, eh?"

"No," I say coyly, matching his decibel. "But thanks for trying, *Kyle*."

He starts visibly shaking when I take a step forward and give him the eyes. In my peripheral vision, I can see the tellers watching us.

"Oh, by the way," I simper, touching my fingers to his chin. "Can I tell you something, Kyle?"

Sweating, he says, "Yeah, Sara?"

"You've got pen on your face."

For the second time in twenty minutes, his face goes bright red. I can hear the tellers laughing at him on my way out.

13.

check my watch as I leave the bank. I have thirty minutes until my next class starts, but the police station is a minor detour on my way back to campus. I decide to go check if my phone is ready.

There's a large, friendly-looking woman working the front desk when I arrive. I blink, adjusting to the low light inside. There's no one else in the waiting room, so I walk right up to her.

"What can I do you for?" she asks cheerfully.

"Hi," I say. "I'm Sara Bhaduri. Is Detective Kelly here?"

"He is not. Is there something I can help you with?"

I hike my purse up my shoulder. "Yeah, actually. He has my phone—"

"Right! Of course, sweetie. He *mentioned* a nice Indian girl might drop by for it. Forgot your name for a second. I asked the detective if I should call you and tell you it was here waiting for ya, and he said, *Sally*, how exactly you going to call her if she doesn't have her phone!"

Sally howls at her own joke as she reaches into a desk drawer and pulls out my phone. She's an over-sharer. I decide to laugh along.

"Thanks so much," I say, taking the phone from her. "Hey, did Detective Kelly say when he'd be back?" I pause, eyeing her. "I can wait."

"You could be waiting a while. I've been waiting for the venti mocha he promised me since my shift started."

"I'm not in a rush," I lie. "I was really hoping to catch him."

"Sorry, hun. I'm not sure when he'll be back." Sally lowers her voice. "You heard about the girl who got killed?"

"I saw it in the paper. It makes me sick just reading about it."

"It's his case, you know. Detective Kelly."

I feign surprise. "*Really.*"

"I tell you what, Sara. Everyone's on edge here at the station." Sally crosses her arms. "The whole damn county will be on edge until they catch the son of a bitch—"

Sally stops abruptly, standing up.

"Oh Christ, he's back."

I whip around, expecting to see Detective Kelly, but through the glass doors I see Dr. Ryan Ellis storming up the path.

"You're not the only one looking for the detective these days," Sally mutters. "You better skedaddle, all right? This isn't going to be pretty."

Ellis's father pushes through the door and I step to the side quickly, turning my head so he can't see my face. I don't know if he knows who I am. That it was my Ride that led Ellis to her death.

"Where is he?" Dr. Ellis shouts when he reaches Sally. "Is he here?"

I bend over and pretend to tie my shoe, gazing up through my hair. Ellis's father is wearing black jeans and a puffer jacket. Blue veins trail down his neck, conspicuous. He looks like he's about to hit someone.

"I already told you on the phone, sir," Sally says calmly. "The detective is not here."

"For Christ's sake, my daughter is *dead*. He should be finding the bastard—"

"And I'm well sure that's the reason he's out, Dr. Ellis—"

"Then I should be with him. I need to know what's going on." Dr. Ellis is barking, like a dog. "Has he been to the college? Did he interview her friends? What did they say?"

Sally opens her mouth to speak, but then she throws me a look that tells me I need to leave. I pretend to finish tying my laces, and then I go outside. I don't realize I've been holding my breath until the fresh air hits my face.

Who *is* Detective Kelly interviewing today? Did he find the driver who took Ellis to my house? The murderer? What if he finds . . .

I drift back to campus, lost in thought. My mind and even my body are consumed by the case, and I'm back in the Commons before I remember I have my phone back. I unclench my palm. Sweat is streaked across the screen, and I wipe it off with my sleeve as I wait for the device to power on and remind myself to breathe.

Slowly, the notifications pop up. Most are alerting me to

things I've already read. Texts from Tina, Ajay and my parents. Emails from a few professors about coursework and assignments. Another one from student administration, reminding me to pay my tuition. I scroll down to see if I have any missed calls, which would not have come through on my laptop. I have one from my parents' work line, and one more from a blocked number.

Hesitating, I click on that final notification. The call came in last night, when I was walking home from Professor Miles's.

He used to call me from a blocked number, but I haven't heard from him in two months, and it has to be a coincidence. This call is from a telemarketer, trying to sell me insurance or a long-distance phone package to India, or offering to clean my air ducts. This call is not him trying to get in touch, having tracked down my new phone number. This is *not* him telling me that he knows what I did.

Right?

I shiver, and instinctively glance around me. There are students studying and eating tuna fish sandwiches at the tables, gossiping and talking on their phones, moving forward and going about their lives.

It's time for me to do the same.

14.

After class, I call my parents to check in, and then I go pick up Benji from school. While he's playing Xbox, I make him a strawberry banana smoothie and bring it down to him. I think about blending one for myself, but instead I make myself a double macchiato with the high-end De'Longhi.

I'm too exhausted to study, and I sit on the uncomfortable wooden bench at the kitchen table to stop myself from falling asleep. It's nice to have my phone back. Normally, I'd sit here mindlessly scrolling through Instagram, but today I find myself clicking obsessively on Ellis's profile, which is still private. Why would I think I'd be able to see it now?

I search her name on Google again. A few more news outlets in Massachusetts have picked up the story of her death, including the *Boston Globe* online, but there's no new information, nothing I don't already know. I wonder if I should tell my family about Ellis, that a girl died right in front of my house, but decide not to for the time being. My parents are too busy to read or watch local news. They are barely up to date with major current events. And what about Tina? She might find out. But if she does, I'm sure I can convince her to stay quiet. I don't want my parents to worry about me more than they already do.

I sigh, standing up, and stretch my arms above my body. I don't trust myself to sit down again, so I wander through the main floor. The stuffy, early-twentieth-century library with the credenza desk. Professor Miles's home office. I walk back through the sitting room, past the baby grand piano, and then linger in the foyer. Down the stairs, I can hear Benji playing some sort of space video game. There are lasers blasting and digital people screaming bloody murder. I tear my gaze away from the basement doorway, glancing upward. I've never been invited to see the top floor. I have ten minutes until I need to go get Benji, so I decide to take a look.

At the top of the staircase, there's a long hallway leading to a bay window at the opposite side of the house. I pad quietly, peeking into the first room on my left. It's a stereotypical boy's room, like the Marvel Universe threw up on it. I keep going, and open the door on the opposite side of the hall.

I know immediately that this is the daughter's room. Brooklynn. There's a Persian rug tucked beneath a writing desk, an antique-looking wooden bed frame. The duvet is mint green, the curtains some sort of thick velvet. The bookshelf is chock-full of Puffin Classics and Harry Potter. A hardcover copy of Michelle Obama's *Becoming*. I run my hand over the bedspread.

After Brooklynn's bedroom, there is another study, then a bathroom, and finally I reach the door at the end of the hall. I'm not sure what I was expecting, but Professor Miles's room is surprisingly normal. All beiges and neutrals, except for a royal blue throw cushion on the unmade bed. I sit down on the edge, taking in the scene.

There are no family photos downstairs, but Professor Miles has a gallery wall above her bed. There are pictures of Benji and Brooklynn filling most of the spots, and a few of them as a family, before Professor Miles's husband died. I wonder what happened to him. Other than the fact that he died four years earlier, she's never told me a thing about him.

Slowly, I move to the master bathroom. The masterpiece. There's a clawfoot tub, a steam shower, a double sink, and rows and rows of expensive creams, masks, toners and makeup fill the medicine cabinet. On tiptoe, I check out the top row. I spot a box of tampons, some wax strips and, right behind them, several pill bottles. They're all open, all half empty.

They are all prescriptions for Ambien.

Pop culture is pharmaceutical culture, and even though I've never had good enough health insurance to take meds, I know all about Ambien.

I glance in the mirror, hesitating. My skin is clear, but gray with fatigue, and staring at myself, I wonder where I'd be right now if I'd grown up in a house like this. If I'd had someone to make me a smoothie, and buy me small luxuries, and had the space to stretch and grow into the best version of myself.

Life wouldn't be so much of a fucking struggle, but would I still be me? I blink. The image of Saraswati Bhaduri blinks back.

There are four bottles of Ambien. Without hesitating, I take one pill from each of them and slip them into my pocket.

It's nearly time to grab Benji. I turn off the bathroom lights and close the bedroom door behind me. Briskly, I walk the length of the hall in sock feet, glancing in each doorway as I pass it. I reach the top of the stairs. I step my right foot forward, to go down the first step. I feel two hands firmly on my back.

And suddenly, I'm falling.

15.

SARAH ELLIS
Two and a half years earlier

My class is the biggest bunch of assholes.

We all used to eat lunch together every day in the cafeteria, but then the scholarship students arrived and everyone started avoiding eating with Nathan and Andrea, which is pretty harsh. Nathan's objectively handsome and all, and if you showed me a picture I would say "cute," and nod, and not think much of it, but he's what my mother would call an "odd duck," which just makes him super unattractive. And Andrea is fine, like she seems kind of dull and earnest, and sometimes cannot understand social cues, but she doesn't deserve to be excluded.

Nathan and Andrea clued in pretty quickly and started eating lunch by themselves at one of those tables by the bathroom that nobody uses, and Tommy's started sitting there, too. Some of the bitchier girls hollered at Tommy from across the cafeteria to come sit with them instead, because everyone *loves* Tommy, like freaking *loves* Tommy, but he's a loyal guy and made it clear to everyone that the new kids come as a package deal.

If it's possible, I think I love Tommy even more.

It took me a while to work up the courage, but a few months ago I decided to sit with them over by the bathrooms. Journey and Felix ended up tagging along too, and it ended up being really . . . *fun*. Like, it was a nice dynamic with just the six of us, and everyone must have felt that way because now we sit together every day. We even teamed up for Ms. Haley's new group project on Shakespeare. Journey, Felix and Andrea have *The Merchant of Venice*. Tommy, Nathan and I got *Macbeth*. I read it over the weekend. Actually, I read it twice, because I didn't really understand it the first time, and I'm glad I did, because today Ms. Haley called on everyone in class to tell us something about the play we read, something that jumped out at us or that we might want to focus on for our presentations.

I took notes diligently because I know this is the kind of thing that's going to end up on the final exam. Our group was up last. Tommy said something about the three witches that I'm pretty sure he got from Wikipedia, and then Nathan took the position that Macbeth wasn't at fault for what happened to him. Can you believe it? That Macbeth was a *victim* of circumstance.

"What do you mean by that?" Ms. Haley asked him, perching on her desk. "Convince me."

"It was Lady Macbeth's fault," Nathan said. "She manipulated him into killing Duncan. She made him do it. She was . . . like, *crazy*."

Ms. Haley stayed quiet, studying him, and Nathan went star-eyed and swiveled around to Tommy for support.

"Right?" Nathan asked, and Tommy shrugged and said, "Sure, I guess."

I was practically sweating through my shirt, and I think Ms. Haley could tell I did *not* agree, because she asked me if I had a response to Nathan and Tommy's position, and I kind of went off the rails a bit. Now that we're friends, I'm not so nervous talking around Tommy and saying what I actually think, and I told the whole class that Nathan and Tommy were one thousand percent wrong, and that Lady Macbeth is totally misunderstood and vilified for her ambition, and if she was born now, *she* could have killed Duncan herself and become queen, but back then she knew a man had to do it. I said that if anyone was crazy, it was Shakespeare, who couldn't write a strong woman character without giving her a fatal pseudo-crazy flaw because he was goddamn sexist.

Honestly, I don't know how long I talked, but when I was done the whole class was dead silent and Ms. Haley was smiling ear to ear and writing a few of my points on the whiteboard. I was feeling pretty pleased with myself, and Ms. Haley was suggesting we all consider our assigned plays with a feminist lens, when out of the corner of my eye I saw Tommy whispering to Nathan.

"See?" Tommy said, pointing at me beneath the desk. "*Crazy.*"

Nathan howled so loud Ms. Haley interrupted the lecture to ask the class what was so funny. She asked me, really, because I was the one with a red face who was trying not to cry, but I didn't want to get Tommy in trouble, so I kept my mouth shut.

I'm home now. I've had a good cry, a bowl of cereal, and my copy of *Macbeth* stolen out of my locker, which is annoying because I'd written notes in the margins.

I'm starting to realize that even Tommy can be a dumb guy, and not that I'm making excuses for him, but I really think he was just trying to make Nathan feel better for his odd-duck comment about Macbeth being a victim.

If that weak-willed little man was a victim, then it was Macbeth's choice to become one.

16.

I'm halfway down the stairs, disoriented and flat on my ass on the landing. My left hip and thigh are throbbing where I fell. I start to move my limbs, one leg and arm at a time. I sigh in relief. I don't think anything is broken.

When I come to my senses, I look up. My heart is pounding in my ears. I don't know what or who will be standing there. But it's just Benji. He's at the top of the stairs, staring down at me. He's grinning.

"What the hell, man?" I say, massaging my leg. I know I shouldn't swear in front of a child, but I'm too angry to care about that right now.

"I was just kidding. I didn't know you'd fall."

"You were kidding when you pushed a woman down the

stairs?" I hold his gaze as I sit up. His grin disappears into a smirk. He *meant* to push me.

I am babysitting a little psychopath.

"You aren't supposed to be up here." He crosses his arms, taps his sneaker on the hardwood. "I'm telling Mom."

"Go ahead and tell her," I say slowly, picking myself up. "I guess I can tell her about how I fell."

He furrows his eyebrows at me. "It was an accident."

"Has your mom ever taught you about tort liability?"

"No."

"Really? We talk about it all the time in class."

"My mom does?" I nod, and Benji continues. "What does it mean?"

I walk up a few stairs, until we're eye to eye. "It means if I get hurt in somebody else's house, *even* if it's an accident, I can take them to court. Do you know what court is?"

He nods. He looks scared.

"And then the judge gets to decide what happens."

I crouch down slowly.

"Will I go to jail?" I hear him whisper.

"No, Benji. Don't be silly. You're just a kid." I pause. "But . . ."

"But?"

"Your mom might," I lie, biting my lip. "And if the judge is *really* mad, she'll make her pay me a lot of money, too. She might even make your mom sell this *house*."

He looks terrified. Good.

"I won't tell Mom you were upstairs," he says. His voice is small, scared.

I've won. Then again, I always win.

"I think that's a good idea, Benji," I say, after I make him wait a beat. "Now. I think it's time you go practice piano."

My ass is sore, but at least I'm awake. While Benji bashes away at the piano, I start dinner and then read through Ajay's notes on corporate financing on my laptop. I manage to get through most of it. I've never bothered to connect to Professor Miles's Wi-Fi and don't have any distractions.

"Smells good," she exclaims, waltzing through the kitchen. "Did you catch the six o'clock news?"

I close my laptop and watch Professor Miles unravel the scarf from her neck. She always looks like she's in a hurry, even when she's getting home from work.

"I didn't."

"They talked about Sarah Ellis. Do you want to go look?"

Professor Miles loves having the upper hand, but I don't want to give her the pleasure of it. As casually as I can, I stand up from the table. Inside, my heart is racing.

I follow her into the living room and she turns on the local television station. The news is on again. A reporter is standing outside the Windermere police station, and says three times that he has an exclusive with a "source close to the case" before revealing the new information: Ellis's purse, which contained her wallet and phone, is still missing.

"Do you think she was mugged?" Professor Miles asks me, even though I'm still trying to listen to the reporter. "I suppose it wasn't the Ride driver. Surely he would have been arrested by now."

"I'm not sure," I say, still glued to the TV. The reporter

is describing Ellis's purse, the Marc Jacobs cross-body, her white Chanel wallet, and her phone—an iPhone XS with an emerald-green case. He is pleading with the public to contact the Massachusetts State Police if they find any of it.

"Everyone on campus is talking about her," says Professor Miles. "They think she was on Hillmont Road to buy drugs."

I cross my arms, turning to her. I wonder if Professor Miles told "everyone" she was talking to that Ellis was in a bad part of town because she'd gotten into the wrong Ride.

I wonder what everyone will say about me if they find out the truth. I wonder if they'll blame me.

17.

My shift at Gavin's starts at seven, and it's already packed when I arrive. Friday night is pizza night. The guys in the kitchen pump out cheap, edible meals for five dollars a pop. It pairs well with the piss we keep on tap.

"Sara!"

I look up when Gavin calls my name. He's behind the bar with Cassidy, another bartender who I don't work with much. I wave hello as I shrug off my backpack, but she's taking customers' orders and doesn't see me.

Gavin calls my name again and I maneuver through the crowd toward him. When I get to the bar, he gestures to the back hallway without looking at me.

"We need to talk. Go to my office."

He's in a mood, although resting-pissed-face is his default expression.

"It's swamped," I holler back. I'm reluctant to leave Cassidy alone on bar. "Do you want to talk after—"

"Office," he barks. "*Now.*"

I wait until I turn around to roll my eyes. Gavin's office is at the far side of the bar, near the kitchen and bathrooms. I hesitate as I walk past the women's. A part of me wonders what would happen if I pushed open the door. I press my head against the greasy wooden frame, remembering the way Ellis's legs were splayed outside the stall. I shudder, pushing away the memory of her lying there, of us smoking outside, of—

"What are you doing?" A voice startles me, and I whip around. Gavin is standing right behind me.

"Nothing," I snap. "Waiting for you," I try again.

Gavin doesn't answer, brushing past me. I follow him a few paces to his office. As soon as I take the seat opposite him, he tosses an envelope at me.

"What's this?"

"Your final paycheck."

My jaw drops.

"You're fired, Sara."

I sit up in my chair, fuming. "Why the hell are you firing me?"

"Do you know," he spits, "how far up my ass the police are crawling right now?"

"This is about the girl?"

"I don't have CCTV, Sara, in contravention of about ten municipal and state regulations, or so that fucking detective keeps telling me." He wipes spittle from his lips. "I'm screwed."

"But there are cameras everywhere—"

"Do you know how expensive it would be to hook them up? How expensive this whole place is to run?" He slams his palm against the desk. "No. You wouldn't. Because you're a goddamn idiot who took that girl out the back way, and now she's dead."

I want to tell him he's a dick and where to shove it, but I need this job. I need to make rent. I need to eat. I need to pay my fucking tuition.

"Gavin, please." I force out a smile. "It's packed out there. You need me—"

"Don't kid yourself. I could have another little hussy out here in an hour to replace you."

I breathe out, hard. I don't want to sound desperate, but I am. "*Please.* I'll do anything. This isn't fair—"

"You've worked here two months, and you're still on probation," he says blandly. "I don't need a reason. And it definitely doesn't need to be fair."

"I—"

"So get the fuck out of my bar."

I clench my hands so hard they hurt. There's nothing more to be said, or begged. It's over. I allow myself the brief fantasy of slamming my fist into his jaw. And then I leave.

18.

There are students everywhere on Main Street. I kick a loose stone, swearing to myself. Some of them are probably on their way to Gavin's, and a part of me is tempted to call that reporter from the local news and tip him off about where Ellis was last seen alive, tell him there is no security footage of the evening because Gavin is a fucking con artist. The press would skewer him, and if Ellis's parents didn't already know there was no CCTV, they'd sue the shit out of him.

Tort liability applies to tavern owners, too. I learned that on my very first day of law school.

I fucking hate Gavin. He's the scum of the earth, and as much as I want to screw him over, I know involving myself with the press would only make my life more difficult. The last thing I need is my name printed in the papers for my family to find.

I think about going home, but then decide to walk to campus. I'm wired from the double macchiato. I should study. I should concentrate.

I should not let my mind keep wandering back to Ellis.

Gavin blames me for taking her out the kitchen exit. I wish I could remember why we left through the back, but when I picture us leaving, it's like watching a silent movie. I can see Ellis and me together, our arms wrapped around each other like girlfriends, but I can't hear what we're saying. I was exhausted and my mind was elsewhere. At that moment, I was still so desperate to get rid of her; I just wanted to go home.

I stop at a street corner, waiting for the light to change. I'm not far away from the police station, and I wonder yet again where Detective Kelly was today. Was he looking into the ex-boyfriend, Tommy Eagle? Ellis's friends from the bar?

I wish I knew the truth, and if he was on the right track. If Ellis's death was purely by chance, a random encounter, or if someone was after her. If someone is after *me*—

No.

No. I need to buckle down. I need to get Ellis out of my head. Tuition was due today, and I will go to student administration first thing next week to plead for an extension, but even that won't help me if I fail my classes this term.

Shivering, I jog the last block to the law school. I grab a chocolate bar from the vending machine and then make my way to the law library, eating quickly. The space is modern compared to the rest of the building, an extension that juts out the back and gives us blessed law students our own little sanctuary. There are long rows in which to study, each desk separated by a divider and with its own lamp. The walls are all windows, so the books are kept downstairs.

There are just a handful of other students around, so I get the far row to myself. I take the desk square in the middle and spread out my computer, notebook, pens, highlighters and water bottle. For the next two hours, every time my mind floats back to Ellis I pinch my thigh and force myself to think about the task at hand. I have an essay due Monday, but I have a ton of reading to do before I can even start writing it, so I flip through case after case, retaining as much as I can. Intellectual property law is tough at the best of times, and as the coffee and sugar start to wear off, it becomes even harder to grasp. I flip back a page, scanning the text. I read it a moment earlier and don't recall a word of it.

I look up, yawning. Only a handful of students are left. I decide to take a break from the essay and switch back to studying for Professor Miles's corporate financing seminar. I still haven't been able to buy the textbook, but a quick search of the library database tells me there's one available to check out.

I rarely go to the basement. It's poorly lit and hot, and smells like wet dog. Once I'm downstairs, I walk past a small cluster of desks and make my way down the hall between the long, tall shelves, looking for row QD. I stop, glancing behind me. Nothing echoes down here, and as soon as I stop moving, it's dead silent.

I find row QD and run my hands along the shelf until I find the right textbook. I tuck it under my arm, and when I glance up, I catch a shadow of something brushing past the far shelf.

A cold shiver runs down my spine as I realize I am not

alone down here. I hold my breath, clutching the textbook harder. I'm staring down the row of shelves, waiting for the other student to show themself. But nothing happens. No one appears.

I take a step forward, and then another. I can feel sweat sticking beneath my armpits. Was the shadow in my imagination? Could it have been my own shadow? But then—

It happens again. Another shadow. I glance up at the lights, trying to figure out from which direction the shadow was cast, but the halogen bulbs are all pointing in different directions.

"Is someone there?"

I'm quiet, but it's loud enough that anyone within a row or two would hear, would come out and make themselves known. When no one appears, hot dread runs through me like a wave of nausea.

I am not alone down here. I am being followed *again*.

I hold up the textbook like a shield and walk briskly down the hall. I'm at an intersection now, shelves running perpendicular. I glance in each direction, waiting, listening.

"Don't tell me you're scared," I say into the silence.

I don't expect a response, but am infuriated when I don't get one. I swallow the bile in my throat and break out into a brisk walk, ready to fight. Ready for whatever the fuck lies around the corner.

I'm racing down the central aisle, away from the staircase. My eyes dart left and right each time I pass a row. I will whoever it is to appear so I can face them. Finally face *him*. I'm nearing the last row, and I slow my pace when I hear something. A murmur, maybe. A sob.

It's on the other side of the bookcase. I'm sure of it. I hold my breath, ready, and I whip around the corner. My heart nearly gives out at what I see, but it's not what I expected.

The boy's eyes bulge at the sight of me. He leans forward, tapping the girl's shoulder. I avert my gaze, backtracking.

"Sorry . . . "

She gets up from her knees, staring at the floor. Her face is beet red.

"I'm so sorry." I turn around, blushing myself. "As you were."

I can't help but smile as I leave the couple. They look young and in love, and this sexual escapade is probably something they've been working their way up to for months. He won't tell a soul, and she will only talk about it when drunk at a bachelorette party, trying to prove to her friends that she is not vanilla, even though with one glance I can tell that she is.

Upstairs, I find a librarian behind the return desk. It's too late for small talk, and she only opens her mouth to remind me to bring the textbook back within the week, that I have late fees past due on my account. The interaction is regular, and calming, and I feel like myself by the time I return to my seat. I was being paranoid before, racing around the basement like a panicked child.

I yawn, settling into my cubby. I'd left my phone on my desk, and I quickly glance at the home screen. My heartbeat quickens.

I have a missed call from a blocked number, and just then, my phone starts to vibrate.

It's the blocked number again.

I close my eyes and take a deep breath to ward off the panic. Is it him? Does he know? Did he come over to my house that night, and in the dark mistake Ellis for me? Did he—

I flick my eyelids open, blink until I can see straight. I am being paranoid, I repeat to myself. I am overtired, and confused, and nobody is following me. Nobody wants to kill me.

My phone is still vibrating, and I hover my thumb over the green button, willing myself to confirm the truth.

But I can't. I click decline. I pack up my things, and as quickly as I can, I leave.

19.

SARAH ELLIS
Two years earlier

Adam isn't home this summer because a big-time prof hired him as a research assistant, but I needed to talk to him, urgently, so today I called him over and over until he finally picked up.

"What is it?" he barked. "I'm at work."

"Do you have five minutes?"

"No."

I rolled over on my bedroom floor, which is where I spend most of my time these days since the world is on fire and the last four months of my junior-year classes were virtual. On the bright side, my parents tell me, I have had plenty of time to study for the SATs.

"Fine," I said. "Bye—"

"Sorry, Ellis." Adam softened. "I'm here. What's up?"

"How did you know you wanted to be a physicist?" I asked him.

It's August, and my SATs are in one week, and I'll be heading off to college in one *year*, and it's starting to hit me that whatever decisions I make right now are going to change the course of my whole life. I can see myself going in so many different directions, multiple timelines of Ellis where I'm a doctor working for my mother's practice in Windermere, or somebody's housewife in Boston, or building bridges in faraway countries, or being a magazine editor in New York City . . . or a million other things that seem both possible and impossible in the very same breath.

"I just knew I wanted to study physics," Adam answered thoughtfully. "It feels like I was born to be in this field. Do you feel that way about anything?"

I laughed.

"How were your marks this year?"

I'd already emailed him my transcript, but he must not have read it, so I told him how I killed it in English and the social sciences, but scored pretty average in math, chemistry and biology.

"What did Mom say?"

"What do you think she said?"

Adam grinned. "If you don't want to be a doctor, then don't be a doctor, Ellis. Just figure out what you want to do, and have a plan before you tell her. OK?"

I smiled into the phone. Adam was so fucking smart. He just knew how to handle things—our parents, school, girls, stress. He knew *me*.

"OK," I said. "I miss you."

"I miss you, too, Ellis."

I don't know when my face got all wet and salty. I put the phone on mute while I grabbed a tissue and wiped my nose.

I do miss Adam, but I kind of hate him, too. I hate how easy everything is for him. I hate how my mother worships the ground he walks on. I hate how he just left us, and never calls, and never even pretends like he wants to come and visit.

I hate how my big brother hasn't even met my new boyfriend.

Yeah. Tommy finally asked me out. After he called me crazy in class, I stopped making an effort to get him to notice me that way. It wasn't hard. Like, three days later, we went into lockdown and classes went online and I couldn't even freaking *see* Tommy. I pretended like I was OK just being his friend, satisfied by our group's dumb "Zoom hangs," a member of the Journey-Felix-Nathan-Andrea-Tommy-and-Ellis clique that we've sort of turned into. We even have our own WhatsApp group.

But then last month, Felix convinced his parents to let him throw an outdoor party and I finally got to see everyone in person. Normally, I spend the first few hours at parties joined at the hip with Journey, but she recently confessed she has a crush on Felix—I know, *vom!*—so I stayed away in case she wanted to make a move. I was flying solo, and had slipped into the kitchen to make myself another drink when Tommy joined me behind the counter.

"Are you following me?" I asked him. Felix lives on a palatial estate on the edge of Windermere, and the room is so marbled and tall my voice echoed.

"Do you want me to be following you?" Tommy asked me.

I shrugged, and returned to mixing my gin and soda. I thought Tommy was just being his drunk, hot-and-cold self again, but the next thing I knew, I felt his hands on my waist.

"What are you doing?" I whispered.

"Do you want to go upstairs?"

My cheeks reddened as I whipped around to face him. The week before, I bumped into this meathead from Bishop Bailey when I was getting groceries for my mother, and he'd been telling *everyone* about what we'd done in the parking lot. I hated that Tommy had heard. I hated that he'd assume I'd be willing to do that with him, too. I hated that Tommy, who was supposedly my friend, was treating me like trash.

He was standing so close to me, but he still felt far away as he leaned in for a kiss. I missed seeing him so much, and I'd been wanting him to do that for so long, that when he pressed himself against me, I almost forgot myself. I nearly didn't push him off.

"What's wrong?" he asked when I managed to squirm away.

"Fuck off, Tommy."

He laughed. He was drunk.

"Come on, Ellis. I know you want me—"

"I don't want you like that, you asshole." I grabbed my drink, downing the liquid so I wouldn't cry.

"What's your problem?"

I still didn't answer. I'd finished my drink, so I started making myself another one.

"Seriously—"

"I don't want to go upstairs with you."

He took a step closer to me, and when I didn't push him away, he put his hand on the small of my back. "Then what do you want?"

I turned to face him, looked him dead in the eye.

"I want to go on a date."

He didn't flinch, and I wondered why I'd never tried honesty with him before.

"I want you to . . ." I trailed off, trying my best not to stammer. "Be nice to me, and not call me *crazy*."

Tommy's face split open. God, he was handsome when he smiled.

"Still mad about that, huh?"

I crossed my arms.

"Is there anything else you want?"

I bit my lip. I wanted Tommy. Oh, sweet Jesus, I wanted him so bad.

"I want to go on a date," I repeated. "A real one."

"A *date*." Tommy smirked. "I guess we could manage that."

He leaned in, and that time when he kissed me, I let him.

Maybe I am a little crazy. I am crazy about *Tommy*.

20.

I'm outside in the Commons when I hear someone call out my name. I keep going and ignore it.

"Saraswati!"

I stop at the sound of my full name, turning on my heel. It's Ajay, rushing up behind me.

"Sorry," I say, when he's close. "I didn't realize someone was calling me."

"Just another Sara?"

I smile. "What are you doing here?"

"Studying."

"You study on Friday nights?"

"*You* study on Friday nights?" he fires back.

"Touché." I laugh, my body unclenching. "Were you in the library? I didn't see you."

"I was right by the front," Ajay says. "You walked right by me."

We fall into step and head toward Main Street, and I allow myself to forget about the missed calls and what they might mean. I talk to Ajay in that easy way we've gotten the hang of over the past few years. During the last four hours, I've babysat a psychopath who tried to hurt me at one job and gotten fired from another, but Ajay's been at school studying the whole time. No wonder he's at the top of our class.

"How's the essay going?" he asks me. We have the same essay on intellectual property rights due Monday.

I hesitate. "Getting there."

"I summarized all the prep reading just now, if you want it. It'll save you a few hours."

"Ajay," I sigh. "No . . ."

He waves me off, pulling out his phone. After a moment, he looks up and smiles. "There. I just emailed it to you."

"You're too nice."

"There's no such thing as *too* nice."

I shake my head, smiling like an idiot. There is such a thing as too nice. Ajay is the definition.

He asks me if I've eaten as we pass a popular twenty-four-hour diner just off Main Street, and when I take more than one second to reply, he rolls his eyes and makes for the door. We share a milkshake, and although I insist I don't want dinner, he orders us both omelets, hash browns and toast. I think he can tell I'm struggling, that I don't have the funds this year to feed myself properly. Last week, he caught me eating chocolate bars for breakfast two days in a row, and he wasn't able to conceal his shock. Ajay grew up solidly middle class and has the sort of Indian mother who doesn't have anything to do all day except to dote on you. She has freshly made *pakora*, chicken curry and *naan* on the table whenever he waltzes through the door. Now that he lives away from Boston, she also drives in twice a month to fill his freezer.

Ajay doesn't let me pay for dinner, even though I give it a shot; he tells me a gentleman always pays. After, we both sit comfortably in the booth, gazing out the window at the passing students, on their way in or out for the night. I catch him looking at me. When I meet his eye, I expect him to glance away. He doesn't.

"Will you let me walk you home?"

Ajay lives in the opposite direction from me, in a condo development a few blocks toward the rich side of town: Ellis's side. Normally, I'd say no, but today I don't. I'm not afraid—rationally I know *he* is not trying to hurt me—but I still don't want to be alone.

Ajay starts fidgeting and rambling as the streets change and we get closer to my house. He's nervous, although I don't know if it's from the prospect of going to my house or my sketchy neighborhood. At the corner of Hillmont, I remember the police tape quartering off my house. I stop dead in my tracks.

"This is good," I say. "I can walk the rest of the way."

"Do you walk alone at night?" When I don't reply, Ajay grimaces. "Sara, it's dangerous for a woman down here. I'm going to walk you home."

"No. Don't."

"Sara . . ." He kicks a loose rock with his toe, and as we watch it skitter down the street, I can tell that I'm hurting him.

"I'm not trying anything on, I promise. I know you just think of me as a friend."

It's true, but I'm not sure why. A younger, naive version of me might have swooned at the fantasy of a gentleman insisting on paying for my meal and walking me home at night. One that thought about my health and safety, and not just my body. One who cared about me, even if it was only a shell of myself who he truly saw.

I glance up at Ajay, soaking him in. He has laugh lines around his eyes, sprinkles of gray in his pitch-black hair. He is the kind of man you can bring home to Indian parents. He is kind, and hardworking, and true, and . . .

He is everything I am not.

"That's not why I said no." I glance down the road, shivering. He must notice, because suddenly I feel his large, warming hand on my shoulder.

"You know that girl that got killed? Sarah Ellis?" He's nodding when I look back him.

"What about her?"

"I met her the night she died. At Gavin's."

"You did?"

I don't want to say what happened out loud, again, but I do.

"Sara," he whispers, after I've finished, "I'm so sorry." He wraps me in his arms, tight, rocking me right there on the sidewalk. I bite the inside of my lip, and try not to think about the way his body is pressing into mine, how many months—or is it years?—have passed since I've been physical with someone.

"I'm surprised you're still . . ." He releases me from his grip, and suddenly I'm cold. "Functioning."

"I'm not functioning," I say with a laugh. "Not really."

"Do you feel safe?" He hesitates. "Do you want to stay with me for a while? Pack a bag. I'll go pick up my car and come get you."

I'm tempted, but I know I can't. Because it would be admitting I *don't* feel safe. That he might still be . . .

"I'm fine." I smile brightly, to show Ajay I mean it. "Honestly."

"Well, I'm still going to take you all the way home."

Ajay asks me more about what happened to Ellis as we walk the last few blocks, although I don't have any of the answers. I tell him that, last I heard, Detective Kelly had gotten the Ride driver's details from my phone, that it sounded like he was interviewing all of Ellis's friends. I don't mention her mother's theory that it was the ex-boyfriend, Tommy Eagle.

The police tape is still there, as I suspected, and when I glance up to the second floor of the house, I see Zo's bedroom light is still on. I wonder how she's doing, handling the fact that a girl died on her property. I think again that I should really go up and visit.

"This is me." I retrieve my house key from my backpack as we walk toward my entrance. "I know it's not much to look at."

"It's weird," I hear him say. "We've been friends for two years, and I've never been over here."

"Don't worry. I've never had anyone over."

Ajay catches my eye, and I wonder what meaning he's attaching to my statement. Am I leading him on? I've spent two years trying not to, but now my judgment feels clouded. I wonder if giving him hope will make me feel hopeful, too.

"Do you want to see my place?" I ask.

He nods and follows me inside, and I give him the quick

tour. I offer him my desk chair and I sit on the edge of my bed, opposite him. I feel self-conscious that I forgot to make it this morning.

"Tea?"

"I'm OK, thanks." His gaze drifts from my wall art to the mess of papers on my desk to me.

"What do you think?"

"It's cute," he says, his eyes locked on mine. "Just like you."

Cute.

I feel like I'm floating. I don't know if I'm annoyed or flattered by his word choice. I don't know if I want him to stay or leave; if what I'm feeling is longing or exhaustion.

Ajay stands up and so I do, too. He closes the gap between us, and I think he's going to kiss me, but he doesn't. He wraps me in a hug.

"Do you . . ."

I trail off as he holds me. I can hear his heartbeat against my chest. It's steady, like a drum. Mine is out of control.

"I better go," he whispers. His lips brush my forehead as he pulls away. "Good night, Sara."

There is something in my throat that stops me from replying. I wave goodbye, and without another word, he walks out the front door.

There is such a thing as too nice. At least, there is for me.

21.

After Ajay leaves, I collapse onto my bed. My eyes are closed, but suddenly I'm wired. Now that it's nighttime and I'm home, I can't even think about sleep.

I haven't checked my phone in a few hours, and my heart lurches when I see that I have another missed call, but it's not from a blocked number. It's from Detective Kelly. And he's sent me a text, too.

> Hi Sara, this is Detective Kelly. I tried calling you. I'd like you to come down to the station tomorrow. We have a few more questions. Ten am? Thanks.

I type out "I'll be there," but I hesitate before pressing send. As curious as I am about the case, I suspect that Detective

Kelly doesn't know much more than I do. I fetch my laptop from my backpack and google Ellis's name again. A few more articles have gone live over the last few hours, including another one from the *Boston Globe*. It's a think piece about Sarah Ellis the devoted daughter, sister, student and friend. It has a quote from Windermere's mayor, who lambastes the state police for allowing such a tragedy to happen, for not having a single lead to share with the public.

I read everything I can find, again and again, and for the next hour, I'm lost. I'm looking for *something*. I'm down the rabbit hole, and every time I take a breath I'm gasping, unable to think clearly.

There were no cameras, and therefore there's no way for the police to identify who Sarah Ellis was talking to at Gavin's, who might have followed her to my house and killed her. I am one of the few people who could have an answer. I dig my fingers into my temples, praying something is in there. Did Ellis say something to me that would help them with the case? Did she tell me who the killer was—and I just don't fucking remember?

But what if . . . I gulp. What if Ellis's death had nothing to do with *her*? What if—

I stand up so fast my head spins. I cannot go down this road again. I cannot float around this space like a zombie, sleeping on and off as my mind allows, burying myself into a hole. Darker. Colder.

I think about all the things I need to do this weekend, like study, and write that intellectual property essay, and *sleep*, and I toss my phone to the side. I will not respond to Detective Kelly. Ellis is dead. It's a fact and something I cannot change. I need to walk away. From her, from everything. Yet again, I know I need a fresh fucking start.

I dig into my pocket and pull out the four Ambien pills. I don't know if taking one makes me weaker or stronger, but I lack the energy to care. I hide three of the pills in the change purse of my wallet, and I pop the fourth into my mouth. I've never taken Ambien before. It's bitter on my tongue and I nearly gag as I chew it. I hop off the bed and chug down a glass of water, bent over the kitchen sink. I can still taste it, so I grab the whiskey from above the fridge and pour it over ice. Three sips, and it's gone. I refill the glass, and then take it into the bathroom.

A hot shower is what I need. I stand beneath the stream until my skin burns. After, I wrap myself in a plush towel and wander back into the main room.

It can't be hitting me yet. It hasn't been that long. Yet I find myself smiling, even giggling. I don't know if I've ever giggled.

I close the window and then set my half-drunk whiskey down on the floor in front of my wardrobe. I touch each hanger, every garment. My scarves, T-shirts, jeans and fall jackets. The blouses I wear to law school events. My one pair of smart trousers.

My hands stop, and then slide down smooth fabric. A silk kimono, rose and mint green, hand-embroidered in Japan. I brush the hanger aside, and gaze at the next piece. A cocktail dress, strapless and pitch black, with a balconette-style bodice and an asymmetric hem. I lick my lips, remembering, and then pull out the next one, the Saint Laurent maxi in champagne. Mock neck, sleeveless, with crinkled gauze that drapes over my figure like magic.

I push garment after garment aside, until I finally reach the masterpiece. My midnight-blue gown with a high-low hem, embellished lace and halter neckline.

I pull it out from the wardrobe. Letting my jeans pool at my ankles, I step into the dress, then I tug off my shirt before lifting the gown and fastening it around myself.

Everything sways. The room. My hips. I'm in front of the mirror. My body lifts. My back arches as I tie the halter around my neck. I pull the material until it's hard to breathe. Until I can barely feel a thing.

As if in slow motion, I fall back onto the bed. It's like I'm landing in a cloud. The plush, soft duvet. The texture of the dress. I run my fingers over everything, laughing, relishing every curve and touch. I tickle my belly. I shiver as I pull up my skirt and my hands slip beneath fabric. I'm tingling all over, panting. And when I come, finally, I can sleep.

22.

Saturday, October 1

S ara, *where* have you been?"
   I don't remember waking up and answering my phone, but when I blink, it's in my hand and Tina's voice is blaring through the speakerphone. I reach for my jeans lying nearby, tuck them beneath my head. I'm disoriented. I've been sleeping on the floor.

"Hello? Are you there? Where have you been?"

Tina's voice is louder than usual. I clear my throat. It's full of phlegm.

"What do you mean?"

"You haven't called me in a few days."

"I haven't?" I yawn. "Well, why do I always have to be the one calling you?"

"True." On the other side of the line, I can hear Tina rummaging around in the background. "Man, it's dead in here. What are you doing?"

I glance at the clock. It's 11 a.m. Tina always works Friday and weekend mornings to give my parents a break.

"I was sleeping, thank you very much."

"Still?"

"I was studying last night. Late." I swallow, sit up from the floor. "Anyway. What's new? How are classes?"

Tina rambles a bit about her chemistry lab, her hard-ass calculus teacher. She wants to be an epidemiologist and has her heart set on Yale. If we lived in a just world, Tina would be a shoo-in. She has a 4.0 and has been passionate about public health since her first preschool flu season, but it will be hard for her to stand out against those legacy kids, whose grandfathers donate millions to build a new library and ensure their descendants never have to work hard.

Even if Tina doesn't get a scholarship, she says she's still going to go. I worry that means she'll soon be drowning in debt like me.

"Anyway," Tina says, switching topics so suddenly it makes my head hurt. "I have something to tell you. It's very important. I'm coming to visit."

I freeze.

"How about one day this week? After class—"

"Wait, what do you mean you're *coming*?"

"Sound more excited, would you?" Tina scoffs. "Mom and Dad say it's fine with them if it's fine with you. I can come after school, stay the night, and I'll take an early bus and be back in time for class—"

"Tina," I say, a little too forcefully, trying not to sound panicked, "why do you want to come?"

"To *see* you, Sara. You've never invited us to Windermere, you know." She pauses. "I miss you. And *you* haven't been home to visit us . . ."

In months. Since the summer. Since before . . .

"Anyway, if *you* don't miss me—"

"Of course I miss you." I sigh. She is so good at the guilt trip. Mom must have taught it to her. "I'm just surprised."

"Does this week work? Thursday?"

I have no desire for Tina to see my tiny basement apartment, where a girl got killed just a couple of days ago. I don't want her to know about Ellis. I don't want her to see my life here, or know anything about what I have to do to survive.

"No," I say quietly. "This isn't a good time. But I'll come home soon."

"What do you mean it's not a good time?" Tina shrieks. "You're like an *hour* away. And if you have to study, I'll just study next to you—"

"I have to work, too, Tina."

"You mean your research job? Can't you do that whenever?"

I clear my throat. I'd forgotten about the lie I told my family last year to explain where the money was coming from. "Actually, I'm babysitting for a professor right now, too. It's just . . . pocket money . . ."

"Doesn't your scholarship give you a stipend now?"

Fuck. Another lie. I am still groggy and not used to so many missteps.

"The real world is expensive, Tina—"

"You know what *isn't* expensive?" Tina asks. "*Bus* tickets. It's twenty bucks for me to come visit. Why don't—"

"I said no!"

My voice reverberates around the apartment. Tina sulks and doesn't reply. I feel a breeze, and as I shiver, I catch sight of the window by the door.

It's open.

I stand up, racing over. It's chilly outside and I could have sworn I closed it last night. I stick my head out and look out to either side. It faces an alley overrun by weeds that leads over to the garbage bins. There's nothing there. I turn around, trying to recall if I opened it last night when I was tripping on Ambien.

My pulse quickens as I try to calm myself. No one was here. I am being paranoid. I smile. Judging by the state of my room, I *must* have opened it. There are clothes over everything. The bottle of whiskey has lost its lid and is much emptier than it was yesterday. I have no idea what I did or didn't do in here last night.

"Are you still there?" I ask Tina, after a moment.

"Uh-huh."

I can hear her tapping a pen against the counter, rapidly. I open my mouth to say something, but Tina beats me to it.

"I love you. Talk to you later?"

I sigh in relief. "You, too. And yes. I'll call you, soon."

23.

I pick myself up off the floor, tidy my apartment, and after just one sip of coffee, I feel like a new woman. I forgot what it feels like to have a good night's rest.

Detective Kelly texts me Saturday evening, and then again on Sunday, wondering why I haven't turned up at the station. I need to get my life back on track, and ruminating about the night Ellis was killed isn't going to get me—or the police— anywhere. I don't know anything more that will help them. No matter how much I obsess or talk about it, I'm not going to remember or change anything about what has already happened. I decide to ignore the detective's texts and get back to my own life.

I spend the weekend in a trance, deep in thought. I read the notes Ajay shared with me and write my intellectual property essay in record time. I even manage to do the required readings for a week's worth of classes. Although I don't sleep much more over the weekend, I don't feel like I need it. Just one night of good, solid rest was all I needed to keep me going.

First thing Monday morning I hand in my essay over email. It's sunny outside, perhaps one of the last warm days of the year. I pair a summer dress with my denim jacket and head over to campus. Student administration is on the top floor of the law school, a dank room at the end of a long hallway of professors' offices. I'm waiting outside at 9:01 a.m. when the clerk opens the door.

"Do you have an appointment?" he asks. I follow him into the room and watch him take his position behind the reception desk. There's a large mug of coffee right by his keyboard, and I wait until he throws some back before speaking.

"I don't," I say. "But I'm hoping to make one."

The clerk sips his coffee again, and I smile widely. There's no one else around, but still I'm whispering.

"I haven't been able to pay my tuition yet. And I'm hoping to apply for . . . special dispensation."

He nods. He's clearly heard this before.

"Does someone have time to chat?"

The clerk cranes his neck around. "What's your name? I'll pull up your file."

"Saraswati Bhaduri," I say. "But I go by Sara."

"Got it." He scans the screen, and then furrows his brow. "Uh, you're all sorted, Sara. Your payment came in over the weekend."

The blood drains from my face.

"Pardon?" I manage. "I don't think I heard you."

He looks up at me. "I said, you're all sorted. Your tuition for the year has been paid in full."

Can he hear my heart pounding through my chest? I crack a smile, to prove I am calm.

"Oh, that's . . . unexpected." I bat my eyelashes. "I thought it was going to a bit delayed—"

"Well, it arrived Saturday, so you were a day late." The clerk grins. "But we're not going to charge you a late fee for that."

I can't breathe. I suck in air, slowly. In for three. Out for three.

"We sent your benefactor a receipt, but would you like one, too?"

My pulse slows a touch, and I force myself to form words.

"By chance, is it from the same bank account as last year?"

The clerk looks back at the screen and then nods. My stomach sinks.

"It is. Exact same account."

"I'm . . . OK, then—"

"Is something wrong?" The clerk frowns at me. "You look like you're going to faint."

"I'm fine." I beam at him, and then press the back of my hand to my cheek. "Low blood sugar. I forgot to eat breakfast this morning."

I leave the office as quickly as I can and go out into the stairwell. Light floods in from the windows and I squint, sitting down on the top step. It's empty in here and I can hear myself panting, gasping for breath.

This can't be happening. This *can't* be happening.

My cheeks are on fire as I pull out my phone. I swallow hard, typing in the phone number I once knew all too well.

what do you want from me?

A full minute passes before my phone buzzes his reply.

I want you, Sara.

And then again, a beat later.

Did you really think you could walk away that easily?

I did think I could walk away. For two months, I thought
I had.

I stand up, my knees trembling. He figured out what I did.
He has been hunting me ever since. And I would bet my own
life that Sarah Ellis is dead because of it.

24.

His name is Jason Knox.

You would look twice if you came across his profile picture on LinkedIn, or brushed past him on Beacon Street, or served him his Americano on his way to the office. You would find him attractive and take comfort in his broad shoulders and white skin. The gold band on his ring finger. If you flirted, he would mention his wife, Lacey, and show you a picture of the two of them at a benefit last weekend, smiling. Happily married. You would sigh and think how lucky she was to snag a man like that. You would think about him from time to time, until the next daydream flashed you a smile.

Eventually, you would forget he ever existed. Trust me. You are the lucky one. For me, there is no forgetting Jason Knox.

I was halfway through my first year of law school when he

showed up in Windermere. After a term of so-called hybrid learning, the college had resumed in-person classes just in time for the first-year moot court competition, which was an opportunity for us to show off what we'd learned so far about advocacy and the art of persuasion. Jason was among several dozen Massachusetts lawyers in town to guest-judge the competition, and everyone, even Ajay, claimed I was lucky to have *the* Jason Knox assigned to my case.

He was a silver fox with a silver tongue, and a hotshot partner at the most prestigious law firm in Boston. If I impressed him—which I did, of course—then I was supposed to have it made.

"You were fantastic today," Jason said to me at the cocktail hour later that evening. I'd just spent a good half hour schmoozing him, along with a handful of other students, but the rest had finally given up and left us alone. "You blew me away, actually."

"Thank you," I beamed. I already knew I'd impressed him, but it was nice to hear it again. He'd praised me so much during the formal review, my moot partner had gotten jealous and stormed off.

"Have you thought about where you might apply to be a summer associate?"

"I'm from Boston." I took a sip of my red wine and held his gaze. This was the moment I'd been waiting for, and I didn't want to seem desperate. "I'd like to go back."

"Is there an area of law that interests you?"

"I'm a first-year law student," I said drily. "I'm supposed to say it all interests me."

Jason laughed, and emboldened, I continued.

"I understand you practice corporate financing? I'm very interested, and if your firm is hiring, I'd love to be considered—"

"We only hire second-year students," Jason said abruptly. "Maybe next year."

I pursed my lips, annoyed. Out of the corner of my eye, I caught sight of another lawyer who worked at a different Boston firm, not quite as prestigious, but among the top five.

"Well, then," I said, getting ready to make a move, "I hope we can connect next year."

"Is that it?" Jason asked me. I was about to leave, but something in the tone of his voice made me stay. "You'll talk to me next year?"

I laughed, feeling awkward.

"You're done schmoozing me?"

I crossed my arms. "I've already impressed you, and you made it clear you're not going to hire me this year."

"And you want a job *this* year, huh." When I didn't respond immediately, Jason laughed. "You're bold."

"Does that surprise you?"

"Should it?"

"I don't know." I shrugged. "I take it you don't know a lot of women like me."

"Indian women?"

"That." I gave him the up and down. "And women who don't *fawn* over you. Sexually, emotionally." I paused. "Intellectually. You're used to being the first one to walk away. Am I right?"

"Well, when your mother leaves you at the age of five, I suppose that's . . ." Jason trailed off, and suddenly, his demeanor changed. I was enjoying the banter, flirting with the hot older man who'd already ruled me out for employment, but now I was uncomfortable. I couldn't get a read on him.

"I didn't mean to say that," Jason said, after a long pause.

A veil had slipped, ever so suddenly, startling us both. People had the tendency to overshare with me—family, friendly acquaintances, even strangers. But I had the feeling that Jason Knox wasn't the type to go belly up so easily. He guarded his vulnerabilities in a vault.

"And I didn't hear a thing."

"Thank you," he said.

I glanced up from my wine and made eye contact. He was studying me, carefully, and the crazy thing was, it was like he could truly see me. To break the tension, I said, "And even if I did, I'm not giving you any sympathy. We all have mommy issues, and you got pretty far in life despite yours."

Jason laughed again. Loud enough that the group standing nearby turned to look, their ears perked with curiosity.

"I should clarify what I said earlier," Jason said quietly. "The firm does not *officially* hire first years."

I leaned away from him, unsure I liked what he was implying. "And unofficially?" I asked.

"I'm looking for a new assistant."

At the beginning, I really was just his assistant.

Jason emailed me legal questions and I was overflowing with excitement to answer them. I stayed late in the library using Westlaw or LexisNexis to look up the latest precedent set by the Securities and Exchange Commission or investigate a gray area in the Bank Secrecy Act. I compiled my research and analysis into pithy memoranda, and I always delivered early, because I didn't have the luxury of making a mistake. I didn't have any connections, like the mediocre white men in my class, and I wasn't going to graduate in the top percentile, like Ajay. If I wanted a chance at a big-time firm, Jason was my way in. I needed to impress my way through the grunt work until he could offer me a real job.

So I ignored the red flags. I didn't ask Jason why we corresponded by text or his private Gmail rather than his firm account, or even why he paid me, generously, from his personal bank account. I didn't even blink when he asked me not to tell anyone I was working for him remotely, saying it would "look bad" if the legal community knew he and his staff weren't capable of handling their own work. I told my parents I was working for a professor, and Ajay and my other acquaintances at law school that I was doing work for a relative. I played along. I did what I was told. And then Jason told me he needed me in Boston.

He sent a black car to pick me up, and I wore the only suit I owned, which wrinkled as soon as I slid into the back seat. The driver wouldn't speak to me, and I spent the next hour irritated at Jason for having summoned me to the city on short notice. It was late spring and final exams were close. With all the work he'd sent me over the last few months, I'd barely had time to study.

I should have walked away when the driver dropped me off at the Four Seasons on Dalton Street. I should have sprinted when Jason texted me his room number and I realized it wasn't a conference room that I was meant to join him in.

I should have known it was my last chance to escape.

"What are you wearing?" Jason asked me when he opened

the door. He was wearing a plush white robe, and presumably nothing else underneath. Dread creeped over me like a burning-hot liquid.

"A suit," I said stiffly. "Where are we going?"

Instead of answering, he pulled the door wide and beckoned me to follow him inside, which I did despite my better judgment. After the door swung shut behind me, I watched as he grabbed his wallet from the nightstand. He fished out a credit card. I nearly vomited when he threw it on the bed.

"Fuck this, Jason." I shook my head, backing away. "No. I don't know what you think . . ."

I trailed off when I felt his hand on my forearm, holding tight.

"Will you calm down?"

"I'm not a hooker."

"No," he said, "you're not. You're better."

He grinned at his own joke as I withdrew from his grip.

"In my line of work, sometimes I need some assistance."

I gestured at his robe. "I bet you do—"

"I said. Calm. Down."

It was the first time I didn't feel safe around Jason. It was the first time he looked at me like he could hurt me, like he could do so without so much as blinking.

"Where do you see yourself in five years, Sara?"

I grimaced at the question, which was one law students were always told to prepare for in interviews.

"I'm working at the best law firm in Boston," I said evenly. "I'm your senior associate. I'm in the running for partner."

"Is that it?"

"No," I quipped. "I'm a shoo-in for partner."

Jason smirked, grabbing the credit card off the bed. "I find you very charming, Sara. And I invited you here to help me win over some . . . clients tonight. This credit card is so you can buy something decent to wear. That's it."

"You think I'm 'charming'?" I asked, both insulted and overwhelmed. "You don't know me."

"Don't I know you?"

I ground my teeth, watching Jason watch me, and an eerie realization crawled over me like an insect. Jason had judged me that day at the law school, but not just for marks. After one moot court, he knew that I could argue, and coax, and drop into a difficult line of questioning and land on my feet. One glance at my suit, and he understood that I didn't come from much and needed money wherever I could get it. One look at my skin color, and he recognized that I could code-switch as well as I could breathe. One flippant conversation, and he'd learned that I was more than the sum of my parts. I could be a chameleon.

Nobody knew me, not really. But somehow, maybe Jason had figured me out.

"I don't tell anyone about my mother," Jason said. "But I told you."

"That's not my fault—"

"No, that's your power. You see, I'm getting the feeling that you are capable of manipulating anyone you want." He paused. "You always get what you want out of people, don't you? By that expression on your face, I'm guessing I'm right."

I took a step backward, disoriented. Sure, I understood how to read people's fears and desires with a single glance, and yes, from time to time, I used that knowledge to my advantage. But it *wasn't* manipulation. It was a manner of speaking. It was never deception, rather *per*ception. It was not exploitation, but emotional fucking intelligence.

"Take a compliment, Sara," Jason continued. "I'm offering you a chance to work for my more lucrative dealings. To actually put your skills to use. After you graduate, do you want to push paper around and make just enough money to pay your mortgage?"

I could feel my heartbeat pounding in my ears. He was goading me and I didn't like it.

"Or. Do you want to work for me? Where the real money is?"

I let the carrot dangle for a moment. I didn't want to seem as desperate as I felt.

"*If* I come with you," I crossed my arms, speaking slowly, "what will I do exactly?"

"You'll eat dinner. You'll be charming."

"Who are the clients?"

Jason said the names and a knowing glance passed between us. I'd heard of two of them before. The first was a Massachusetts state senator frequently under suspicion for campaign finance violations, although each accusation had gone unproven. The second was the chief executive of a major pharmaceutical company, who had been named in the Panama Papers.

"Dinner," I repeated. "That's it, really?"

"Just be charming."

He beamed at me, his beautiful mouth turning up into a smile. "That's it."

I wondered if that was really all I'd be expected to do, and then how I would pay for next year's tuition if I turned the opportunity down. Jason had kept me busy the last few months with legal research work. Because of him, I was not prepared for final exams, and there was no way I'd be getting another scholarship.

"You promise?" My voice cracked, making Jason grin.

"I'm not going to try to fuck you, Sara."

My skin crawled as he stepped forward, pressed the credit card into my palm.

"Believe it or not, I love my wife." He paused, eyeing me. "Besides, your tits are too small."

Some people say that, at the time, they didn't realize when they were at a momentous crossroads, but I knew.

I knew who his clients were, and what working with them would make me. I knew that if I stepped into that deep, murky pool, there would be no going back. I'd get wet, and I might be ruined. But, back then, I thought I might never get anywhere if I didn't try.

25.

Monday, October 3

I arrive at class fifteen minutes late and slip into the empty seat next to Ajay.

I open my laptop. I keep my eyes fixed on the PowerPoint presentation projected on the front screen, and although I can hear everything the professor is saying, my mind is far away. Racing. In a dull, dreamlike panic.

Why did I think Jason would leave me alone, that I could go back to the way my life was before?

The professor is talking about mergers and acquisitions, but in my head, I'm imagining Jason standing there in the dark, outside my house. Waiting for me.

Was it him? Did he realize too late that he'd grabbed Ellis instead of me? But if he wanted me dead, then why had he just paid my tuition? Why hadn't he come for me yet?

I press my palms against my face until it hurts and think back to when I woke up to an open window. To the footsteps trailing me home from Professor Miles's house. The shadows in the library basement.

I shake my head, trembling.

Jason likes to play games. I wonder which one we're playing now.

I can feel Ajay staring at me throughout class, but I keep my head down, taking notes as best I can. The class drags on endlessly, but finally, it's over.

"How was your weekend?" he asks me, as soon as the professor wraps up.

I turn to him, stuff my belongings into my backpack. "Fine. You?"

"It was all right." He smiles. "I thought I might see you at the library."

The class clears out around us, but Ajay keeps talking, jabbering. About the essay we just handed in. The nonfiction book on evolution he started reading the evening before. I want to get up and leave, too, although I'm not sure where I'm even going. I tap my foot, smiling. He's mumbling something now. I'm distracted. I have no idea what we're talking about.

"So, what do you think?"

I hesitate. Shit.

"About?" I ask.

"Dinner, Sara." Ajay pauses. "Tonight maybe? My place?"

He must notice the look on my face. He flinches.

"Sorry, never mind." Ajay stands up, and I rush to join him. "I misread this. Seriously. Forget I said anything—"

"Wait." I tug on his jacket sleeve until he looks at me. "Don't be sorry, Ajay. I'm just . . . surprised."

"Right . . ."

"I'm having a weird day," I say finally. "Can I take a rain check?"

"A rain check," he repeats.

I nod, trying to appear earnest. Right now, I can't think about whether or not I want to have dinner with him. I just need some air. I need to leave.

"Ask me again, OK?" I insist. "Just not today."

Outside the lecture hall, I slip away from Ajay when he turns toward the library. There are students everywhere, clusters of them clogging up the hallways. I weave through them until finally I'm outside.

It's a warm morning and the Commons are just as packed. I turn away from everyone, desperate to be alone. I need to walk. I need to *think*. But when I look up, I realize that isn't going to happen.

"You were right. She got into your Ride." Detective Kelly offers me a lukewarm smile as I stop short in front of him. Less than a week ago, he needed to "verify" my version of events. Today, I wonder if I'm the only hope he has.

"You didn't show up," he says.

"I told you everything I know."

"Besides the driver, you were the last person to see Ellis alive." He pauses. "You could know a lot more than you think."

"How? I was high."

"You know as well as I do there's no CCTV footage." The

detective crosses his arms. "We need to know everyone who was at Gavin's that night, who Ellis might have talked to."

"I don't work there anymore. Ask Gavin—"

"We already have," Detective Kelly snaps. "I understand he let you go. A real class act, your old boss."

"You're telling me," I mumble.

I know Detective Kelly won't leave me alone until I agree to the interview. I have several hours until I need to pick up Benji from school, so I give in and follow the detective to his car. It's unmarked and he lets me sit in the front, but we don't talk. We listen to NPR.

We enter through the back entrance of the station. Apparently, there are reporters hanging around out front, trying to get a lead. Detective Kelly takes me to the same room I was in before and brings me a cup of coffee. He remembers the milk. I drink it while I flip through a binder of photographs he lays out in front of me, tells me to flag any that ring a bell. There are no names, just faces. They are college-aged and mostly white. After a few minutes, they start to look exactly the same.

"She looks familiar," I say, a few pages in. I tap on the girl's memorable red hair.

"Did you see her with Sarah Ellis that night?" Detective Kelly asks slowly. "What was the interaction like?"

"I don't know."

His face drops.

"I've definitely served her before. But that night? I have no idea if she was there, or with Ellis."

Detective Kelly ruffles his hair. He looks pained, and I can tell just by looking at him that the police don't have any leads. There isn't a single photograph in here that I was supposed to identify, or confirm. They are fishing.

"What about Tommy Eagle?" I ask after I get to the end of the binder. I wonder if I flipped past his photo.

Detective Kelly looks at me strangely. "Why do you ask?"

"I overheard Ellis's parents yelling at you the morning after she died."

Detective Kelly stands up quickly. I think he's about to leave, but when he gets to the door, he closes it.

"What do you know about Tommy?" he asks.

"I don't know anything. But I heard her mom tell you she thinks it's him."

"You shouldn't have been listening."

"The door was open."

"I suppose it was."

Detective Kelly returns to the chair next to me and blows air through his teeth. He seems exhausted. He also looks like he's in the mood to have a chat.

"If we're done, can I get a ride?" I ask.

"Sure. Back to campus?"

I nod. "Yeah, I have to study before work."

The detective looks over quizzically, and I shrug.

"Gavin's was my second job. I also babysit in the afternoons."

"Why am I not surprised?"

"We do what we gotta do, right?" I shrug. "My parents run an ethnic grocery store. I don't want that kind of life."

"Grocery store, huh?" The detective glances over at me. "Mine have a gas station."

"Here in town?"

"No. It's quite remote. Windermere is the big city for me, if you can believe it."

I swivel to face him, carefully, so our knees don't touch. "Are you happy here?"

"Not really. You?"

I shrug. "I thought so. I thought . . ."

Detective Kelly drums his fingers on the table, waiting for me, and I coyly glance down at my lap. I, too, am fishing. But for what—the truth about what happened to Ellis? For an answer that will absolve me of the guilt that she died instead of me?

"What are you thinking, Sara?" the detective asks. He leans forward, chin in hand. Elbow on the table.

"I guess I'm thinking about Ellis. I can't stop thinking about her."

For once in my life, I'm telling the truth.

"You and me both."

"I just want to know what happened to her." I pause. "I suppose if you have me in here looking at photographs, then it wasn't the Ride driver."

"Nope. He couldn't have done it. His GPS shows he didn't stop for more than fifteen seconds to drop off Ellis. He rushed her out of the car and then went to pick up another customer."

"*Detective*," I chide. "Were you supposed to tell me that?"

"No."

He looks serious for a moment. Did I miscalculate? I wait for him to look up at me.

"I'm not going to tell anyone," I say. "Who would I even tell?"

"I suppose you haven't told reporters that she was at Gavin's and took your Ride back to Hillmont. And you could have. You know more than most."

I scan his face, calculating. He meets my gaze.

"You were the one who tipped off the local reporter, weren't you?" I smile. "You leaked the information about Ellis's missing wallet and phone."

Detective Kelly smirks at me but doesn't confirm. I know I'm right. I know I'm pushing my luck.

"I understand why you did it." I shrug. "But what I don't understand is why you're not investigating Tommy." I lean forward, hunching. "You said it yourself, Detective. It's usually the ex-boyfriend—"

"Can you keep a secret?" Detective Kelly interrupts.

"Of course," I whisper.

He throws a quick glance at the door before answering me. "Tommy—the ex-boyfriend, the only real lead we had—couldn't have done it. He was at a Bruins game. The night Ellis died, there's stadium footage and several alibis that show he was miles away."

My knees start to quake.

It isn't the Ride driver. It isn't Tommy Eagle. It's not one of the obvious choices, and therefore it's becoming more and more likely that Ellis died because of me.

"Anyway, I better get you back to campus," I hear Detective Kelly say. "Ellis's parents are due to drop by again for another *chat*. I don't want them to see you."

"Do they know about me?" I ask quietly.

"They know Ellis mistakenly switched Rides with another Sarah, but they don't know who you are." The detective smiles at me, gathering his papers. "I won't be telling them your name for the time being. You never know how grieving parents will behave."

"They blame me," I say quietly, and the detective doesn't respond.

I lean my weight into the table as I consider my words. Ellis's parents deserve to know what happened to their daughter, and the police may never figure it out if I don't tell them the truth.

But what is the truth? Jason might have killed Ellis by mistake. Jason very well might kill me next.

Jason isn't the only one with their hands dirty.

"What if . . ." I trail off as my armpits start to dampen. I want to lead the detective in the right direction, but I'm not ready to give myself up.

"If?" Detective Kelly prompts.

"What if Ellis wasn't murdered by anyone she knew, but it wasn't a random attack, either."

"I'm not following."

I look up. "She was killed at my house, Detective. She was in my Ride. We were basically wearing the same jacket—"

"So?"

"So. What if I *am* to blame? What if it was supposed to be me who died?"

Detective Kelly's face splits open, a smile. I'm baffled.

"Are you feeling survivor's guilt? Is that what this is, Sara? You have nothing to feel guilty about."

I narrow my eyes at him. It's the first time I've heard him sounding confident about the case.

"Look," he says, lowering his voice, "between you and me, Ellis was nothing like what her parents have been telling us, or what they're saying in the papers. She would meet up with men, sometimes much older, and go with them willingly. She wasn't a nice young lady, if you know what I mean."

"Isn't that victim blaming, Detective?"

"Not at all. Look at the facts. Ellis was wild. She was never where she was supposed to be. She lied to her parents constantly." He pauses. "And she was known to spend her time with unsavory characters."

"*So?*"

"We looked into you, too, Sara. We know all about you."

My pulse quickens.

"And what did you find out?"

"That this *case* has nothing to do with you." Detective Kelly barks a laugh. "You are nothing like her. Christ, Sara. You're a law student. You're making something of yourself." He pauses again, studying me. "You're a good Indian girl who got into the wrong Ride."

My body clenches as I try to stay calm.

Good Indian girl?

Beyond understanding the basics of my blue-collar immigrant background, he hasn't investigated a thing about me. But I'm the reason Ellis is dead. My lies. *My* "unsavory characters." Who cares who she was and what she did—that girl didn't deserve to die.

"You're not listening to me," I say. I can't hide my exasperation, but he doesn't even seem to notice it. "I'm the one who was supposed to die."

Detective Kelly stares me down, his face unreadable. Is this it? Is this the moment I come clean?

"Can you think of a reason someone would want you dead, Sara?"

Yes, I can think of a reason. A very good reason.

A dangerous man has me in a choke hold. We are playing a game and I don't know how to beat him, which pieces are in play, when he'll make his next move.

But I do know he might have killed Ellis. I know that if I tell the detective my suspicion, I could bring an end to all of this right now.

The words are right there, on the tip of my tongue. But I let them sit, growing sour and stale. I swallow the bile in my throat and avert my eyes.

"I didn't think so," the detective says, after a full minute goes by and I don't speak up. "Now let's get you back to school."

26.

Tuesday, October 4

I toss my laptop away from me. It lands with a bounce at the foot of my bed, and I lie back, sighing. It's the middle of the night and I haven't slept a wink. I can't.

All I can think about is Ellis.

Deep down, I knew Jason wouldn't let me go. I already knew that I could be the reason Ellis is dead.

The detective thought I felt survivor's guilt; that doesn't even begin to describe it. Ellis had no part in this story. She is supposed to be back home in the Orchards, living a foreign life that was hers to live. She wasn't supposed to die. I was.

I am desperate to know who she was. I wonder if it's my way of punishing myself.

I retrieve my laptop and go back online, but nothing has changed. Her social media is still private, and except for the funeral announcement, the newspapers keep running the same old story in different words: The death of such a promising young woman is a tragedy. The police have no leads. Our beloved little Windermere will never be the same again.

Sleep finally comes to me, but it's full of dreams of Ellis. We're walking hand in hand down Main Street, in silence, in the middle of the road, and then suddenly we're in Boston. In my childhood bedroom, which I shared with Tina, whispering beneath the duvet on my twin bed.

I toss and turn. What is she telling me? What don't I remember?

I wake up in a cold sweat before dawn. I take a shower and nearly text Ajay to let him know I'll be missing class that day, but I don't. He'll ask me why.

He'll question if it's a good idea for me to go to Ellis's funeral.

The church is on the edge of campus. A plaque out front states it's the oldest building in town, more than two hundred years old. I've walked by here hundreds of times and I've never even noticed it.

I arrive just five minutes before the service starts, and most of the pews are already full. I take an empty seat at the end of the third-to-last row, my head down. I don't know what I'm doing here. Almost everyone is white, well dressed, the bread and butter of upper-class New England. I can hear laughing among the murmurs somewhere off to the side. It's like nails against a chalkboard. It's disturbing, out of place.

It's exactly how I feel.

The minister begins the service. I'm not religious by any means, but his voice calms me. His prayers—ever so briefly—bring me some peace. After, he invites a red-headed girl named

Journey up to the pulpit. I recognize her from the detective's photo album. Crying, she tells the audience how much she misses her best friend, and shares stories about them growing up—tales that are more meaningful now that they're over. I don't know if I've felt that strongly about anyone other than Tina. I wonder if she's faking it.

Next, the minister calls on Dr. Ryan Ellis, and I squirm forward, leaning slightly into the aisle. Up at the front, I see him unwrap his arm from his wife and stand up. She whimpers, and a young man on the other side, who must be Ellis's brother, Adam, grabs her, holds her weight. I can hear them both crying from the back of the church.

The father takes his position at the front. He paints a picture of Ellis and I wonder how much of it is true, what can and cannot be seen through a father's rose-colored lens. Ellis as a young girl with pigtails, playing happily on the seesaw. Ellis, a first-rate tennis player and future pediatrician. Ellis, who has a caring and loving spirit that now belongs to god.

I shake my foot, impatient. But what about the real Ellis? I want to know her, but I can't understand why. What could I possibly learn that would make me feel better that she died instead of me?

Or maybe I don't want to feel better. Maybe I want to feel worse.

Suddenly, I feel the hairs on the back of my neck stand up. It prickles, and instinctively I crane my neck around. A man sits behind me in the very last row, and he averts his eyes when I look at him.

He's not so much a man as a boy, someone floating between his early and mid-twenties, adolescence and adulthood. He has brown hair and eyes, a jawline that marks him as convention-ally handsome. He looks familiar.

I study him, as discreetly as I can. I definitely recognize him, but from where? Have I served him at Gavin's?

Was he in the detective's photo album?

I wonder if he was looking at me. I wonder who he was to Ellis.

Gasps from up front make me whip around. Ellis's dad has collapsed into the podium, sobbing. The minister is holding him up, and Ellis's brother is up there in a flash. He's crying, too.

I can't breathe, watching all this sadness. The space is too cramped. There are too many people, and they're all here because of me. The whole church is murmuring in concern, watching Ellis's father being taken back to his seat. Their atten-tion diverted, I slip out the back.

The boy who was sitting behind me is already gone.

There are reporters with news cameras waiting outside the church. I pull my hood up and dart across the road when one of them spots me. I hear her calling after me, asking me how I knew Ellis and if I'd like to offer a quote. I ignore the voice and keep going.

On my way back to Hillmont Road, I text my parents and Tina a friendly, vague message checking in. With all the media coverage of Ellis's murder, my family is likely to hear about it. I don't want to be the one to tell them, but when they do find out, I want them to think I am safe.

When I'm standing in front of my house, I don't take the side path leading to my basement suite. Instead, I walk right up to the front door and ring the bell.

Zo takes a full minute to answer the door. It creaks open, one inch at time, and it's so dark inside I can only see her silhouette. Hunched over like that, she's even tinier than I am.

"Rita?" Zo steps forward into the light. She smiles at me, her whole face crinkling into a complex pattern of laugh lines. "You're a sight for sore eyes."

"It's Sara." I smile. Rita is Zo's former tenant, who moved out years ago.

"*Sara*. Sorry, hun. Of course!"

"How are you, Zo?"

"Never better." She widens the door and I step into the foyer. "Although the doctors disagree."

I follow her into the sitting room, politely declining her offer of tea. She turns off the TV and sinks into her recliner.

"I saw your name in the paper," I say, taking the sofa opposite. "I'm sorry I didn't come earlier to check on you."

"Nonsense. I'm doing just fine. It's that poor girl that's . . ." She shakes her head. "I should have rung *you* to see if you were OK. Are you, dear?"

"I'm OK," I say.

"Please tell me you don't walk home alone anymore at night—I've never liked it. This area is fine for us seniors, who keep the door locked and never go out much to begin with, but you youngsters—"

"I'm careful, Zo. Don't worry."

"Well, I hope so." She sighs. "My sons aren't too happy with me right now. They've been bothering me since the *nineties* to sell this house, and this poor girl's death—well, they're right on my case again. They want me to move in with one of them. In *Boston*."

She makes a face of disgust and it makes me laugh.

"Fat chance of that happening, Rita. I wasn't a law-abiding citizen for eighty-one years just to get locked up on death row!"

"*Zo.*" I roll my eyes.

"I lock the door at night. I close the windows. And I say a prayer. That's all the protection I want—let the bastards come."

"No one would go up against you," I say. "If they know what's good for 'em."

"Don't *I* know it."

"Zo," I say, sitting forward, "I gotta ask. What did you see that night?"

She holds my gaze and I wonder what the hell I'm doing here, bothering a forgetful old woman. But I can't stop myself. I'm desperate to know Ellis, to see clearly what happened to her.

"I'm sorry," I say. "I don't know why I'm asking. You've probably gone over it a million times."

"Don't apologize. It's disturbing, being so close to something so horrific. Of course you're curious." She places both of her hands in her lap, slouching. "But to be honest, I don't know any more than what I said to the police and those reporters."

"I see."

"I heard the shouting. It sounded like a fight—what do you call it—a *domestic* disturbance." She nods. "And then I fell back asleep and was woken up by all those police sirens outside."

"What were they shouting about?"

"Heavens, I'm not sure. I wasn't listening all that close. It was quite upsetting."

"I'm sure it was." I pause. "Could you see anything?"

Zo shakes her head. "I couldn't see *them*, if that's what you're getting at. I've shrunk, you know. Even on tiptoes I can't see out those damn high windows, and the police wouldn't let me out the door. The officers came inside to take my statement, and then told me to go back to bed. Can you believe it? As if I could sleep after something like that."

I gaze softly at Zo, thinking about that night. Wondering what happened on our doorstep before I arrived home.

"The tea!" Zo exclaims. She attempts to stand up, but halfway up her knees give out and she falls back into her seat. "You wanted tea," she says weakly. "Didn't you, dear? I can't remember."

"Only if you let me make it, Zo."

I return from the kitchen a few minutes later with two souvenir mugs full of orange pekoe. Zo has drifted off, and when I set the tea down on the coffee table, she wakes with a start.

"*Rita?*"

Zo stares at me blankly as I remind her my name is Sara, that she invited me into her house.

I want to know Ellis, but Zo is not the answer. Even if she is, and she saw something that night that would help the case and my conscience, I doubt she realizes it.

27.

Wednesday, October 5

Every time my phone rings I jump. A shiver shoots down my spine, and cold dread runs through me as I check the call display. I wonder if it will be the blocked number, Jason finally telling me my time is up, but it never is. It's my parents, checking in on me. It's Tina, wondering what I'm up to. It's Ajay, wondering where I was all day, if I need anything, if I'm OK.

I am not OK. I am a mess. But I don't want Ajay to come over, so I don't reply.

In the morning, I slip on a Windermere campus hoodie and walk south along Main Street until I get to the Orchards. Dr. Ryan Ellis and Dr. Beverly Ellis are unlisted, but the neighborhood is small. I easily find my way back to the house with the cherry-red door and shutters. There is a giant oak tree in the front yard, half of its leaves in reddish piles on the lawn. I don't know what I expect to find here, but I walk up the front path and ring the bell before I have a chance to back out. I'm sweating under my clothes. This is not a good idea, yet here I am.

My phone buzzes in my pocket. It's Ajay, wondering why I'm not in class again. Just then, the front lock clicks. I put the phone away.

"Hello?"

Ellis's mother answers the door, and I'm momentarily speechless. She's wearing yoga pants and a loose, flowing cardigan that drips down to her knees. Her nose is red and there are dark circles underneath her eyes. What the hell am I doing here?

"Do I know you?" she asks.

"Sorry. Hi." I clear my throat, force myself to continue. "Dr. Ellis?"

"Yes?"

"I was a friend of your daughter's," I say. "I'm . . . so sorry for your loss."

"Were you at the funeral?" she asks.

"I was, yes. But I didn't get a chance to offer my condolences." I pause. "In person."

Dr. Ellis nods, touching her fingers to her cheek. She studies me like she's trying to place me.

"I'm Saraswati," I say.

I hold my breath as she studies me. She knows that a girl with the same name as her daughter mistakenly took her Ride home. I wonder if she'll deduce my nickname and put two and two together.

"Saraswati," she repeats, pronouncing my name perfectly. "It's nice to meet you. Please. Come in."

Inside, the curtains are drawn. The house is grand and spotless. She points me to a sofa in a room just off the main foyer. She sits on the floor, stuffing a cushion beneath her bum.

"I've been making a scrapbook." She flips open a photo album, points to a picture of Ellis at maybe nine or ten, in a paddling pool with her brother. "This was taken at our old house," Dr. Ellis says. "Did you ever visit us there?"

I shake my head. "Ellis and I met . . . recently."

"You're a college friend?"

"Yeah."

"That's why I don't know you." She pauses. "Did the police interview you?"

I don't know what she's really asking me, but I decide not to lie. I will stay as close as possible to the truth.

"They did," I say. "Detective Kelly, I think his name was?"

She looks relieved, turns back to her scrapbook. "Good. He said he would talk to everyone, but I don't trust that man. He's in way over his head."

I take a seat on the couch, eyeing her.

"You know that she wasn't actually on Hillmont Road to buy drugs, right?" She flips a page of the scrapbook, roughly. "I'm aware that's what everyone is saying about her. I want to tell the reporters the truth—about that damn *Ride*—but Detective Kelly said it will affect the integrity of the investigation. *What* investigation? Idiot . . ."

She goes on for a while about the incompetence of the state police, and I don't interrupt. She says Ellis's purse and phone are still missing, and that while investigators have most of her photographs, emails and text messages, they don't have access to any content she didn't back up to the cloud. Next, she tells me that her husband is out calling in a few favors, trying to go above Detective Kelly's head. I don't need to think very hard about what favors she means. Political favors. A household like this isn't just well-off, they have inherited wealth. Clout. Their privilege is as old as history itself.

She stops talking at some point and I don't prompt her to keep going. It wouldn't feel good to manipulate a grieving mother, someone going through such unimaginable pain. Dr. Ellis continues working on the scrapbook, and eventually, I kneel down on the ground on the other side of the coffee table. She nods, signals that I have permission to join her. The smooth wood is covered with albums and tall stacks of photographs of Ellis. I pick up the pile closest to me.

In every picture, she is smiling. Dimples, full cheeks and those show-stopping blue eyes. In most of them she's wearing a pleated skirt, loafers, a white polo and a cardigan: the uniform of well-bred, private-school girls. Her hands are always linked with a friend's, or waving at someone off camera, or playing the cello, or holding a tennis racket.

She is full of joy. She is absolutely radiant.

I press my hand over my mouth. And she's dead.

I ask myself again: *Why* did I come here? To find out more about Ellis, or to punish myself? To force myself to see what *I* caused?

Quickly, I set the pile of photos down and pick up another. The one on top is a class photo, with three rows of uniformed teenagers standing with good posture. Quickly, I scan the faces and find Ellis's. She's in the middle of the bottom row, and she's standing very close to a handsome boy with brown hair who is not looking at the camera, but gazing over fondly in her direction. His lips are in a half smile, as if he's whispering something to her, distracted by her presence. I squint, studying him, and my hand starts to shake when I recognize him. He was the boy sitting behind me at the funeral.

He is Tommy Eagle.

"That one is from her senior year," I hear Dr. Ellis say. I look up. There are tears in her eyes. "She was so excited to go to college."

"I bet." I smile.

"When she was a little girl, she wanted to go to Duke, like me and her father." Dr. Ellis shakes her head. "He may not have killed her, but he ruined her life."

I gesture at the boy in the photo, setting it down. "Tommy?"

She nods. "Before Tommy, she used to *talk* to me. We used to be best friends. But then they started dating and it was all 'Tommy said this,' and 'Tommy said that.' 'Tommy is going to stay in town for college, so I'm going to, too.'"

I nod, unsure of what to say.

"It was puppy love. Infatuation. I get it. I went nuts over the first guy I dated, too. But she wouldn't listen to reason. She made her whole life about this useless, ignorant boy—and then last year, out of the blue, Tommy dumps her. Tells her he doesn't love her anymore."

Dr. Ellis's voice is as cold as ice.

"I could have killed him."

I swallow hard, meeting her eye. "It's hard to let go. When someone has a hold on you like that. It can feel like a noose."

Dr. Ellis holds my gaze, nodding. "That's exactly it."

She thinks I'm talking about an ex-boyfriend. She thinks the man who has a hold on me is just a nuisance, a stupid little boy like Tommy.

"Were you able to walk away?" she asks me.

Yes, I want to say, because I did. Two months ago, I'd finally had enough and I left. I did what I needed to do, and I let myself believe that I had gotten away with it. That I could leave the ugly past where it belonged.

"I'm working on it," I say.

Dr. Ellis turns back to her album, and after a few minutes, I leave her in peace.

Deep down, I know Jason is coming for me. Maybe tonight, or next week, or maybe he'll make me wait. It's just a game to him, but my life is at stake. I cannot lose. Whenever he shows up, I need to be ready.

28.

Wednesday, October 5

I nearly forget that I have to pick up Benji from school, but I remember in time to arrive only ten minutes late. Later, I bail the minute Professor Miles walks in the front door, with an excuse about having to leave on time, because I don't have the bandwidth for her chitchat, to yet again speculate about who could have killed Ellis.

I walk toward campus as I check my voice mail. Ajay has called seven times and left seven messages pleading for me to call him back. He just wants to know if I'm OK. He'll be studying right now, so I avoid the law school and cut straight through campus toward the student center. I buy a sandwich from the cafeteria and find an empty table. My fingers tremble as I unwrap the sticky plastic wrap.

I am not OK, and if Ajay were to confront me with that terrifying question right now, I might just tell him the truth.

I'm reluctant to go home. I don't want to be afraid of Jason, but I am. He is coming for me, and there is nothing I can do about it. He could be waiting for me in my apartment right now.

I go through the motions of eating. Bringing the sandwich to my lips. Biting. Chewing. I don't taste a thing. When it's done, I throw the plastic wrapping in the bin and sip my coffee. I think about pulling out my laptop or a textbook, but an hour passes and I never do.

My neck is getting stiff. I shift uncomfortably and reach my arms back, stretching. As I swivel my head from side to side to loosen the muscles, I catch sight of a familiar face one table over and back.

I squint. Are my eyes playing tricks on me? I scan his brown hair, his eyes, his jawline. He has a generic face, but it's definitely him. It's Tommy Eagle. I recognize him from the funeral, the photo from Ellis's house. I wonder how long he's been sitting there.

I angle my body slightly toward him, trying to get a better view. He's wearing dark denim jeans, a gray hoodie zipped partially open, revealing a white T-shirt. He's reading a book, sitting alone and hunched over the table. My curiosity gets the better of me, and I lean over to look at the cover.

"Can I help you with something?"

My face turns red as I recoil away from him. He's smiling wryly, still looking at his book. He flips the page, bookmarks it and then sets it down on the table.

"I wanted to see what you were reading," I say sheepishly. "Sorry."

"*Macbeth*." He turns to look at me for the first time. "Have you read it?"

"A long time ago."

"Did you like it?"

I'm surprised by his directness. "I think so. Can I be honest with you, though?"

He nods.

"I can never remember which story is *Macbeth* and which one is *Hamlet*. They both die at the end, though, right?"

"Right." He looks bemused. "Although the hero's death is inevitable. In tragedies, at least."

"Is English lit your major?"

Tommy hesitates before answering. "Can I be honest with *you*?"

I nod.

"I'm reading this for fun. Shakespeare is what I do for fun. Are you judging me?"

"I wouldn't dream of it." I smile, and it suddenly occurs to me that we're flirting. I slump down, confused.

"What's your name?"

"Sara," I say, after a beat passes. "It's nice to meet you . . . Tommy."

He looks shocked that I know his name, and all I can do is shrug.

"I saw you at Ellis's funeral. You were sitting behind me, right?"

"Right." There's an edge to his voice, sadness in his eyes. "I thought you looked familiar. I left early."

"I noticed. Why?"

"Nobody wanted me there." There's an awkward pause before he speaks again. "You're a new friend of Ellis's?"

"Not really. I only met her once."

"Just once?" He smiles. "She must have made quite the impression on you."

"She did." I smile. "She . . ."

Tommy stares at me curiously, and I tell myself to stop talking. To stand up, pack up my bag, wave goodbye and leave. Ellis is dead, and talking to her ex-boyfriend won't get me anywhere. It can't change the past.

Then why do I want to stay?

I find myself telling Tommy about the night she died. It's the fourth time I've said the story out loud.

I was numb when I told Detective Kelly the morning after. I recounted what happened like I was telling him about a novel I'd read, remembering the events only as I said them out loud. Professor Miles and Ajay both got nothing but the facts, in as few words as possible. Sentences that conveyed information but not emotion. Only the bare bones of reality, of what happened to Ellis.

But with Tommy, it's different. Somehow, I can remember the twinkle in Ellis's eye as she lit up the joint. The sound and texture of her voice. The heat of her hand as I helped her up from the bathroom floor. The pressure of the drunken, chaste kiss she left on my cheek.

It's like Ellis is sitting there with us at the table. Her denim jacket is rolled up to her elbows, and she's resting her chin in her palm, watching us. She wants me to know who she is. She wants me to know about the girl I let die.

She knows that Tommy is the one who can tell me.

• • •

Tommy is quiet while I talk, and I don't blame him. A girl he's only just met won't shut up about his dead ex-girlfriend. When I tell him that Detective Kelly let it slip to me that they've cleared his name, Tommy grabs my hand and suggests we talk somewhere quieter. Again, I don't blame him. If I'd briefly been suspected of murder, I wouldn't want to be overheard, either.

Everything on campus is starting to shut down for the night, and so we go to the physics building. The foyer is empty and there's a long bench that runs the length of it. We sit in the very middle.

We stay silent for a minute and only then do I realize how much I've been talking. I am not a chatty person, and I am never vulnerable or desperate, but until this moment, I hadn't realized how badly I needed to talk about Ellis. About how her life, now over, has somehow melted into mine.

"What is it?" Tommy asks me.

Our eyes lock onto one another for a moment, and it makes my heart beat faster. Tommy's gaze is piercing, and I can't help but wonder what it would feel like to run my hands through his hair. Down the sharp edge of his jawline. But he belonged to Ellis. I can't let myself think of him like that.

I avert my gaze, glancing at the floor. For the first time in more than a week, even years, I feel calm. I feel like I'm where I'm supposed to be. "Nothing."

He knocks his shoulder against mine. "Seriously. What were you thinking?"

"*Honestly*, I was thinking this is weird."

Tommy laughs. "This *is* weird. But you know what?"

I look at him. "What?"

"It's also not weird?"

"Tommy Eagle," I tease. "A regular Shakespeare."

"I'm not actually that into Shakespeare," he says, his cheeks reddening. "I lied to you earlier. I was trying to impress you or something."

"Oh?" I smile.

"I . . . *we* had to read it for class a few years ago." Tommy pauses. "I never really understood what the fuss was about, but Ellis—she was really into it."

"You miss her."

He doesn't respond, and I'm racked with guilt. The tension, the fact that Tommy wanted to impress me. I wonder how Ellis would feel about that, and so I clear my throat and decide to stop. I slouch farther away from Tommy, so I can't feel his heat. He is much younger than me, but inexplicably, I'm finding it hard not to be attracted to him.

"So. What happened between you and Ellis?" I ask. If I keep her here between us, then maybe I'll behave. "Her mom hates your guts, you know. She was convinced you killed her—"

I stop talking when Tommy's mouth tightens.

"Sorry," I whisper. "I don't know why I told you that."

"It's fine. I don't care what Ellis's parents think." He pauses, leans forward on the bench. "Did you think I killed her?"

A twisted part of me wishes it was Tommy. That the answer was that simple.

"No," I say.

He tilts his chin, looking back at me. "Really?"

"Until Detective Kelly told me about your alibi, maybe I did." I shrug. "I don't know. Men find all sorts of reasons to murder the women they love."

"We haven't been together for a while." He pauses. "It's been nearly a year."

"Why did you break up with her?"

"The real question is, why did she pick *me*?" He laughs angrily, leaning back against the wall. "Everybody at school wanted her. Ellis shouldn't have gone after me, but she did."

"Well, she saw something in you—"

"She didn't see a thing. She was wrong."

I'm surprised by the coldness in his voice, but I recognize that Tommy is feeling guilty. He's punishing himself and he wants to suffer; I want to tell him I know how he feels.

"Hey," I say quietly. I'm holding his hand and I don't know when that happened. "She loved you."

I didn't know Ellis, but somehow, I know this. I scan his face, searching, wondering why I'm holding his hand. Why I'm still here. He looks up and his gaze is piercing, almost off-putting. But it only seems to draw me in.

"Will you tell me about her?" I shuffle in closer until our thighs are touching. I watch his mouth as he speaks. He tells me about the first time he saw her, the way she lit up a room. The way she could cast a spell on everybody around her.

Time passes, and under the fluorescent lights, it ceases to have meaning.

We have both hurt Ellis. We have both done things we cannot take back. We've both lost someone we have no claim over. The despised ex-boyfriend has no more right to mourn, and me—the one with lead for a heart, and blood on her hands— well, I never had the right at all.

29.

Thursday, October 6

When my eyes flutter open, I realize that I slept through the whole night. I tilt my chin up so as not to disturb the boy beside me. Tommy's arms are wrapped around my waist. We're on top of a thin polyester blanket, and we're both fully clothed. I'm still wearing my jacket. My neck feels sticky and hot from his breath.

I shift slightly and glance around his room. It's a single dorm, with a twin bed, a desk and a wardrobe. The walls are gray-white and there's nothing hung on them except an empty corkboard pierced with seven bright-blue pins. There's a window to my left and I roll toward it, unlatching myself from Tommy. From here, I can see the physics building, where we stayed talking late into the night. The path we took in silent agreement, after the janitor kicked us out, that cut through the gardens and led us back here.

I feel Tommy stirring behind me. His hands brush against my back.

"Good morning," I say.

"Morning."

I can't read his tone, and suddenly I feel self-conscious, guilty. Nothing physical happened and I don't even remember falling asleep, but I'm suddenly furious that I allowed it to happen.

"Sorry." I sit up as fast as I can, rubbing the sleep from my eyes. "I shouldn't have slept over."

He doesn't answer straight away, but then he says, "*Weird night.*"

He's teasing me for calling him Shakespeare, and so I smile. "Yes, it was."

"But a good one, too. Right?"

I hesitate. "Right."

I stand up from the bed, not too quickly, but fast enough so he knows I won't dawdle. I'm trying not to feel the things I'm feeling. Guilt and confusion are at the surface, but deep down, there's a rumbling in my core that I find troublesome. I know myself, and I wouldn't have gone home with a guy I'd just met if I didn't want to. I wouldn't have fallen asleep here if there wasn't a reason, as unclear as that reason is to me now.

We talked, and then fell asleep, because neither of us wanted to be alone. Neither of us wanted to say goodbye to each other, or to Ellis.

Is that why this happened? Because of her? Or is it more? It's strange to feel close to someone you shouldn't, who twelve hours earlier was only a silhouette filled in by speculation.

My hand reaches out as if it has a will of its own. I want to stay in bed with Tommy; in a very visceral way I want to be with him, but I know I shouldn't. It wouldn't be right.

"I'm glad I ran into you yesterday," he says, sitting up.

"Me too."

"Can I see you again?"

I waver.

"Sara, it's OK." Tommy smiles at me, weakly. "She's gone. You don't owe her anything."

If Ellis and I had been friends, then it would be a betrayal to be here with her ex, the guy who broke her heart.

We were never friends, but still, I owe her. I owe Ellis the truth.

30.

What is the truth?

It depends on how you look at it. In hindsight, everything is as clear as day. But at the time, I couldn't see the truth even when I was staring it in the face.

The summer after my first year of law school was one of the hottest on record. And that dinner Jason wanted me to attend in Boston was only the beginning.

I took the credit card, reluctantly, and bought myself a Saint Laurent maxi from Saks. Jason waited in the lobby while I changed, and then a black car took us from the Four Seasons to a private members' club near South Station.

Jason and I had dinner with the state senator, the pharmaceuticals CEO and three other white men, all of whom seemed to know Jason and one another from their college days at

Harvard, or through their country club. At first, I didn't really understand why Jason had invited me along, but these were his clients and he wanted them charmed, and so that's what I did. Over dinner, we talked about politics, and I dazzled them with witty one-liners on the state of the world. We talked about money, and I conjured up anecdotes about the time a made-up ex and I got stuck in the Maldives during monsoon season.

We talked about sex. What they liked, and what their women liked.

"A lady doesn't tell," I said firmly, when I refused to answer and the senator wouldn't let up.

"Are you a lady?" he jeered.

"I'm not your lady," I fired back.

They all laughed, even that disgusting politician, who later followed me to the ladies' room. He was waiting for me in the hall when I came out, his hand pressed against the doorway. We were alone back there and I didn't know what he was capable of, so when he reached for my ass, I drove my knee straight into his crotch.

"Are you going to fire me?" I asked Jason, after I told him about the incident on the drive back to the Four Seasons.

"Why would I fire you?"

"I assaulted the client," I said.

"It sounds like he got what he deserved."

I was staring out the window, at the streetlights of Boston twinkling in the night. I turned back to Jason. "He's thinking about running for governor, you know. He's interviewing campaign managers next week."

"Is that so?" Jason said.

I nodded, recalling the client's lackluster non-apology as he nursed his groin by the restroom and pretended groping me was a misunderstanding. Our hour-long private conversation afterward in the lounge, where he drank and divulged way too much. "He also offered me a job. Apparently, there's room on his team if I ever want to jump ship."

"Do you think you'll take it?" Jason smirked.

I held his gaze. "Do I have a better offer?"

Jason didn't respond, but a beat later, I felt him toss something onto my lap. It was a wad of cash. He told me to use some of it to buy a new dress, because he needed me again tomorrow.

After that first night, it all started to fall into place. The fact that my employment with Jason was off the books, rather than through the firm. That the legal research questions he sent me had nothing to do with his established corporate financing legal practice, but rather, a foreign government's oversight on cash transactions of a certain size. Methods by which midsize corporations could embezzle without triggering a German bank's anti–money laundering whistles. Our U.S. Attorney's burden of proof should, let's say, a certain individual be indicted for racketeering.

You see, the clients Jason introduced me to weren't strictly clients, and his legal advice to them wasn't strictly legal. Money flows in mysterious ways, and Jason was happy to usher it along, to handle the law like the nuisance it was. The "clients" didn't care how Jason did his work, as long as he did it, and as long as they trusted him. Because who doesn't need to trust the man who's advising you on how to match your suit and tie with your white-collar crime? The one who carries your wealth, your livelihood and even your freedom around in his briefcase?

The only problem is that trust, in this world, is getting harder to come by. We may still live in the rich white man's America, but his house of cards isn't as sturdy as it used to be. Not when the wealth gap is widening in plain sight; the fairness of our tax regime is under media scrutiny; and every Tom, Dick and Harry at the Department of Justice wants to skewer the next Michael Cohen. Our esteemed former president trusted *his* lawyer to handle his affairs, but all of Cohen's talk about taking a bullet for his buddy Donald was bullshit. And all it took for him to cave was a federal investigation.

You always hope the house doesn't catch on fire, but if it does, it's a race to cooperate for prosecutorial immunity, to be the first to betray your clients, partners or lawyer for the chance at a fresh start. Every dinner, every hushed phone call, every email put Jason on the chopping block. He understood the danger of crawling into bed with other bad men, and even though a healthy and trusting client relationship wasn't a guarantee, it mitigated the risk. Jason needed to believe that if one of his clients was going down, they'd do their best not to bring him with them.

So where did I come in? Why did Jason want *me* by his side?

Jason was right when he observed that I had a power, that I could be—let's call it—*useful* to his practice. If I want something from you, chances are I'll get it. If I play a game, I always win. And if I wanted his clients to trust him, he figured out that I would get the job done.

That summer, I started going in to Boston more and more, and it was always the same song and dance. "Business" was handled, quietly and without an audience, and then I showed up. It was my turn to work. Jason's clients were old-fashioned, unabashedly misogynist, and therefore predictable. I knew exactly what to say and what subjects to avoid, how to be feminine enough for them to relax around but tough enough to keep their respect. How to appear as if I'd let my guard slip, so they in turn would expose their own vulnerabilities. How to make them like me, care about me and, therefore, trust me.

Jason kept his cards close to the chest. He never told me what exactly he did for his clients, but I thought it boiled down to money, blended into one of the many shades of capitalism. My parents' unwavering belief in the American dream is nonsense. Life isn't fair, and for people like us, working hard isn't enough.

So I thought I could play along. I thought I was finally getting my dues.

I also thought nobody was getting hurt.

31.

Thursday, October 6

I don't want to go home, so I use a spare toothbrush Tommy finds in the wardrobe, and by the time I wash my face and freshen up in the co-ed bathroom, the halls are busy with undergrad students. It's time for me to go to class.

Tommy and I exchange phone numbers and I promise to call him this afternoon, but I don't know if I will. Being around him feels all-consuming, and as soon as I've left the dorms, and the autumn wind is brisk on my face, I feel like I can breathe.

I grab a coffee from the cafeteria and then cut across campus toward the law school, trying to remember what day it is. Wednesday? No. Thursday. Even though I'm walking forward, going to class, I feel like my life is on a loop, in an endless limbo, and I don't know when it's going to stop.

I don't know when Jason is going to come for me, or what I'll have to do when he gets here.

Ajay avoids me during class, choosing a seat several rows behind me. I would have been surprised if he wasn't upset with me. He's been texting and calling for two days, worried, and I haven't replied to a single message.

As soon as class is over, he bolts. I have to jog after him.

"I'm sorry," I say, when I catch up to him in the Commons. "I know you've been worried about me."

He stares at the ground. "The only reason I haven't called the police is because I saw you last night. You were walking . . . somewhere."

I catch his eye and it clicks. He must have seen me with Tommy.

"I've been having a rough couple of days."

He's not satisfied with my answer.

"I'm sorry I made you worry," I try again.

"Sara." His jaw tightens. "You're not mine to worry about."

"Ajay . . ."

"I asked you out for dinner, and you freaked out. I knew it was a mistake. I knew you . . ."

He trails off, but then looks up, hoping. He wants to be consoled. He wants me to tell him that this is all just a big misunderstanding, that I haven't given up on him. Because even though he's been looking at me like this for more than two years, I can tell he hasn't given up on me.

"This isn't about you," I say eventually. "I'm sorry that I ignored you. Maybe you're right. Maybe I freaked out."

His face changes. It's the answer he wanted, and I hate that I gave it to him.

"I'm not—"

"I found you!"

The voice calls out from just behind me, and my heart stops. It's loud and bold, almost shrill. It can't be . . . But when I turn around, I see her.

It's my baby sister, Tina.

I'm dumbfounded as she closes the gap between us and throws her arms around me. She's a good four inches taller than I am, and when she squeezes me, my nose squishes into her chin.

I pull away from her, examining her top to toe. She's wearing wide-leg jeans and the alpaca wool sweater we found at a thrift store in Boston, the one we fought over at first but that I eventually said she could have. I vaguely remember the conversation we had last week, when she told me she wanted to come visit. I told her *not* to come. Why didn't she listen to me?

"And who are *you*?" Tina pulls her sunglasses down as she takes in Ajay. "Are you who Sara has been hiding all this time?"

"You must be Tina," Ajay says, grinning. "Nice to meet you. I'm Ajay."

"Damn, Ajay—"

"What are you doing here?" I interrupt.

Tina ignores me, still looking at Ajay. "Sara hasn't invited me up to visit her in two years. Can you believe it? I don't even know where she lives, so I had to come find her here."

"Shouldn't you be in school?" I ask.

"Mom and Dad won't care if I skip *one* day to see you." She beams. "I have a 4.0."

"I bet you do," says Ajay. "Are you going to go to Windermere after you graduate? Do you want a tour?"

"Maybe," Tina replies. "But Yale is my first choice. Their epidemiology program is first-class."

"I have a friend who went there," says Ajay. "I can introduce you."

Ajay grills Tina on her plans for university. I zone out of their conversation as I try to catch my breath and take stock.

Fuck.

Tina is here, and I need her to leave. It's not safe to be anywhere near me.

Tina follows Ajay and me to our next class. My Civil Procedure professor says he doesn't care, as long as she sits in the back and stays quiet, which she does. After that, it's nearly time for me to go pick up Benji from school. I say this out loud to Tina and Ajay. I tell her she needs to come with me.

"That's boring," Tina whines. "Why don't you give me your keys and your address? I'll wait for you there—"

"No!"

Tina and Ajay stop dead in their tracks. They weren't expecting me to scream; I didn't foresee it myself.

"Why don't you come back to my place while Sara's working?" Ajay suggests. "The weather isn't bad. I have a balcony."

I sigh in relief. By the way he's staring at me, I can tell Ajay knows I don't want Tina to be alone at my house. Ajay doesn't know the half of it.

"Are you sure you don't mind?" I ask, throwing him a look of gratitude. He smiles and wraps his arm around Tina's shoulders in a brotherly way. "Not at all. We'll have fun."

"We sure will—"

"Tina," I snap, "don't hit on him. OK?"

She giggles as Ajay awkwardly pulls his arm back. I can't help but laugh, too, momentarily at ease. I know Ajay would never let anything happen to Tina.

Time crawls by slowly this afternoon. Ever since our confrontation on the stairs, Benji has largely stayed quiet and out of my way. He doesn't complain about the snacks I bring him or use the most excessive curse word he can muster when replying to a simple question. In gratitude, I'm letting him play on his Xbox for forty-five minutes instead of thirty.

I sit at the kitchen table and stare at my coffee. It's my fourth of the day. I know I need to cut back, but I have bigger problems.

Like what the hell I'm going to do with Tina.

I can't bring her to my house. I haven't heard from Jason in a few days, but he could be anywhere. Maybe he came for me last night, when I was out with Tommy. I almost hope he did. I wish I could have seen his face as it got later and later and he realized that I wasn't coming home. That I had moved on. That he hadn't rattled me, and I wasn't afraid of him.

Because I am not. I won't be.

After a few minutes, I work up the courage to open my messages app and scroll down to Jason's last text.

Did you really think you could walk away that easily?

I've been living on borrowed time, but Tina showing up has made me realize that I can't do that anymore. I sit up straight on the bench.

I need to make a move. I refuse to take whatever's coming lying down.

> Yes. Are you too much of a pussy to prove me wrong?

My thumb hovers a moment before I press send. I can feel myself falling already, back into his orbit. The gravity that kept me bound for far too long. I will do what I must, but it won't be for him. It will be on my own terms.

I don't have to wait long for his reply. It arrives less than five minutes later, while I'm sipping the dregs of my coffee.

> I love it when you bite.

Before I have time to think of a reply, he texts again.

> Is it a family trait?

The blood drains from my face.

Jason knows Tina is here. Is he watching me? Is he watching *her*?

My leg shakes uncontrollably as the fear sets in. At first it prickles, like an itch on the back of the arm, or behind the knee. And then it spreads.

> If you touch her, I will kill you.

I wait one minute, my palms sweating. When Jason doesn't reply, I call Tina, but it goes straight to voice mail. I can feel my heart beating in my chest, pounding as if it's trying to burst outward from my body.

I call her again, and when she still doesn't answer, I call Ajay.

He doesn't pick up, either.

32.

SARAH ELLIS
A year and a half earlier

My mother and I had the biggest fight we've ever had. It started out pretty regular, one of her run-of-the-mill rants about Tommy, how he's aloof and never wears a mask and isn't a good influence on me, and how my grades only started slipping after we started going out. I told her correlation did not equal causation, and then she told me not to "be smart," and then I told *her* I thought me not being smart was the whole reason she was yelling at me in the first place.

I thought I was being pretty funny, but then she tried to slap me. Can you believe it? In the *2020s*? I'm eighteen. It's not even child abuse. It's basically assault.

Anyway, I'd smoked a joint earlier and wasn't thinking clearly, so I told her that I never submitted my application to Duke and was going to stay in Windermere for college, which is where Tommy is planning to go, too, and then I grabbed my backpack and left so she couldn't murder me.

Tommy and Journey are both out of town this weekend, so I ended up walking to campus. Even though the town is small, I don't actually come down to Windermere University that much. I picked out this really pretty spot with tables and benches right outside the law school, trying to figure out what to do, and then called Felix, who said he was drinking with his brother's (sketchy) friends down at Abbey Lake. I knew I shouldn't go to a party like that alone, so I called Andrea and guilted her into coming with me. I told her I'd order us a Ride and pick her up in an hour.

I have time to kill, so right now I'm in the giant church at the edge of campus. I haven't been here since Grandma's funeral. The door was open and I took a seat at the back, and I thought I would cry, but I didn't, because, honestly, I'm happy she's in a better place, and if heaven doesn't exist, then at least she's out of her misery, right? At least she can't look down from the afterlife and see how nasty I am to her daughter, or that I never visit her grave, or what Tommy and I like to do in bed.

When Adam still lived at home, he used to watch these space documentaries. He was obsessed with this British scientist, Brian something, who rambled on about far-away planets and black holes and how the sun is just one of hundreds of billions of stars, among hundreds of billions of galaxies, which means that Earth, our precious little world, is just an unfathomably tiny speck of dust in all that chaos.

Adam thinks he was born to study the cosmos, but if I think about the universe too much, I just end up wondering why any of us exist at all, and what the point is of even trying.

My phone buzzed just now. My heart lurched, thinking it was Tommy, but it's just Andrea. She's bailing on Abbey Lake because she's tired and wants to get up early to study for our civics exam on Monday, which I forgot about until now. I grip my phone tight, tempted to skip the party myself, but then I think, *Fuck it*, and I tell Felix I'm on my way.

33.

Thursday, October 6

Thank god Professor Miles answers on the first ring. I tell her it's a family emergency, and she pulls into the driveway less than ten minutes later. I'm already outside with my sneakers on, ready to run. I race past her as she pulls herself out of the car.

"Benji's still downstairs!"

"Sara, are you—"

"I'm fine," I call, without looking back. "I'll see you tomorrow!"

I sprint the whole way to Ajay's house. I try calling him and Tina on the way, when I'm catching my breath at stoplights, but neither of them pick up. Has something happened? Is Jason there right now?

Finally, I arrive at Ajay's building, but I don't have the code to get inside. I press his call button once, twice, but nobody answers. I bang on the glass door.

"Hello!" I scream. "Is somebody in there?"

"Are you OK?" I hear someone ask. There's an elderly man standing behind me, fumbling with his keys.

"My sister," I step aside, panting. "I need to get in the building."

The man nods. My panic seems to have thrown him off and he opens the door for me, a total stranger. I thank him and then rush through the door. I run up the stairs two at a time until I get to the third floor.

"Ajay? Tina?" I'm sucking air as I bang on Ajay's door. I can't hear anything but the sound of my own breath. I wait one second, and then try the handle.

It's unlocked.

Quietly, I push the door open and close it behind me. Ajay's kitchen is empty, spotless. Tina's school bag is sitting on the kitchen counter. My heart stops.

"Tina?" I call.

I peer into the living room, but there's no one there. The balcony is empty, too. I backtrack through the kitchen and make my way down the hallway toward the den. On tiptoe, I creep past the bedroom, and then stop outside the last door, which is partially closed. There's something happening on the other side, but I can't make it out. I muster up the courage and take a deep breath. And then I fling open the door.

I sigh in relief when I see them. Both Ajay and Tina turn around and give me a big, smiley wave. They are lined up in front of the television, headphones on, bouncing around on twin white mats with colorful squares beneath their feet.

"*Dance Dance Revolution!*" Tina shrieks. I wince and she pulls down the headphones and lowers her voice. "He's old school. I like him!"

I laugh as relief crashes over me. I look over at Ajay, who glances back at me, smiling. I've never been so happy to see him, to know that he's kept Tina safe.

"He's OK, I suppose." My eyes are locked on Ajay's. "Is he any good, though?"

"I'll have you know, I was DDR high-school champion," Ajay says.

"Really?" I say. "I wasn't too bad myself."

Tina hops off her mat. "She's seriously good, Ajay. I don't know if you want to challenge her. She'll eat you alive."

Ajay's eyes don't leave me when he says, "She's already eating me alive, Tina."

We play DDR for an hour straight. I win. I always do. Before the arcade next door to my parents' grocery store went out of business, the owners used to let Tina and me play for free.

Later we order pizza and eat it on Ajay's balcony. I forgot my jacket at Professor Miles's house, and when Ajay spots me shivering, he brings me one of his hoodies. It's maroon and threadbare and smells exactly like him. I feel almost paralyzed wearing it.

"I should probably give this back to you," I say, pulling at the zipper in his front hall. Tina has already said her goodbyes and is waiting for me in the hallway. She seems to be under the impression Ajay and I need some privacy.

"Keep it," he says, leaning against the closet door.

I shrug in thanks, zip the hoodie back up to my neck.

"I like you in it."

He's watching my face, wondering how I'll react. I'm wondering this myself.

"I . . ."

When I trail off, Ajay steps forward and places his hands on my arms. His grip is gentle but his gaze tears right through me, and I can't tell if I want to throw myself at him or make a run for it.

Was it only last night that I fell asleep in Tommy's arms? A guy—a *boy*—who doesn't make any sense. Then why did it happen? Did I imagine everything between us?

"I'll see you in class tomorrow?" Ajay finally asks.

"Maybe," I say, "although you never know with me . . ."

He laughs, a full one straight from the belly.

The only thing I've ever cared about is getting out, getting ahead, and pulling my family up with me. I was going to be the one to make it. To change our fate. To earn a place for us so we can finally belong. With Jason, I was willing to do whatever it took.

But where would that road have taken me? To what end would it have led? Now I'm back to relying only on myself.

Not once have I ever dreamed of being happy. It never even occurred to me. I wonder if it's even possible.

34.

Tina won't shut up about Ajay.

Ajay is so cute. Ajay is so intelligent. Ajay is *such* a good guy.

"Why haven't I heard about him before?" Tina asks me, as we turn off Main Street. "Don't worry, I didn't tell him I had no clue who he was. But you should have told me there was a *guy* in the picture. Is he going to be my brother-in-law?"

"No," I say, double-checking the directions on my phone. "We're not dating."

"Will you be?" She giggles. "Because Ajay is *definitely*—"

"Tina," I warn. I look over to find her sulking. "What's wrong?"

"What do you mean, 'What's wrong?' What's wrong is you never talk to me. I tell you everything. I text you when a cute girl even *looks* at me, but I have no idea what's going on with you."

I sigh, trying not to seem frustrated. "Well, what do you want me to say?"

"I don't know. Anything? Tell me *something* about your life? You call all the time, we talk all the time, but *you* don't say shit. Even Mom and Dad say so."

"Oh yeah, and what do they say?"

"How you're like a ghost sometimes. Even before you left. And now that you're away it's like, oh, does she even *exist?*"

I swallow hard, stopping at the pedestrian crossing. I don't know how to react to what she's telling me, so I don't react at all. I call home practically every day, or text at the very least. Even if I am a ghost, I'm a good daughter. Everything I've done is for them. For *our* family.

I stare at the lights across the road. The numbers count down, changing from green to orange as they draw closer to zero.

"Can you at least tell me one thing?" I hear Tina say. I nod stiffly, and she continues.

"Have you and Ajay ever banged?"

I groan and then dart onto the street, even though the light is still telling me to wait. There are no cars on the road, and Tina jogs behind me until she catches up. We pass by the police station and hang a left. Tina slows down as we approach.

"I thought we were going to your place . . ." She trails off, and I look up and catch her eye. "No. Fuck no. I'm staying with you tonight."

I keep my pace, despite her whining, and only stop when

we're right in front of the bus terminal. It smells like gasoline and piss.

"Mom and Dad already know you're catching the 8:45," I say, turning to face Tina. I texted them while she and Ajay were deciding what kind of pizza to order. "They're going to pick you up from the downtown terminal. You have ten minutes before your bus leaves, so you might want to use the bathroom."

"No," she stammers. Her lips are quivering, but I don't budge.

"Yes."

"I said *no!*" she screams, so loudly that a passerby turns to gawk. "I'm staying with you. I came all this way——"

"And I said yes! You are going home right now——"

"Is this about that dead girl?"

My legs start to tremble. When I don't say anything, Tina continues.

"Yeah. I heard last week. It's all over the news."

I pause, looking down at my shoes. "Do Mom and Dad know?"

"No. They haven't watched television since Kamala Harris was elected." Tina laughs. "I figured you didn't want them to worry."

"You figured right."

"Well, we'll go straight to your place and lock the door. You don't need to worry about *me*."

I do, actually. Tina can't be here. She doesn't know that the dead girl was found on my doorstep. She doesn't know that it was supposed to be *me*.

"So, which way is——"

"I said *no*, Tina."

My voice is low and hoarse, and Tina narrows her eyes as she studies me. She starts to yell at me. She tells me I'm acting like an "effing bitch."

My sister has never called me that before, at least not to my face. I don't want to be a bitch. I don't want my baby sister to look at me the way she is now—like she hates my guts. All I want is for her to be safe, and around me, she isn't. Not yet. Not until I deal with Jason.

"Are you done?" I cross my arms, interrupting Tina's tirade. "Your bus leaves in eight minutes."

"I hate you," she spits.

I roll my eyes. "I love you, too, Tina."

"No." She bangs her shoulder against mine as she brushes past me toward the terminal entrance. "You fucking don't."

I hate that Tina is mad at me. I consider texting her to apologize, but I don't. I can't think about that right now. She's safe and on her way home.

And I need to come up with a plan.

My earphones are at the very bottom of my backpack. I plug them into my phone, pick a playlist and then hit the pavement. I stick to Main Street and the busier roads around campus. I don't know where to go, but I'm not ready to go home. Jason hasn't replied to my threatening text. Does he think I'm bluffing? I don't think I am. If he came anywhere near Tina, I would kill him. I would do whatever was necessary.

Windermere is a small town. There are only so many streets. And eventually I find myself walking by Gavin's. It's busy outside. Students are clustered in groups, smoking, waiting to go in or leave, or maybe they haven't decided yet. It appears the news of Ellis's death hasn't affected business. I wonder if anyone knows that it all started here.

"Sara?"

I can barely hear my name over the music, but I stop dead in my tracks and look around. It's Cassidy, one of the bartenders, smoking by the garbage bins. We don't know each other that well. I only worked at Gavin's for a few months, and our shifts rarely overlapped.

"Hey," I say, pulling out my earphones. "How are you?"

"How are *you*?" She sucks on her cigarette, blowing smoke out her nose. "I heard Gavin fired you."

"Yeah, he did."

"Douche!"

I nod, studying her. Cassidy wasn't working that night. I wonder if she knows about Ellis.

"It's busy tonight," I prompt. "A good crowd, considering . . ."

"Is it?" She glances behind her, through the large window. "Seems pretty average to me."

I nod. It appears as if Cassidy doesn't know a thing. No one knows the dead girl everyone in town is talking about was here before she died.

"How's Gavin?" I try instead.

"An asshole, as usual." Cassidy throws her cigarette on the ground, stepping on it. "He's been in such a mood lately. I think it has something to do with the police being here."

"The police were here?" I ask, keeping my voice cool.

"Yeah, they've been around at least three times, but no one

seems to know why." Cassidy lowers her voice. "Well, the guys in the kitchen do, but they won't say a word. Said Gavin will fire them if they talk."

"Oh, really," I say with a smirk.

"Do you know what's going on?" Cassidy gasps. "Oh my god. Is that why he fired you?"

This is the fifth time I say what happened out loud, and with Cassidy, I play with the truth. I tell her Ellis was at Gavin's the night she died, but I leave out my involvement. I don't tell her we switched Rides.

"Oh my god. She was underage." Cassidy wipes her brow after I tell her the story. "Why didn't he hook up the cameras? Isn't it, like, the *law*, though?"

I smile. "It is the law, yeah."

"What a scumbag."

"I know, right?" I pause. "You won't tell anyone, will you?"

Cassidy shakes her head adamantly. "Of course not," she says, even though I know she will. It's the reason I told her.

"Anyway, do you want a beer?" Cassidy asks, shaking out her hair. "It's on the house."

"I probably shouldn't go in."

"Come on. Gavin isn't even here tonight."

I glance inside. I'm not much of a drinker, but a beer sounds like exactly what I need.

Cassidy laughs. "There are no cameras, right? He'll never know."

"Right." I smile at Cassidy and then follow her inside. "Just for one."

35.

There's an empty stool at the far end of the bar, and I force myself not to look down the hallway that leads to Gavin's office, to the bathroom where I first found Ellis. Cassidy slides me a pale ale and then moves on to a girl nearby waving her credit card in the air. There's a big crowd waiting for drinks, fighting for the bartenders' attention. It's just Cassidy and some new girl on bar tonight. There should be three, even four, front-of-house staff for a crowd like this. It was even busier the night Ellis died, and it was just Gavin and me up there, as well as the three guys back in the kitchen, who he treated even worse than me.

I introduced myself once, during my first shift. The kitchen guys are all international students. The two from China and Nigeria didn't say much, but the guy from Bangladesh was friendly in that slightly assuming, South Asian way I'm used to. He told me he was raised near Dhaka and had moved to the U.S. to study, that he had nearly completed his master's degree in organic chemistry and was trying to give up smoking. He must have guessed my heritage, because at some point he started speaking to me in Bengali, and we chatted until Gavin yelled at me for messing around and summoned me back to cover the bar.

I'm halfway through my beer. Lethargy spreads through my limbs as I try to remember the kitchen guys' names and decide if I should go find out what they know. Every shift, I always thought about going back into the kitchen and saying hello, but never did. Maybe they won't even talk to me. Maybe they think I'm a snob, that I'm too westernized to have had the decency to be friendly with them.

I lean forward against the bar, resting on my elbows. The alcohol is making me think less clearly, but I know I can't stay here forever. I need to make a move, and soon. Whether it's tonight or next week or next month, Jason is coming for me. I've provoked him, but I can't just sit here and wait for it.

I glance toward the window, past the busy barroom and outside onto the street. This is an undergrad bar, and the smoker's pit right next to the door is full of toddlers puffing on joints, cigarettes, sipping out of soda bottles not so secretly filled with alcohol. They are laughing, carefree. It makes me nostalgic for a time I've never experienced, and I'm about to turn back to my beer when I see someone. He's wearing a different jacket, and a black beanie partially covers his forehead, but it's definitely him.

It's Tommy.

He's leaning against a brick wall, face blank, his hands stuffed into his jeans pockets. I think about going out there to say hello, but then he notices me.

I smile at him through the window. A beat later, he comes inside.

"What are you doing here?" I ask him, after he's maneuvered through the crowd. He unzips his jacket and stops short right behind me.

"I'm meeting up with friends." He checks his phone, shaking his head as he slips it back into his coat. "If they ever show up."

"Well, it's probably past all of your bedtimes."

"You're making fun of me again," Tommy says. "You think I'm too young for you."

The beer has loosened my tongue, and I press my lips together as Tommy throws me a lazy grin. I'm embarrassed about teasing him about his age, that I'm flirting with him. That I'm sitting here talking to him to begin with.

"You didn't call me," he says.

I sit up straight and avoid his gaze. "I didn't have the chance."

"You know I'm twenty-one, right?" he continues. "I'm not too young for you."

"Tommy, stop—"

"Just hear me out." He rests his hand against the curve of the bar, leaning forward. "We should do something. I don't know. Let's go on a date, Sara."

He looks so young and earnest, and I wonder if he's ever been on a real date before, with and as an adult, and it isn't just something he's seen people do in the movies.

"I don't know," I say, stalling. "I don't know anything about you—"

"What do you want to know?" The girl next to me leaves, and Tommy slides onto the free stool. "I'm a history major. I like beer. I like *you*."

I laugh. I have to hand it to him. It's not every day that someone makes me laugh.

"What else do you want to know?"

"Well," I say, "why aren't you on social media?"

"Bishop Bailey Hall forbade it." Tommy shrugged. "And after we graduated, a lot of us never bothered. It seems like a waste of time."

I nod, agreeing.

"Wait, how did you even know?" He smirks. "Oh, I see— you looked me up, you little stalker."

Playfully, I shove him. "Hey!"

"You can't get enough of me, can you?"

"If you must know," I say pointedly, "I looked you up before I met you. Back when . . ."

I trail off and a knowing glance passes between us. I didn't creep Tommy online after I met him in person. I looked him up before I knew about his alibi and thought he might have murdered Ellis.

I turn back to my beer, and we don't say much as Tommy orders his own. I've ruined the moment, but maybe that's a good thing. I was letting myself get derailed from planning my move against Jason. This isn't important, and Tommy Eagle is just a distraction.

Or is he?

In my peripheral vision, I see the bathroom door open. It stalls halfway, as if there's someone on the other side who was about to come through but then decided otherwise. My whole body stiffens.

"Sara?"

I don't respond to Tommy. I'm frozen, my gaze fixated on the door, suspended in time. I feel his hand on my forearm, and just then the door opens fully. A girl stumbles out, and another one after her. They look both irritable and giggly in equal measure. I'm holding my breath, and I finally let it out.

"Sara?" Tommy repeats. "Are you OK?"

I turn to him. "I don't think so."

He nods, glances at the bathroom door and then back at me.

"You said you found her in there," Tommy says eventually. "And now you're wondering if you could have done something different. If you could have saved her."

"I—"

"You couldn't have saved her, Sara," he interrupts.

I shake my head, press my eyelids tight.

"Sara." Tommy's standing up next to me now. I can feel his arm on the back of my chair, his hand firmly on my shoulder. "Listen to me. This isn't your fault."

"And what if it is?" I open my eyes. "What if it is my fault?"

Tommy's breath is hot against my ear. He's a kid, innocent, just like Ellis. I need to walk away. I need to get up and go home. My reckoning has nothing to do with either of them. But I'm paralyzed. I've lost control.

"You need to let her go, Sara." He's whispering in my ear, his other hand brushing against my thigh. "We both do."

I drink two more beers, and for the second night in a row, I don't go home. Instead, under cover of darkness, I walk back with Tommy to his dorm. His large hand is dry and soft, and he doesn't let go of mine until we're in front of his door and he fishes out his keys.

Inside, I sit at the foot of his bed and watch him kick off his shoes. He kneels down in front of me. We're eye to eye. I put both my hands on his cheeks.

"Kiss me."

He does, but it's too gentle. Infuriated, I pull off his T-shirt and run my hands over his chest, his arms, pulling him closer to me as he fumbles with my jeans. I hear myself groan as his body slides against mine, and he pushes me back and down onto the bed.

Our bodies move together, like one body. Our clothes come off, piece by piece, until finally we're both exposed. I don't have a condom, but Tommy does. After he puts it on, he places his hands on the bed on either side of me, shifting forward.

"No," I say.

"No?"

I shake my head and wrap my legs around his waist as I kiss him, contorting my body around his until it's Tommy who's on his back. The blood rushes to my head as I climb on top, as I dig my fingernails into him and he sinks back into the bed.

"That's better."

He smiles, and I wonder what I look like from down there. I close my eyes as I press myself on him. I rock back and forth, and my hands slip up around his neck.

I push down on his throat. I grip harder.

I squeeze until I come.

36.

SARAH ELLIS
One year earlier

got off the wait list today, but only because Daddy called a friend of a friend at Windermere University. It's a few weeks until classes start up and I hadn't heard anything, which isn't surprising, considering how I fucked up my senior year marks and only stand a chance at a decent college because I did well on the SATs. Anyway, this morning he said enough was enough and he was going to call in a favor, and I exploded. Clearly, I said, I didn't deserve to be there, and I didn't want to take anyone else's spot, and then *Daddy* exploded, which he never does. He turned sunburned red and said what I deserve has nothing to do with anything, and I had made their lives miserable enough with the whole Duke thing, and I said I wanted to go to Windermere, so that's where I was "going to fucking go."

Three hours later, I got the email confirming my acceptance, and I spitefully forwarded it on to my parents and then switched off my phone. I was halfway to Cape Cod with my friends. The six of us are splitting up soon. Felix's dad went to Harvard, so guess where Felix is going, and Journey got into Georgetown, where she's wanted to go ever since she watched this old TV show I'd never heard of, *The West Wing*. (She's also dated three guys over the last year to make Felix jealous, but the guy is too much of a stoner to even notice.) Journey and Felix are my oldest friends, and it'll be weird not to see them every day, but at least I'll be with Tommy, and also Nathan and Andrea. They're staying in Windermere, too. It's not Ivy League, but it's rated pretty well these days. It's rated well enough that my parents won't consider me a total embarrassment.

Back to my day: Journey drove us down in her dad's Escalade. Cape Cod was stupid busy, and we found a sliver of empty beach and hung out and smoked and made this funny TikTok for Journey's new account. I'm not into posting there myself—I just have an anonymous account to watch TikToks when I'm bored—but I love Instagram and have admittedly gone a little crazy since we graduated and were allowed social media. So next, Journey, Andrea and I did that jumping thing in the waves while Nathan took photos for us with my new iPhone. We all agreed on who got to post which photo, and I know it's superficial, but it's so fun because it's such a novelty.

Afterward, I wandered around the boardwalk looking for Tommy, who had disappeared during the photo shoot, but I couldn't find him anywhere. When I got back to the beach, Journey, Felix and Andrea were in the water, and Nathan was chilling on his beach towel.

"Where's Tommy?" I asked Nathan, sitting down next to him.

Nathan grunted a response, and I looked over to find him muttering under his breath.

"Well?"

"I don't know. What are you, his babysitter?" Nathan rolled his eyes, and when he reached into his grimy backpack and pulled out a book, I grabbed it and tucked it under my legs.

"What are you trying to say?" I asked him.

"I'm trying to read, Ellis."

"I'm not his babysitter. I'm his girlfriend, and I'm just curious. Am I allowed to be curious?"

Nathan smirked, and it made me want to hit him.

"Am *I* allowed have my book back?"

My breath caught because of the way his hand was reaching for his book, gliding against the bare underside of my thigh. I was frozen, and it took me a full two seconds to realize what was happening and move away.

"Nathan," I said quietly. "That was weird."

"What was weird?" He stood up, holding the book he'd retrieved. "Oh look. Your prince charming has returned."

Nathan dropped his book and went to join the others in the ocean, and a beat later, I caught sight of Tommy waltzing toward me, a skip in his step.

"Where have you been?" I asked him.

"Nowhere." Tommy sat next to me on the beach towel. He was wearing sunglasses, so I couldn't read his expression.

"Well, guess what happened while you were gone." I paused. "Nathan . . . touched me."

"What do you mean?" Tommy asked.

I explained how he'd slid his hand against my thigh, and I thought Tommy was going to lose his shit, but he didn't. He just smiled.

"Ellis, you took the guy's book. *You* put it under your leg. He was just getting it back."

I hesitated. "You think so?"

"Yeah." Tommy lay down on the towel and put my sunhat over his face. "It's no big deal. Why do you always have to be so dramatic?"

I was about to spaz and say that the touch made me feel uncomfortable and I wasn't being dramatic, but that would have been dramatic, so I stayed quiet.

"I got into Windermere University," I said instead.

Tommy took the sunhat off his face, although his eyes were still closed. "So. Your dad finally made the call, huh?"

My jaw clenched. I didn't want to cry. This was good news. Tommy and I would be together, just like we planned. Why didn't he seem happier?

"Something like that." I cleared my throat. "Hey, let's take a picture for Instagram."

"Didn't you just take a thousand?"

"I mean of *us*." I pulled Tommy over to my towel and made him lie down next to me on our stomachs so we could take a selfie with the ocean in the background. I knocked over my tote bag in the process. As I stuffed everything back in, I found a cheap-looking bangle among my things. It wasn't real silver, and it looked like the blood-red fake rubies had been glued on by children. I looked up. Tommy was watching me.

"Oh." I smiled. It looked like the kind of jewelry sold up on the boardwalk. "Is this from you?"

"No."

I blushed. He sounded embarrassed.

"You know I don't care how much it cost, right?" I slipped the bangle onto my left wrist. "I love it—"

"Ellis," Tommy snapped, "that's not from me."

"Yes, it is," I teased, but then I stopped, because Tommy had that aloof, pissed look back on his face, and I realized the bangle wasn't from him, and when I asked Tommy who he thought it was from, he accused me of buying it myself to try to make him jealous. Can you believe it?

We had it out right there on the sand. Tommy called me pathetic, and I yelled that he was gaslighting me, and that it wouldn't hurt him to buy me a bangle or something sentimental once in a while, and he was just starting to convince me that I really had bought myself that fucking bangle when our friends got back from the ocean and we had to shut up.

We're all home from Cape Cod and Tommy won't answer my calls. It was just a stupid little fight. Now who's being dramatic?

37.

"Y ou have to call me this time."

"I'll think about it," I joke.

Tommy's still in bed, watching me dress. Now that the sun has risen, now that what's happened between us has happened, I don't know what the hell I'm doing here in this sad, washed-out little dorm room. What I'm doing here with Tommy.

"Do you want to hang out tonight?" he asks me.

"Can't."

"Why not?"

I'm desperate to leave, but to be nice, I put on a smile. "Because I've got to *study*."

Around Tommy, I feel myself dissolving, and I need to get away from him. He sits up in bed and pulls on his jeans. I step toward him and he grabs my ass and pulls me down until I'm straddling him. He's forceful. I don't like it.

"Do you want me to drive you home?"

I shake my head. "I like walking."

"But—"

"Tommy," I warn. "No. But thank you for the offer."

I let him kiss me, and after I pull away, I finger his neck.

I've left a bruise.

It's already late morning by the time I manage to get away. If Tina wasn't so mad at me, I would call her and ask her to explain the chemical reactions that occur when a woman has good sex. I'm not even sure I like Tommy anymore, but last night my body was attracted to his body. And now that I've screwed him, my brain has released endorphins or something, and I'm feeling good. It's almost against my will. It's fucking biology.

I think about going to the law library, but Ajay is likely to be there, and I don't think I can face him after what I did last night. Instead, I go to a hipster coffee shop and pay twenty-seven dollars for coffee and steak and eggs. I can't afford it, but I need the calories. Overnight, I have missed three more calls from a blocked number.

And I still don't have a plan.

I haven't been home in two days, but I know I can't avoid it forever. Maybe Jason is there. Maybe he's not. Maybe the missed calls really are from a telemarketer and I'm just going fucking crazy.

The barista is glaring at me. I'm done with my breakfast and he wants me to give up my table to another customer. I sit there five more minutes to spite him, and then I walk to the police station.

There are at least four reporters camped out in front, drinking coffee and smoking and throwing nasty looks at the harmless, homeless drunks loitering nearby. I lean against an empty storefront, watching. I imagine myself going inside and asking Sally, the overly friendly receptionist, if I can speak with Detective Kelly. I imagine following him into that miserable, windowless little room and telling him the truth, the whole truth and nothing but the truth.

So help me god.

But then what?

Detective Kelly didn't believe me at first when I told him Ellis took my Ride home; would he listen to me now?

I imagine him trying not to laugh in my face, the edges of his lips pursed tight as he takes my statement on a legal pad. I imagine the questions he would ask me, the proof he would demand in order to "verify my story"—proof that I do not possess.

The only truth I have is what I saw with my own eyes and heard with my own ears, and that's not enough to go up against a man like Jason Knox. Detective Kelly and the law are not on my side. They will not be able to save me.

Only I can save myself.

When the reporters notice me, I turn on my heels and walk north toward Hillmont. Since I was last home, the police have taken down the yellow caution tape sectioning off the house. The street is quiet, barren. Clouds cover every inch of the sky, and a sense of calm washes over me as I stand out front. Everything is as it should be. The lawn is brown. Zo's lights are on. There's recycling in the garbage bin.

But I know something is off.

I reach into my purse and pull out the steak knife I pocketed during breakfast, gripping it as I follow the path down to my entrance. The door is ajar, even though I remember locking it, and I push it open with my free hand. I take a deep breath, stepping forward, and then I flick on the light. My stomach drops to the floor.

Jason is here, flipping through papers at my desk. His hair is gray. His eyes are dead. And he doesn't flinch when he stands up to meet me.

"Have you been waiting long?" I ask coolly, masking my terror.

"Long enough."

I hold the knife out in front of me, pointing it at him. "I hope you got some sleep. My bed is pretty comfortable."

"You don't sleep in your own bed these days?"

"That's none of your business."

"My money paid for that bed." Jason looks blandly at the knife, and then flicks his gaze back up at me. "It is my business."

I'm playing it cool. I'm playing his game. But inside I'm screaming. I have no real plan. I have no way to escape.

And I'm standing in front of the man who wants to kill me.

PART II

38.

Go online and stalk me. Comb through my social media and look for the bread crumbs, the clues. Go to Boston, the block where I cut my teeth and learned how to swim. Survey the neighbors. The childless couple next door. The Punjabi family across the hall. Call my parents, call Tina. Talk to everyone I've known over the years. All the people who thought I was their friend.

Mention my name, and a smile will appear on their lips. Ask them what I'm like, and they will tell you I'm as sweet as an autumn plum. That I carry in their groceries, or am a comfortable shoulder to cry on, or that I'm worthy of my namesake, Saraswati, the Goddess of Knowledge. They will praise me like fools and repeat to you what Detective Kelly called me at the police station.

They will say I am a good Indian girl.

By now, you know that's not true. But it's easy to play the role you are born into. When something is expected of you, it's the only part of you other people can see.

Jason Knox was the first person to see me for my potential. To stare into my eyes and know that I was capable of anything.

It's the reason I first followed him into the shadows. It's the reason I am going to find my way out of this alive.

The summer between my first and second year of law school passed by quickly. Being Jason's assistant was an immersive occupation. It swallowed me up. By Labor Day weekend, I could barely remember what my sad little life was like before we met.

"Friday night," Jason said, in a black car on the way out to dinner. The heat refused to let up that September, and the air conditioning was on full blast. "Pack a suitcase."

"Again?" I groaned. The weekend before I'd reluctantly accompanied him on our first trip out of state. We flew business class to Newark, but we were back by breakfast the following morning.

"Where are we going?" I asked.

"Vegas."

I was applying my lipstick in my compact, and craned my neck to look at him.

"Have you been?"

I shook my head.

"It's even hotter down there." He grinned. "Pack light."

I rolled my eyes, ignoring his remark. "How long? Overnight?"

"As long as it takes."

"Sure. But class starts soon—"

"You'll be fine." Jason angled his phone toward his face and the screen flashed to life. "Pack enough for a few days. We'll buy you more clothes if you run out."

I was grinding my jaw, and I could feel tension setting in. I had a feeling I was about to cross another line. I just didn't know what it was yet.

"Can I ask you what we're doing there?"

"We're meeting a new client. Ollie Cullen. There will be lots to discuss."

"Right." I paused, not understanding. Jason never included me in meetings that were actually to do with business. "Then why do you need me?"

Jason looked over. "Like I said. He's a new client—"

"And?"

"*And* he's bringing his wife."

I scoffed. "Why can't you bring Lacey to babysit her?"

"She's not a good sport like you."

"*Meaning*, you don't want to get her involved in whatever you're—"

"Ah ah ah." Jason waved me off. "No need to be crass."

I tossed my lipstick and compact into my purse, annoyed. "Well, what the hell am I supposed to do with the wife when you're busy? Take her shopping?"

I was being sarcastic, but Jason nodded.

"Perfect. She's a woman. Women love shopping."

I scowled, watching him text on his phone. I hated how he spoke to me, how he spoke about women. I dug my fingernails into my palms until I didn't feel so angry.

"I'll give you cash when we get there. Buy whatever you

like." He looked up. "But for appearances, we'll have to stay in the same hotel suite."

"Excuse me?" I balked. In New York, I'd had my own room at the Roosevelt and made damn sure I had the only key. "No—"

"*Yes*. And there are two bedrooms in the suite." He smirked at me. "So don't get too excited."

"You want them to think I'm your *wife*?" I asked icily.

"Of course not." Jason winked, and my stomach bottomed out. "Not my wife."

I turned forward in my seat. The dark glass partition was up, so I couldn't see the driver, and suddenly, I felt trapped.

I'd played the part of Jason's assistant so far, but nothing more, and I dressed up for him and the clients, but not like a slut. I had my dignity. No cleavage. Absolutely no touching. I was elegant and aloof. I flirted back, but only when I wanted to. Only when I was in control.

Now he wanted me to act like his mistress. What next? Would he—*no*. Jason had been clear about that. He wouldn't expect anything more of me, if only because trying to fuck the girl who helped win clients' trust wasn't good business.

I exhaled sharply, imagining where I'd be a year from now. And for the first time, I questioned what kind of life Jason was leading, and why I had agreed to be a part of it.

Jason had implied he would hire me at the firm after I graduated, but when that happened, would he still expect me to assist him off the books? Would he ever let me off this path?

"You're being a buzzkill, Sara," Jason said, interrupting my thoughts.

I looked over. He was on his phone again.

"I don't think it's a good idea for me to come with you," I said, after mulling over my words. I didn't want to go to Vegas, but I couldn't afford to get fired, either.

"And why is that?"

"My classes are starting. Second-year marks are important—"

"Forget your classes. I'll pay you well—"

"It's not about the money."

"Interesting." He cocked his head to the side. "Because if you agreed to Vegas, I was going to pay your tuition this year."

I froze, my head doing the math while my gut screamed at me to get out while I still could. In addition to buying me a new bed, laptop and clothing, Jason had paid me quite a lot over the last three months. I'd diligently saved every penny, but I still didn't have enough for tuition. Not even close.

"Is that a yes?" Jason asked me.

His tone irked me. He thought I didn't have the luxury of saying no. But the truth is, I could have walked away. I could have said no and avoided all of this.

I simply chose not to.

39.

Las Vegas was exactly how it's portrayed in the movies, and I hated every second of it.

The city felt like an amusement park version of America. A thrilling microcosm of sex and violence and money and power. Jason didn't like it, either, I could tell, but I suspected for different reasons. Up in Boston, he was a big fish in a small pond. He was Jason Knox. Here, he was just another guy. He had to share an elevator with teenagers wearing sweatpants and glittery masks, friendly Southerners who wore T-shirts that said "FBI: Female Body Inspector," the people who cleaned his hotel room.

There were the rich and the poor and everyone in between, and the only thing they seemed to have in common was that very human trait of poor decision-making. It was everywhere, in the casinos and the clubs and the trash cans, and the city was not ashamed of itself. It was giving you permission to do anything you wanted, because everyone else was doing it, too. If you were fucked up it didn't matter. Your personality got lost in the crowd.

Jason gave me an hour to change once we got to our hotel, and then we took a car over to a Japanese restaurant at the Wynn, where Ollie and his wife, Rachel, had made a reservation. They were waiting for us at the table when we arrived.

Ollie was just another man I had pegged the moment I laid eyes on him. A Boston boy about Jason's age, but rougher around the edges. If Jason was the rich kid at prep school who took advantage of the opportunities handed to him, Ollie was the kid waiting outside the gate with a shiv in his pocket. He was uneducated and gruff and not particularly good to look at, but he was sharp. Strategic. And he'd worked his way up from the streets of South Boston to do . . . well, I wasn't exactly sure. But these days, he was filthy rich and owned a handful of opaquely legitimate businesses here in Vegas and back home on the East Coast, so I suspected that Ollie trafficked drugs and Jason cleaned up his dirty money.

And then, of course, there was Rachel. She was the first woman Jason wanted me to win over, and she didn't really take a shine to me at first. She was more complicated, harder to figure out. She looked like she could have been anywhere from twenty to forty, and had chestnut-brown hair that fell in waves down her back. A tight, sparkly dress that hugged her perfect body. A face that looked too perfect to be natural.

I'd gone in hard. I'd tried to act like the woman I thought she would be—ditzy, alpha—but she didn't like her power challenged. Then I went quiet, submitted myself to her as the dominant female in the group. But she didn't like that, either. She wanted me to be like her, but not better than her. It was hard work, balancing the line. It always is.

"How did you two meet?" she asked during dinner, while Jason and Ollie spoke in hushed voices across the table.

"How did we meet?" I echoed. Rachel and I were both on our fifth gin fizz and my head was spinning from the alcohol. Jason never drank much when clients were around, and neither did I, but tonight he'd told me to do what was necessary to make Rachel feel comfortable. "It's not that interesting a story."

"Sara," she snapped, "just tell me."

"We met at my law school," I said to Rachel, choosing my words carefully. "Jason was the guest judge for my moot."

"Your *what*?"

"Like, it's a fake courtroom." I rolled my eyes, as if the competition was stupid. Rachel had mentioned earlier she'd dropped out of high school and used to waitress before marrying Ollie, and I didn't want to intimidate her. "Jason was the fake *judge*."

"I bet he was." She bit on the straw of her drink. "That's kind of hot."

"Right?"

"What happened after?"

"*Well*, he started chatting me up at the cocktail hour." I lowered my voice, widened my eyes, even though just the thought of fucking Jason made me nauseous. "But we couldn't—you know—do anything right there at school."

"Of course!"

"So, I slipped him my address. And an hour later—"

"He knocked on your door?"

"Honey." I crossed my arms. "He didn't even knock. He just walked right in."

"That's quite a story, Jason," I heard Ollie say.

I turned to look at the guys. At some point, Ollie and Jason had tuned in to our conversation.

"You going to leave Lacey?" Ollie asked Jason.

"Ollie!" Rachel swatted him, apologizing to Jason with her eyes. "Don't ask him that!"

"One step at a time," I said, winking at them. "I want to be his associate before I want to be his *wife*."

Rachel laughed. "How many associates can you have at one time, Jason?"

"Four," he said stiffly. "Maybe five."

"And how many wives?"

"One," I retorted, feeling light-headed. "But it's a rotating position."

When we left the restaurant two hours later, unexpectedly, Jason grabbed my hand. I glanced at our fingers, intertwined. His skin was softer than I expected.

"Hey, Sara?"

I was drunk, and I wobbled slightly as I looked up at him. Twenty feet away, I could hear Ollie and Rachel calling out for a taxi.

"Yes?"

From the outside looking in, Jason and I were a couple vacationing in Las Vegas. We were dressed up for a night on the town. The way he was gazing down at me, so very intensely, it might even have appeared that we were in love.

He leaned in, pressed his cheek against my face, but he

didn't kiss me. He gripped my wrist and twisted it so tight it throbbed.

"Don't you dare talk about my wife again."

I didn't understand what had set Jason off. He wanted me to play his mistress. I guess I'd been too fucking convincing.

After all the shit he was putting me through, he *was* going to hire me, wasn't he? I didn't want to be his assistant, or his mistress. I wanted to work at his firm. I wanted to be a real, wealthy goddamn lawyer.

The cab took us to a club on the other end of the strip, which was Rachel's idea. It would be crowded, and I could tell Jason didn't want to go, either, but we had to. It was what the client wanted.

The music pounded in my ears and the alcohol was starting to make me feel ill, so I switched to water without anyone noticing. Rachel liked me by then, and she sat me down next to her in our private booth like I was her pet, the edges of our thighs sticking together. She shouted in my ear much louder than she needed to to be heard. I kept nodding and smiling and agreeing, trying not to wince. Half the time, I didn't even know what she was saying.

Ollie and Jason were on her other side, and I got a moment of reprieve when she scooted over to say something to Ollie. I checked my phone. I thought it was late but only a half hour had passed since we'd arrived.

"Asshole."

Rachel was back by my side. She was scowling. I wrapped my arm around her obligingly.

"Fucking Ollie. What a *fucker*!"

"Aww, sweetie," I said drily. She was ten years past drunk and I didn't need to try as hard. "What's the matter?"

"He's . . ." She narrowed her eyes at me. She was about to say something and wasn't sure she could trust me.

I smiled sweetly. "He's what, hun?"

"He's so fucking judgmental, Sara." She pointed at a bouncer about twenty feet away. "That guy right there? Yeah. We used to work together. I used to *work* here. That guy right *there*"—she was starting to slur, repeat herself—"sells coke, and Ollie won't give me the cash."

I shrugged, reaching for my bag. "Hun, if you want cash, I'll—"

"It's not that." She waved me off. "I got fucked up last night, and Ollie says I can't do it two nights in a row. Says it makes me look like an addict."

I nodded like I understood, but the truth was, in my naive little world, I had never done anything except smoke the occasional joint. Before that night, I'd never been around anyone who did hard drugs, either.

"You know I used to coke up, like, all the time, before Ollie. All the time." Her eyes bulged. "And I was totally fine."

"I know you were," I said blandly. "I believe you."

She lowered her voice, squishing closer to me. "I used to work here *a lot*."

"Waitressing?"

She huffed, shaking her head. I didn't catch her drift, and a beat later she rolled her eyes and sighed.

"Are you going to make me spell it out? How do you think I met Ollie? How do you think I could actually *afford* . . ."

Oh. I nodded.

Right. Rachel was a call girl. That made a lot of sense. She looked like she'd originated the role.

"Are you judging me now, *too*?"

"Not at all, girl." I sat up straighter, stroked her upper arm. "I don't care. We all gotta earn, right?"

"Right."

She didn't say anything. I needed to be obliging, so I continued. I played curious.

"What was it like?"

"It was fun, sometimes." She sipped her drink. "It was safe, too. I felt totally safe. I was always in spots I knew. With people I trusted just outside. It was *good* money. Did I tell you that?"

I shook my head. "You met them in clubs?"

"Often, yeah."

"Well, how does it work? You approach them? They approach you?"

"Either. Both."

"And then what? What if . . ." I trailed off, watching her smile widen. "Like, what if they don't know they're supposed to pay?"

"You make it clear. You *always* make it clear."

I didn't know what she meant, but I nodded and pretended like I did.

"And sometimes, if they don't look like they're going to pay . . ." She lowered her voice. "You make sure they do."

"How?"

"You slip a little something into their drink."

I could feel my insides twisting into knots. She was talking about a roofie. She was talking about drugging men and then taking their money.

"It's not hard. They're so distracted they don't even notice." Our glasses were nearly empty, and she reached for the bottle of gin and poured a bit in each glass. "Mix?"

"Sure . . ."

She added cranberry juice and then handed me a glass.

"Fuuuuck," she whined. "I want some coke. Maybe I should just buy some from Tony and *save* it . . ." She nodded to herself, thinking through the plan. "Yeah! Why don't I do that? I'll tell Ollie to buy some now, and then I can do it *tomorrow*—"

I cut her off. She was starting to sound like a junkie. It was irritating.

"Why don't we play it by ear?" I said dismissively.

"Yeah, but I know Tony's got the goods." Rachel looked flustered. "I don't work the scene anymore. I can't find it so easily—"

I laughed, loudly. She eyed me, prompting me to explain myself.

"Can't you just get it from . . ." I paused. "*Ollie?*"

"Sara," Rachel said, like I was stupid, "Ollie doesn't deal drugs."

I looked over at Ollie and Jason, watching. Wondering. If Ollie didn't deal drugs, then what exactly did he do? What were Jason and I helping him with?

It was easy for them, too, to play the part they were born into. All night, it had been the only part of them I could see.

I had thought the only way a man like Ollie could climb the ladder was by dealing drugs. I had thought a man like Jason, white and privileged and beautiful, couldn't be dangerous.

By now you know that I was wrong. You know that Las Vegas was only the beginning.

40.

Jason is more than a foot taller than me when I'm not wearing heels. His shoulders are wide from years of rowing and rugby. He is a threat to me without even trying.

"Which one are you fucking?" he asks me, standing in my apartment.

"Excuse me?"

"I said"—Jason pauses—"which one are you fucking? The Indian guy? The teenager?"

My jaw drops despite myself. He's been following me. He knows where I've been going, and who I've been with. It was Jason following me home that night, wasn't it? Stalking me like a predator in the basement of the law library. Did he see me with Tina? Or maybe he paid someone else to keep tabs on me.

I grip the knife tighter. "I don't know what you're talking about."

"You look like you've had a rough night." Jason looks me up and down the way he always does, leering. Distant. "Maybe it was both of them—"

"Maybe you can suck my cock, Jason."

I decide not to mention Ellis, not yet, at least. Jason's laughing at my outburst and I need to keep my cool. I need to stay on his level. I've left the door open and I'm close enough to run if I need to, but I don't know where I'd even go.

"This is why I missed you." Jason stops laughing. "You add a lot of color to my life."

"I'm so glad I can be your token brown friend."

"Always with the jokes. Always with the"—his voice gets cold—"sass."

"It's why you paid me the big bucks, isn't it?"

"I paid you to stick around."

He tries to move closer to me, and, panicking, I take a giant step backward. I accidentally bump my shoulder against the door. It swings shut. Now my back is flush against the wall. I'm cornered.

Fuck.

"I've been trying to call you," Jason says. "You're coming with me tonight. It's important."

"Find someone else."

"Ollie's in town."

My gut twists as I try to hide the shock on my face.

"Oh yeah?" I breathe.

"He brought Rachel." Jason grins. "She 'can't wait to hang out.' Apparently, she's 'over the moon.'"

I'm starting to sweat. "I'm not going. Tell them I'm out of the picture—"

"No one walks away from me, Sara."

His words are like ice. Gripping the knife, I steal a glance to the left. The door is closed, and if I lunged for it, there's no way I could fling it open and get out in time. Jason is standing less than ten feet away from me, and he is strong, and long, and he would take me down before I even had time to scream.

He would finally finish the job that started with Ellis.

"What's the next move?" he says, challenging me.

I can't face Ollie again. I can't.

"Get out!" I yell.

Jason laughs. "Are you going to make me?"

Shaking, I wield the knife at him. "I'm warning you."

"You're going to kill me, is that right?"

"Fuck you—"

Before I can move, or even think, Jason has knocked the knife out of my hand and has me pinned against the wall. His left hand grips my neck, squeezes ever so slightly. I'm choking, trying to breathe as I watch him smirk down at me, as the white spots dance in my field of vision. After a few seconds, he lets go. I fall on the floor in a fit of coughs.

"Kill me," I croak. The wind is knocked out of me and my neck is on fire. "Just like Ellis." I'm sucking air. "I don't care . . . I'm *not* coming with you."

A flash of confusion passes over Jason's face, but he doesn't respond. It's gone a moment later when I sit up from the floor.

"You stink." He picks up the steak knife and sets it on top of the dresser. "Have a shower, would you?"

"Kill me, you bastard. Otherwise, I'll go to the police."

I'm still on the floor, limp. I feel like I'm about to throw up. I am a fool. Why didn't I go into the station and talk to Detective Kelly when I had the chance?

"I'll tell them everything," I say, my breath heavy. "We'll *both* go down."

"How about I call the police for you?" Jason pulls his phone from his jacket pocket. "You seem out of breath."

Jason points his phone at his face. It flashes to life and then he keys in a number by memory. While the phone is ringing, he sets it to speakerphone.

My face heats up when she answers the call. I would recognize that voice anywhere.

"Bhaduri's Delights. How can I help you?"

I lick my lips, forcing myself to my knees. I'm shaky, but I need to end this. I need to try.

"Hi, yes," Jason says, clearing his throat. "Who am I speaking to?"

Tina hesitates slightly before saying her name.

"Tina!" Jason's voice is cheerful. He backs away from me as I crawl toward him, my hands clenched into a fist. "Gorgeous name. I bet you're a gorgeous girl, too—"

"Is there something I can help you with that's grocery-related, sir?"

She's impatient, and if I had enough air in my lungs, I would laugh. My sister doesn't take shit.

"Yes," Jason says. "Indeed. I was wondering if you stock adult products."

"Adult products?" she repeats.

"You know," Jason says. "Something that will get you off—"

Tina ends the call and Jason grins down at me. I'm on my knees, just below him. He crouches down to my level.

"I'll kill you—"

Jason presses his palm over my mouth, clutching hard enough that my jaw shakes.

"If you don't get up right now," he says evenly, "I will kill *her*."

41.

"Put your feet down," Jason barks. "Please."

We're halfway to Boston in his spotless white Range Rover. I've never been in it because he always used to hire a black car service to shuttle us around. Reluctantly, I uncurl my feet from beneath my butt and place them on the floor. There's a Nirvana song playing on the sound system.

"Still sulking?"

I don't respond. I haven't said a word to him since we left my apartment, and although he let me take my wallet and change into clean clothes, he forced me to leave my phone behind. I chance a look over. Jason never shows his hand, but he always has an agenda. I wonder if we're really going to meet Ollie and Rachel for dinner. I wonder if he made me leave my phone so the police can't track my final movements after they find my body in a garbage can.

"Sara, cut it out, would you?"

"Cut *what* out?" I snap.

I am acting like a brat, but to be fair, he is holding me hostage. Why hasn't he killed me already?

I run scenario after scenario in my mind, but I can't reach any logical conclusions. If Jason meant to kill me instead of Ellis, then he must have figured out what I did to him and his precious client Ollie. But, then, why am I sitting in his car right now, very much alive? Why is Jason telling me we're about to go have dinner with Ollie and Rachel?

Either he's lying, and he's about to deliver my head to Ollie on a platter, or the game has changed. For whatever reason, he needs me tonight more than he usually does.

But then what? Will Jason just get rid of me when dinner is over?

"You better cheer up by tonight," I hear Jason say. "Ollie and Rachel didn't come all the way to Boston to hang out with a miserable little bitch."

I bite down on my tongue, hard, and push past the urge to clap back. If I'm going to come out of this alive, every second counts. Every *word* counts. I have to find out what's going on.

"If they didn't come to hang out with a miserable little bitch," I say, mocking his tone, "then why are they here?"

"Business."

Jason is firm, and with one glance I can tell he's not going to spill anything helpful—not right now, at least. I need another tactic. I wait five minutes, and then, loud enough so he can just barely hear me, I laugh.

"Yes?" he says quickly. Jason never likes being out of the loop.

"Nothing."

"Sara," he says sternly.

"You won't freak out?" I turn to look at him, and when he doesn't say anything, I speak. "Fine. I was thinking about Lacey."

"What about Lacey?"

I shrug, stalling. Jason doesn't like to wait.

"I *said*, what about—"

"Where does she think you are this weekend?"

"Business."

I chuckle. It irritates him.

"Yes?" he prompts.

"Well, it's just that Lacey is a twenty-first-century woman. She's a lawyer, too, isn't she?" I pause. "Doesn't she mind that you disappear all the time?"

Jason snaps his head toward me. We used to speak frankly to each other all the time, and I know he's trying to figure out if we're back to the good old days or if I'm playing him.

"Not trying to overstep," I say. My voice is tepid, like I don't even care. "I just know that when *I* have a family—"

Jason scoffs. "You? A family?"

"I plan to have a family," I lie.

"Right."

"And I wouldn't be OK if my husband didn't do at least fifty percent of the domestic labor."

"Jesus," he sneers. "This is the problem with your generation. You think you have to hate men to be feminists, huh?"

"I take it Lacey doesn't 'hate men'?"

"As a matter of fact, she doesn't. She practices part-time, so of course she does more at home with Jillian—"

Suddenly, Jason stops talking and I try not to smile. He's surprisingly human and easy to handle, but he's also intelligent enough to immediately figure out what I'm doing. I know he suspects I'm manipulating him—trying to, at least—but right now I don't care. He has never told me a single detail about his daughter before, other than the fact that he has one, and I'm grasping for something—anything—that could be used to my advantage.

"How *is* Jillian?" I ask, pretending I haven't noticed this is the first time he's revealed her name. I've googled the family before, and although there's plenty of information about Jason and Lacey the power couple, there isn't a word about their daughter. They're paranoid. Well, Jason is. I suppose, when you work with dangerous people, it comes with the territory.

"Fine," Jason snaps.

There's tension in the air. Jason is still worried, so I lean forward and change the music.

"That song blows," I say playfully. "Sorry."

Jason's jaw unclenches, and he relaxes ever so slightly. I need to wait for my moment. I don't know when it will come, or what choice it will require of me, but it's going to be my one chance to make it out of this alive.

42.

Jason won't let me out of his sight, even though I tell him that following me around Saks is a waste of his billable hours. He parks the car at the Four Seasons and we go across the street. Usually, he walks one step ahead of me. Today, he's right at my side.

I know being in public with me is stressing him out. He's worried I'll do something stupid, which is very likely, but he knows where Tina is, so I can't let him out of my sight, either. I lighten the mood as we walk through the first floor, and I get him to buy me a pair of nude heels and a clutch, some makeup from Estée Lauder, a new bottle of Dior. He thinks buying things puts him in charge.

We go upstairs to women's evening wear and I take my time. Rack to rack. Dress to dress. I run my finger over every piece of fabric. I wait for Jason to grow impatient, and then I let out a sigh.

"What is it?" he asks icily.

"I can't decide."

He glances at his watch. "Just pick a dress."

"But I don't know where we're going." I cross my arms. "Men get to wear suits for everything, but it's different for women."

"Here we go . . ."

"Is it *formal* formal, as in I need a ballgown? *Yacht* formal—like that cocktail thing last June—"

Jason steps forward, a signal for me to lower my voice.

"Or just dinner formal—"

"Dinner formal," he says, cutting me off.

I cock a hip to the side. "Yeah, but—"

"We're going to Chester's." He exhales, pulls out his phone. "All right? Now just pick a fucking dress."

I nod, grabbing fabric indiscriminately from the rack. Jason could be lying about the plans he has in store for me, but he could also be telling the truth.

"That's perfect," Jason says, without looking up from his phone. "Can we go?"

I blink, long and hard, trying to remember the layout of the restaurant, which he took me to once over New Year's. Is there a fire escape, or is that Cibo I am thinking of? And is there a unisex bathroom or women's only? I bite my lip, mapping it out in my head. Trying to get one step ahead.

"So?" Jason prompts.

I pull out two more dresses. "I need to try them on."

The changing room is empty of other customers, and the

girly girl Mae running the place devotes herself to me entirely. She's wearing a peplum skirt and a silky top, and she has bright-red lipstick on her teeth, which she shows off by smiling at me to no end. Usually, this would be my worst nightmare. Today, she's my best friend.

"What do you think?" I ask her, coming out in the third dress. It's gold and goes to my knees, something you could wear to Cinderella's ball, or dress down with a denim jacket. "Too much?"

She gasps, clapping her hands together. "It's never too much."

I walk over to the full-length mirror, hemming and hawing. Jason is on a lounge seat. He's on his phone, ignoring us.

"Gorgeous," Mae says to Jason. "Don't you think?"

He doesn't hear her, and I roll my eyes.

"Clearly, it doesn't have the wow factor I was looking for—"

"Now, are you *sure*?" Mae smiles at me. This is the most expensive dress I brought back here, and I know she wants the commission. "What does your husband think?"

I giggle, loud enough so Jason looks up.

"Honey, he's *not* my husband."

Mae's eyes widen as her gaze flicks to Jason's left hand, to his ring. She nods, a sly grin spreading on her face.

"He's taking me *dancing* tonight."

Mae's ears perk up. "*Is* he now?"

I nod vigorously. Jason is trying to catch my eye, but I won't let him.

"But I'm not sure I can move in this." I sway my hips to the side. "What do you think?"

"Why don't you dance, and see how it feels?"

"*No.*" I blush. "He won't dance with me."

"*Yes*, he will." Mae turns to Jason. "Won't he?"

I laugh, and just as I planned, Mae pulls Jason to his feet and leads him to me. I throw my head back and wrap my arms around his neck, pulling him in tight.

"Aren't you going to *hold* me?" I chide.

"What are you doing?" Stiffly, he sets his hands on my waist.

"Getting into character." I speak quietly and start swaying my hips. Mae is watching us like we're a reality TV show. "It's been a while."

"Has it?" Jason says, looking down at me. "I thought you got some last night."

"You're incorrigible." I press my stomach against his hips as we sway, hard. His chin knocks against my forehead. He's a loyal married man and I'm making him uncomfortable.

I'm also searching for a gun.

"Are you done yet?" he asks me. He's irritated. I slide my hands down his sides, to his hips. There is no weapon hidden away, nothing I can feel except his phone.

"Do you want me to be?"

"Yes."

I shrug and let him go, but not before I swat him on the bum. Mae laughs.

There's no gun there, either.

"We'll take this one." Jason backs away, nodding. "Can you wrap it up?"

"Of course." Mae winks at me. "Will that be all?"

"No." I cross my arms. "I need a shawl, or a coat. *Someone* made me leave in a hurry today . . ."

"Is there a particular color, or brand—"

"Anything is fine," I say. "As long as it matches."

"Anything?"

"Something nice," Jason adds.

Mae's eyes widen. "I have just the one."

43.

The fact that Jason doesn't have a weapon on him does little to calm my nerves. After all, he strangled Ellis with his bare hands.

We walk back across the street to the Four Seasons and are noticed the moment we push through the doors. Carl is at the concierge desk. No matter what day of the week or what time we stroll in, it always seems to be Carl who's there.

"Mr. Knox," he says formally, rounding the desk to meet us in the lobby. He takes the shopping bags from Jason and then summons a bellhop. This is the kind of treatment a regular gets at hotels like these. I suspect it also helps that Jason pays in cash and tips like a friendly drunk.

"How are we this afternoon? Any luggage we can help you with?"

Jason shakes his hand. "No luggage today, Carl."

Carl doesn't look my way, as if he's barely noticed me. I am one of the personal effects, and later tonight, should Jason ask him to store my body in the luggage room, I'm sure Carl would oblige.

"I'm sorry, sir. We only have you down for one suite tonight." He pauses. "We can make up another room for Ms. Bhaduri—"

"That won't be necessary. We'll be sharing a room."

"Ah. I see." Carl smiles at him brightly. "Very good, sir. Now, if you'll follow me."

I still don't have a plan by the time I shower, change and pack my new handbag. It's just large enough to fit my wallet, new lipstick, and a razor from the amenities basket. At the very last minute, I toss the razor in the garbage. Thank god I do. Jason checks my bag before we leave.

A black car picks us up to take us to Chester's, or so Jason claims. He is tense. I wonder if I overdid it at Saks. I glance out the window, my wheels turning. I don't know if I trust his behavior, in the same way he can't take mine at face value. He's wondering if I'm putting on an act, which I am, and I can't stop thinking about why he hasn't gotten rid of me yet.

Did Jason kill Ellis by mistake when he came after me? And then what happened—he simply changed his mind because Ollie and Rachel were coming to town? Or maybe both Jason and Ollie know what I did to them. I swallow hard. Maybe Jason is leading me into an ambush.

"So, what brings them back to Boston?" I ask Jason, my voice casual.

He doesn't answer, so I laugh.

"You brought me to help you." I narrow my gaze, trying not to panic at the thought that I'm en route to my demise. "Let me help. What's the real reason you need me so badly?"

"Maybe I just missed you," he says playfully.

My heart is beating like a drum, and it calms only slightly when we turn onto Salem Street and I realize we are in fact at Chester's. In front of the restaurant, Jason tells the driver he'll get my door. He walks around the car and flashes me a toothy grin as he extends his hand to help me up.

I purr, "Thanks, sweetie—"

My world spins as he drops me, and a beat later I land hard on the pavement. One of my legs is still wedged in the car, and suddenly, I feel the searing pain of my twisted ankle.

"Sweetie?" Jason exclaims, mocking me from above. "Are you OK?"

I am blinking, pushing past the tears. Breathing through the pain. Finally, when I open my eyes, I see Jason hovering. He's making a show for the passersby, assessing my injuries.

I shoot daggers at him, but let him help me stand up. My ankle is on fire and I have a nasty scrape on my elbow but I'm OK. For now, I'm alive.

I'm shaking as he pulls me in closer, grips my waist so hard that I can already feel the bruise.

"I hope you weren't planning to make a run for it tonight," he whispers. "Or are hiding something else up your sleeve."

I smile, for our audience. "My dress doesn't have sleeves."

Jason stares at me for a moment, and then a slow, devilish grin spreads on his face.

"I'll do whatever you want." My voice shakes. "I promise. Just don't hurt my sister."

"I want you to go inside and make them think we are a happy couple. That everything is absolutely fine. That our friendships are solid. Do you understand?"

"No," I spit, "I don't—"

"There's a lot at stake right now." Jason shuts the car door behind me, his voice low. "One of Ollie's business dealings is in rough waters."

"And he's blaming his lawyer?" I roll my eyes. "He'll get over it."

"I'm not fucking around, Sara." Jason links his arm through mine, helps me hobble toward the front door of the restaurant. "I need you."

I look up at him. Jason is trying to hold it together, but the fear is as plain as day on his face.

"Ollie was arrested this summer," Jason says quietly. "And now he's iced me out."

"Really." I swallow hard, a lump forming in my throat. "Why was he was arrested?"

Jason avoids the question. "You understand the gravity of the situation. Don't you? You understand what this could mean for me?"

I nod, allow him to lead me toward the restaurant. Jason doesn't want to be the next Michael Cohen, plastered on the news for his family and country to see how he wronged them. Ollie got arrested, although I'm not sure for what or when or how long he spent in jail, and now Jason is worried they are both under scrutiny. That Ollie will win the race to the plea deal and throw Jason under the bus.

What does this mean for me? Jason could be lying. But Jason is on edge, and afraid, and it makes me think he's telling the truth about what's at stake. Jason may have figured out what I did, and tried to kill me for it, but for the next few hours, he needs me.

"What do you want me to do?" I ask, even though I already know the answer.

"Find out what's going on," Jason says, as we push through the revolving door. "Fix this, Sara."

Despite my fear, it feels good to be needed. It feels good to know that, for all his power, even Jason Knox can be rendered powerless.

"Fine," I say. "Consider it done."

44.

During my second year of law school, my attendance was so poor that three different professors threatened academic warnings. I had so little time to study, I just barely passed my courses—and only because Ajay gave me all of his notes.

The months flew by like a bad dream. I was sleeping soundly and I had plenty of money, but I also had to be ready at the drop of a hat whenever Jason needed me. Dinners. Business trips. Schmoozing Jason's degenerate "clients" over cocktails, the sort of men who lived their well-bred, lawless lives disguised by their whiteness and wallet size. Ollie was only one such client, but he wasn't like the others, the people who came from money and were willing to do anything to hold on to it.

No. Ollie's money was new. At first, I wasn't sure how he earned it, but I knew he needed Jason to help with the laundering, and that trip to Vegas was the first of several trips the four of us took together that year. It was just the start of something ugly, sinister. It would lead to the night that pushed me over the edge.

Two months ago, when I walked away from Jason, we'd spent the night with Ollie and Rachel. They were in town for reasons I was not privy to, and Rachel drank too much, which happened about half the time we got together. She couldn't find any coke to keep her going, so she was the first one to want to leave, swaying and irritable. I suggested I go with her, and Jason sent us home in the car. Our driver dropped Rachel off first, and I was on my way back to the Four Seasons when my phone rang.

"Where are you?" Jason asked when I answered the call.

I glanced out the window. "Commonwealth and Berkeley."

"Slight change of plan. I'm holding on to something for Ollie, and he wants it tonight." There was noise on the other end of the line I couldn't make out. "When you get back to the hotel, go to the front desk. I've called ahead. They'll give you a key to my room."

I sighed. I'd been looking forward to a nightcap and a hot bath.

"And then?"

"The combination to the safe is 9-1-3-2." Jason paused, then gave me an address. He said, "Go to the front door and ask for Ollie. Do not go in."

"You want me to wait outside?" I laughed. "What is this place? A men's club?"

"Sara," Jason warned, "wait for Ollie to come to you. You hear me?"

Jason's voice was off. I wanted to ask why I was forbidden to go inside, but decided against it. He'd never tell me anyway.

"Sure thing, *boss*." I bit my lip. "Are you and Ollie not together?"

"Something came up. I'll join him later."

Sometimes I forgot that Jason's double life included a legitimate front. That he was a law firm partner and had real clients, too.

"Pretty soon, you'll have to give me a real job," I said, irritated. "You know that, right?"

Jason clicked off, and for the last time, I did what Jason told me to. I wish I hadn't.

45.

Friday, October 7

Chester's is the type of steakhouse that hasn't changed its menu since it opened in the 1960s. The mahogany decor is expensive and timeless. You can almost still smell the cigarette smoke, and testosterone. Their house special is the lobster.

One couple is ahead of us in line, taking their time, gabbing with the host. Jason is emailing on his phone. Silently, I am screaming.

"Shit," Jason mutters, looking up, and I follow his gaze. There is an older gentleman, already seated, staring at us. He waves when he catches us looking.

"A friend of yours?" I ask.

"A partner." Jason adjusts his tie. "If he comes over here, you're a client. Got it?"

"Am I not your mistress tonight?"

"Lacey goes to Pilates with his wife," Jason growls, while he smiles and waves back at the man. "I swear to god, Sara—"

"Wow, man," I say breezily. "Take a chill pill."

There is a speck of lint on his coat and I'm tempted to brush it away, give the law firm something to talk about, but I keep my hands to myself. I suspect the gesture would increase my chances of ending up in a ditch later tonight.

"I'm going to go say hello," Jason says. "Stay here. And I mean it."

Without making eye contact, I gesture at my ankle. "Where exactly would I go?"

He doesn't answer and walks toward his partner, and I thank my lucky stars that, just then, a busboy leads the couple ahead of us to a table. I hobble forward, my pulse pounding. I need to be quick.

"Do you have a reservation?" the host asks, her eyes on a tablet.

"Jason Knox." I speak quietly, soft enough that she's forced to look up.

"Pardon?"

"It's under Jason Knox." I keep my face perfectly neutral, in case Jason looks back my way. "But would you mind helping me with something?"

"Of course—"

"I'm pregnant."

"*Oh*," she beams at me. "Well, congratulations—"

"I'm telling my husband tomorrow." I hazard a glance over at Jason. He's hunched over his partner's table, chatting, but his eyes are on me. I wave. "I have a whole *thing* planned. But he'll be suspicious if I don't drink tonight."

Jason leaves the table. He's glaring at me as he speed-walks back toward us.

"Whoever is serving me tonight, could you make sure—"

The host smiles. "Of course!"

I don't thank her. Jason is six feet away, and so instead I roll my eyes.

"Is there a problem?" he spits.

Jason's back by my side. He's gripping my elbow.

"Yes," I sigh. "She's not sure they have a booth."

The host scowls at me, but I avoid her gaze. If he came back here and I was playing nice, Jason would get suspicious. He knows I'm never nice without a reason.

46.

SARAH ELLIS
Eight months earlier

Tommy and I are over.

I don't know how this happened. I thought we were happy. I thought this morning's coffee date was Tommy making an effort. I thought whatever phase we were going through was, I don't know, an *adjustment*. I'm still living at home, and Tommy's in residence and partying and making new friends, and of course we fought. Who doesn't fight? Who doesn't fight for the person they love?

I have four missed calls from Journey, two from Nathan, and texts from Felix and Andrea. They have all "heard the news" and want to know if I'm OK, but I ignore them all and call Tommy instead.

"I don't understand," I say, when Tommy finally picks up. "Please. Baby. Just tell me—"

"I already told you, Ellis."

I shake my head, licking the tears off my lips. "There must be someone else—"

"Stop, that's not it—"

"So you just don't love me anymore?" My voice is shrill. "No. *No!*"

I'm begging Tommy to take me back when he hangs up on me, and I don't think I've ever screamed so loud, ever felt so alone.

There's a knock on my door. My mother is on the other side, telling me that she loves me, cautioning me not to do something stupid, but I know she's happy he dumped me, so I tell her through the door that I wish she was dead.

She's gone back downstairs now. I wish Tommy was dead, too.

47.

Friday, October 7

Rachel and Ollie arrive at Chester's twenty minutes later. Rachel is all smiles and hugs, reeking of that overpowering lavender conditioner she once forced me to borrow. Ollie, on the other hand, is as stiff as a board. He won't look Jason in the eye as he shakes his hand. When he turns to me, I hold my breath, just in case it's my last, but then he kisses me on both cheeks. I fist pump, mentally. My hunch seems to be correct. Ollie wears his emotions on his sleeve, and if he knew what I did to him and Jason, he wouldn't be able to hide it.

"Traffic?" Jason asks him.

"No," Ollie grunts, sitting down in the booth.

"I see." Jason tries again. He points at the wine list. "What's your poison tonight, Ollie. Wine? Beer?"

"Sure." Ollie looks unimpressed. "Either."

Jason throws me a pitiful glance. The tension is palpable to everyone except Rachel, who is showing off her new Birkin and telling me how she managed to skip the wait list.

"Ollie," I say brightly, after Rachel's finished her story. "Last time we chatted, you were planning a trip to St. Barts. How was it?"

Before Ollie can speak up, Rachel answers on his behalf. She sometimes forgets that a dinner party is not the same thing as being onstage, that decorum requires her to share the spotlight. "What about you?" she asks later, coming up for breath. "Did you get away this summer?"

"Jason did." I roll my eyes. "Where do you go again?"

"Nantucket," he says.

"Ah yes." I beam. "The family heirloom."

"I've never been." Rachel's sitting kitty-corner to Jason, next to Ollie and across from me. She reaches over the table to touch his arm. "Is it really like it seems in the movies? Take us sometime. Do you ever take Sara?"

I laugh. "Sara *wishes*."

"You should take her to India," Rachel says. "She can show you around. Ollie took me there."

"Oh yeah?" I ask, grinding my teeth. I don't bother telling her that I've only been to India once, and know the country about as well as I could carry her. "Where did you go?"

"The Maldives," Ollie says.

"Is that where you're from?" Rachel asks me. "Oh my god. That sand is *so* white. It's fucking paradise, Sara. Why would you leave a place like that!"

I take a sip of my drink. The Maldives is not in India, and

Jason is trying not to laugh. I'm not sure who at this table I want to ram my fist into more.

The tension fades, ever so slightly, as Rachel orders for the table and I pull Ollie into a conversation about the pitfalls of vegetarianism, which I once heard him call a plague. Rachel chooses steak and red wine for the men, and the salmon for us. Next, she orders us both a double gin soda and tells the waiter to "keep them coming." When I take my first sip, I practically sigh in relief. The host came through. My gin soda has no gin.

We're only halfway through our dinners when Rachel leans back in her chair and declares she's stuffed. She flags down our waiter and asks him to take her plate. I'm still famished, most of my salmon uneaten, but I ask for mine to be taken away, too.

"Ladies' room, Sara?" Rachel looks over at me expectantly. Her eyes are glassy and I can tell she's already a bit drunk.

I glance at Jason, my heart racing. He's chewing on his steak, and I can't tell if he's more reluctant to let me go or to be left alone with Ollie.

"You go ahead," I say, winking at Jason. "I'll miss him too much."

"Give Rachel some company." Jason sets down his fork. He's not as good an actor as I am. He doesn't want me to leave, but he has to. "I'll be right here when you get back, *sweetie*."

The ladies' room is on the other side of the restaurant, right between the kitchen and the emergency exit. If Jason hadn't messed up my ankle, I could dart through it while Rachel was peeing, and it would give me a five-minute head start to race across town, get Tina and my parents, and go.

But go where? They have a business to run. Tina has school,

and her future, and so do I. We couldn't just disappear. And unless I do something drastic, we could never get away from Jason, either.

"What happened?" Rachel asks me, as she holds open the restroom door. I hobble after her, shrugging.

"I tripped. I don't know what happened. These heels aren't even that bad."

"They're cute, though."

"Right?"

We both use the bathroom and then stand by the sink while Rachel fixes her makeup. She is yammering on about injectable fillers, but I need to derail this train of thought. I need to find out what the hell is going on.

"Do you think . . ." I start saying as soon as she's finished. I rest my weight on the edge of the counter. "Never mind."

"Don't do that, Sara." Rachel looks at me in the mirror. "It's *me*. What is it?"

I hesitate. "Are Jason and Ollie OK?"

She puts down her lipstick, pursing her mouth. I know asking her for the information Jason needs point blank, without a facade, is a gamble.

"I'm sorry if I'm out of line," I continue, stammering. "I know it's not my business. Jason doesn't want me involved, so I don't know what's going on."

"They'll be OK." She turns to face me. "We're here, aren't we?"

This is all very cryptic. I don't know what she knows, what Ollie knows, or even what *Jason* knows.

"I'm glad you're here," I whisper, squeezing her hand. "If there's anything I can do to help put Ollie at ease. He seems so . . ."

She waves me off. "It's no big deal, honestly. Ollie was only locked up one night. This is more about his ego taking a hit than there being a problem . . ." Rachel screws up her face. "Oh. Jason really doesn't tell you anything, does he? You didn't know."

"No," I say, as I pretend to be shocked. "I didn't. That's horrible!"

"Like I said, it's not a big deal—"

"Of course it is, Rach! He was *arrested*? Is he going to *prison*?" I raise my voice and ramble until Rachel is forced to grab my wrists and shush me.

"You need to calm down. Someone could hear you."

"But—"

"Sara, cool it," Rachel whispers. "There isn't a shred of evidence against Ollie, you hear me? They've got nothing on us. Quit panicking."

"I'm sorry," I say weakly. Jason will be relieved when I pass on the news, although if I had my way, Ollie would die behind bars. "I'm sorry, Rach. I just feel so . . . overwhelmed."

Rachel soothes me, placing the back of her hand on my cheek. "Jason was right not to tell you. I'm sorry. I should have kept my mouth shut."

"Just tell me, *when* did it happen, Rach?" I whine. "How long have the guys been fighting like this?"

I hold my breath, because I think I already know the answer.

Two months ago, the night I fucked over Jason and Ollie. I followed the instructions. I opened the hotel safe, delivered the bag of cash to Ollie, and then—

"He was arrested the last time we were in Boston," Rachel says.

To confirm my suspicion, I have to ask, "You mean, the last time the four of us got together?"

Rachel nods. "That night, after we parted ways, Ollie . . . it doesn't matter, sweetie. That's enough of this talk, all right? It's best you stay out of this."

I watch Rachel watch me pull myself together. I am a faint-hearted mistress on the outside, but inside, I'm reeling. I had tried to walk away and set things right, but my actions only led to Ollie spending one measly night in jail. He got away with it. And because of men like Jason Knox, he'll get away with everything.

"So we're cool?" Rachel asks me. "Can we put this behind us now?"

She sounds impatient. I smile and tell her that we can.

"Lipstick?" Rachel asks me, and I shake my head and open my clutch.

"Got my own." I open the buckle and dig around for my lipstick. My fingers find the edge and I slide it out, and on the way, my nail grazes the outside of my wallet. I smile.

I've confirmed the client's trust for Jason, and now, finally, I have a plan of my own. Or the beginning of one, at least.

"This is new," I say, applying the glossy balm. "Jason took me shopping this afternoon. I thought maybe it would get him off that damn phone for a bit . . ."

I thrust the lipstick into the clutch, shaking my head.

"You OK there, sweetie?"

"He barely pays attention to me, Rach." I crinkle my nose, like I'm about to tear up again. "He's so . . . *stressed* lately."

"Is it his wife?" Rachel asks me in a hushed voice. She is fascinated by Lacey, so I nod. "A bit. *Yeah.*"

"Does she know about you two?"

"I don't know." I throw my hands up. "I don't even care. And it's not just her. With Jason, it's everything. Business stresses him out. This thing with Ollie is stressing him out. He doesn't know how to relax. You see how he is, never drinking more than a few glasses of wine. Never having fun with us. It's so annoying."

"He likes to be in control," Rachel says, nodding.

"And I like that. I do." I pause. "I just wish he . . ."

"Could let loose?"

I nod, and a beat later Rachel grins and grabs my hands.

"Let's go to a club. Let's pretend we're in college and do shots—" She laughs. "Oh, that's right. You *are* in college. You can tell us where to go."

I laugh and pull my hands away. "I wish . . ." I gasp, and then shake my head.

"What is it?"

Slowly, I set my hand on my hip, facing her. "Have you ever done molly?"

"Of course." Her eyes bulge. "Why? Oh my god, Sara. Do you have a hookup? That's a great idea."

I ignore her question. "Jason and I did it once, just the two of us." I linger on my words. "It was . . ."

"I *bet* it was." She swats me, grinning. "It's called the love drug for a reason."

"He won't do it tonight, though. You know, around others." I shake my head. "There's no point even asking."

"Sara." Rachel cocks her hip to the side. "Do you have a hookup here or not?"

I think about the three Ambien pills stowed away in my wallet, and, quietly, I say, "I have it in my purse."

Rachel shrieks, and quickly I shush her.

"I was supposed to go out with friends last night, but then Jason called . . ."

"Girl, get it out. It'll be *good* for the guys—they need to bond and get over themselves, don't they?" She lunges for my clutch. "We're doing it—"

"No, Jason won't agree—"

"Leave that to me, won't you?"

I narrow my gaze, giving myself a full five seconds to catch her meaning. Then I gasp.

"Oh," I exclaim. "I totally forgot!"

Rachel looks at herself proudly in the mirror, and I back away from her, grinning.

Trust me. I never forget.

48.

Wwe were almost starting to get worried," Jason says when we return to the booth. He looks relieved that we've returned.

I scooch into the booth and wink at him, for Ollie to see. "Sorry, sweetie. We had things to discuss."

"Good things, I hope?" Ollie says. "Right, Sara?"

"Of course," I wink again. I can't stand the sight of him. "You're a lucky man, Ollie."

"I'm the lucky one," Rachel coos.

She starts kissing and petting her husband, right there at the table. Jason and I both avert our eyes. The waiter brought me a fresh drink while I was in the ladies' room. I pretend to be bored and take a sip.

"What's that—your fifth?" Jason asks me.

"Do you want me to stop? You're the boss. I'll stop."

Jason ignores me. He's still on edge about Ollie, and he's never in the mood for a flirt. Jason only plays with the edge of seduction as a power move, but at the end of the day, he stays sober and calculated. He would never cross a line. He would never betray his precious little Lacey. The Nantucket-summering family man with mommy abandonment issues keeps the animal in check.

"Did you have a nice chat in the bathroom?" Jason asks me quietly. He's trying not to sound desperate, but I can tell he is.

"Very nice."

"And?"

I wait a moment before answering, but then Jason grabs my wrist under the table and squeezes until it burns.

"You don't need to worry," I say quickly, withdrawing from his grip. "Rachel says the authorities don't have a 'shred of evidence.' Those are her words, not mine."

Jason breathes out heavily as he studies me.

"She also thinks Ollie's ego is bruised. He's getting over it."

"How do I know you're not playing me right now?" Jason whispers.

"You don't."

I maintain eye contact, our gazes searing. Jason doesn't trust me, as he shouldn't, and a part of me wonders if I should kill the elephant in the room right now. I could apologize for what I did to him and Ollie, admit that I know he killed Ellis when he meant to kill me, and pretend to offer a truce. He doesn't tell Ollie my actions led to his arrest, and I keep quiet about the fact that Jason murdered an innocent girl.

But there's no point, because Jason is too smart to believe

me. He's forced me to come here and make sure things are squared away with Ollie, and I'm convinced again that once he accepts that they are, Jason will dispose of me. He knows as well as I do that the banter is just a game for us, intellectual foreplay. He knows that only one of us is walking away from this unharmed.

But there's one thing Jason doesn't know. Rachel is about to slip an Ambien into his drink.

"How's your ankle?" he asks me.

"The one you twisted?"

I don't have to look over to know that he's grinning. That he's smiling at my pain.

"I'm sorry about that," he says curtly.

"No, you're not." Out of the corner of my eye, I see Rachel getting ready to make the move, and so I playfully elbow Jason to distract him. I tip over as we touch—after all, I *am* drunk—and allow my body to fall into his. Ever so briefly, our bodies press together. His muscles tense against mine.

"Sara." Jason clears his throat and quickly slides away from me in the booth. "I didn't mean to hurt you."

"*Right.*"

Jason is looking at me differently, less guarded than he usually is. It's throwing me off.

"I'm sorry I got angry with you today," he says.

"You mean abusive—"

"Don't be dramatic." He laughs. "I know you like it rough."

I stare at him calmly. He is loosening up, but I cannot believe that he's actually sorry, that we could put this fucked-up situation behind us, even though I desperately want to. A man like

Jason is not capable of feeling empathy, or guilt, or remorse. He will say whatever he needs to say to win. It's something Jason and I have in common.

"All right, Ollie, that's enough. We're acting like *teenagers*!"

We turn to look. Ollie and Rachel have come up for air. He's wiping her lipstick off his mouth.

"Should we get out of here?" Rachel asks the group. "Let's go to a lounge or something." She catches my eye. "For another *drink*?"

"I'm game." I shrug as casually as I can, glancing at Jason. "What do you think, sweetie?"

Before he can answer, Ollie speaks.

"If the girls want to go," he says, "I think we should finish our drinks and go."

Ollie winks at me, and my stomach lurches, hoping Jason doesn't notice. There are three Ambien pills in total. The first is in Jason's glass of red wine, the second is in Rachel's stomach (she took it in the bathroom), and the third she slipped to Ollie—along with the plan to drug Jason for his own good—while they sucked each other's faces.

Of course I told Rachel there was a fourth pill. I pretended to swallow it alongside her.

It's risky, bringing Rachel and Ollie into the fold, a plan that I am making up as I go along. They are not playing it cool, and as we get ready to pay the bill and Jason drinks the rest of his wine, they watch him like a hawk. I'm thankful when he downs the last of it and I know the Ambien is in his system.

I don't know what will happen next, but I finally have the edge. I have something on my side.

49.

Friday, October 7

Ollie is in a good mood. As we wait for the valet, he and Jason talk stocks, and quite out of character, at one point Ollie even smiles. The placebo effect of believing you are coming up on a party drug is working for him. Unfortunately, it's not doing wonders for Rachel.

"Is she OK?" Jason asks Ollie when he catches sight of her quietly drooping into my arms.

"She's fine," I say.

"Is she?" Jason asks Ollie.

"You know how she gets," Ollie says quietly. There's a smile on his face and a relaxed ease about him I've only seen once before.

"You good, sweetie? Too much to drink?" I cradle Rachel in

my arms. She's heavier than I'm letting on. "I think I had too much myself."

Jason grimaces. "We don't have to go out—"

"No, I want to," Rachel says, although she doesn't look like she means it. I kiss her on the cheek.

"This doesn't feel right," she whispers to me.

"No?" I peek over at the guys. They are busy chatting and deciding which bar to go to, so we have a moment to ourselves. "I'm feeling *really* good."

"I'm not," Rachel says flatly.

I feel bad about drugging her, and lying to her, as I hold her in my arms. She was expecting a drug that would give her a rush of serotonin, happiness. Instead, I gave her one that will make her fall asleep, and alongside alcohol, could even be dangerous. I think back to when I took Ambien last week, alone, with a few glasses of whiskey. I can't remember anything about that night, except that it fucked me up and I was lucky to come out on the other side of it.

"Do you want to throw up?" I ask her. Suddenly, I'm worried about how much Rachel drank and am desperate to get it out of her system. "You might feel better."

"No. It'll pass." She shakes her head, mumbling, "I'll be fine."

"Throw up," I insist. "I have more. Once you're feeling better, I'll give you some more."

Rachel's twitchy, and her eyes bug out. I can see the shadow of the girl she used to be. The party girl, always desperate for a fix. Always wanting it to last.

We are daughters of two different worlds, but in a way, we are the same. By chance, I was born to blue-collar immigrants in the city, and she, in poor, rural Nevada. We do what we have to do for the life we want. We are not good people. But we are on the same side.

"You don't want to ruin everyone's night, do you?" I say sternly. "You will if you get sick, Rachel."

She frowns, and I continue.

"Go throw up. You'll feel better." I smile at her, still whispering. "Then I'll give you some more."

"You promise?" she asks, and I tell her that I do.

Our car pulls up and Jason calls me over. He puts a hand on my back, helps me into the back seat. I still can't put much weight on my ankle.

I look out the window as we drive away. Ollie's car has arrived now, too, but Rachel has gone back inside the restaurant and he's pacing back and forth on the pavement. I wonder if she'll throw up, like she promised. I wonder if I'll ever see her again.

I really hope not.

Jason told them to meet us at the Chelsea, which is fifteen minutes away by car. On the drive over, I keep looking at him for a sign that the Ambien is kicking in. I'm so anxious I almost forget that I'm supposed to be acting drunk.

"I haven't been to the Chelsea before," I say casually. "What's it like?"

"Hell if I know. But if they want to go, then——" He stops, looks over at me. "Is Rachel OK? She looked off."

"She's drunk."

"No, that wasn't it."

My pulse quickens. Four minutes have passed, meaning I

have exactly eleven during which I need Jason to pass out and not figure out that I drugged him.

"So," I say, turning to look at him, "Ollie seemed in good spirits by the end of the night."

"Yeah." He's texting on his phone, and doesn't look over. "It appears I owe you another apology. You were right. Ollie mentioned . . ."

Jason trails off, and I pretend not to watch him as he takes a deep breath and leans back in the seat.

"Are you feeling OK?" I ask breezily.

"Yes." He swallows hard, even though I can tell he's not. "Are you?"

"Sure." I force out a laugh. "A little drunk, I guess."

Jason goes quiet. He's swaying from side to side, blinking fast and licking his lips. It's hitting him, and I need to find something to restrain him once he's down. There might be something beneath the seat or the center console, like a tool kit. I pretend to yawn, and with my elbow, I unfasten my seatbelt.

"What are you doing?" Jason asks sharply.

I freeze. He is staring, viciously, and I'm caught red-handed as we both watch the seatbelt slide across my body and snap back into place.

"Nothing." My breath is shallow. "What are you talking about?"

"You *bitch*."

In a flash, his face goes dark, and I don't have time to think. I don't have time to move. He lunges at me. He hurls his full weight on top of me.

I scream. Jason grabs me by the hair and pushes me against the window, pressing my cheek flush to the glass.

I choke, sputtering. I can't breathe. I can't get a word out.

"What did you put in my drink?" He shakes me, and my head whips back so hard it shakes the window on contact. "Did you put Rachel up to it?"

I gag. My mouth is dry and my jaw is on fire where he's gripping me. He loosens his hold for a moment, and I gasp for air. I try to scream again, but before I can, he fastens his claws around my neck.

"What are you going to do now, huh?" He's starting to slur. His eyes are loopy. He pulls me down on the seat. I want to fight back, but I only have one chance. I have to wait for my moment.

"You think you're so smart. You think . . ."

He's squeezing my neck, but his grasp is slipping.

"Stop," I sputter. I still can't breathe. He is a giant, towering over me. I'm panting for air. My hands are clenched in fists at my side. At the ready. If I try to run, he'll catch me. If I hit him, he'll only hit me harder. I am small and he is big. I am a woman and he is a man. He thinks he's everything. He thinks he's won. But I can't let him.

I won't.

Jason is high, and losing his balance. He unfastens one hand from my neck, but before he can press it firmly down on the seat, I hook my leg around his arm. I pull, as hard as I can. His weight gives. He starts falling, crashing forward toward me. I roll onto the car floor just in time. And Jason falls headfirst into the glass.

50.

Jason is unconscious for only a few seconds, but it's enough time for me to catch my breath and scramble for my next move. He blinks, coming to. I contort my body away from him as he reaches for me, but before he can touch me, I hit him with the crowbar I found wedged far under the seats.

This time, he's out like a light.

I glance out the window. We have just passed Fenway Park and I calculate that we are five minutes away from the Four Seasons. I press the intercom button, summoning the driver.

"Yes, sir?"

"Hi," I say, quickly. "This is Jason's date. He had a bit too much fun tonight and, well, he's passed out. Whoops."

"Will he require medical attention?"

"No," I say, like I'm annoyed. "He'll be *fine*. But we better

254

take him back to the hotel. I might need help getting him to the room." I scoff. "He was supposed to take it easy. He promised me he'd take it easy—"

"It's no problem, ma'am. I can help you."

"Do we have to use the front entrance?" I ask. "He'll be so embarrassed—"

"Let me find out, ma'am. I'll let you know."

When we're thirty seconds away from the hotel, I bash Jason on the head one more time for good measure. I don't want him waking up on me. My throat is still burning and I need some water. I need to think. And before Jason comes to, I need to tie him up.

Our driver takes us to the hotel's service entrance. He goes inside and tells me to wait in the car. I'm just starting to worry when he reappears.

I open the door a crack and stick my head out. "Everything OK?"

"There's no one around," the driver says. "Let's get him upstairs."

"I'm not sure how much help I'll be." The driver holds my hand as I step out of the car, careful not to put much weight on my left leg. "I tripped earlier—"

"Yes, I remember."

We're face-to-face. He won't look me in the eye, and I have no idea how much he does or doesn't know, or if he even cares. I think about asking him his name. I decide against it.

Somehow, the driver gets Jason upstairs. When we get to the elevator, Jason starts groaning, mumbling incoherently, but his eyes stay shut. After the driver flops Jason onto the bed, I tip him three hundred dollars from the cash in Jason's wallet.

He tries to wave me away, but I insist. I press the money into his hands and force him to look at me. I tell him how much I appreciate his discretion.

I don't waste a moment after the driver leaves. I'm not sure how long Jason will be unconscious. With great effort, I flip him over and rip the duvet and top sheet out from under him. I take the points at opposite ends of the sheet and roll it until it's a long cord, and then I fasten his hands together, tying it as tight as I can. I tie the ends of the sheet to the headboard, locking him down.

I hold my palm an inch under Jason's nose. When I feel his breath, steady, I step away, evaluating my surroundings. I spot the closet and rush over to it. There are two white terrycloth robes, and I take the belts from both of them, using one to reinforce his hand ties and the other to bind his feet. It wouldn't hold him down awake and sober, but it's enough for the time being.

But *now* what? I drag the armchair to the foot of the bed and sit down, gather everything that could be useful. The makeup I left in the bathroom. My shoes, my dirty clothes. I open my purse. There's the lipstick and my wallet. There's Jason's wallet with cards and cash. There's his phone. Jason is too smart to leave incriminating evidence lying around, but it's a start. Right now, it's my only hope.

I have no physical proof of what Jason really does for a living. The other, illegal side of his law practice. Even my old phone, which I ditched months ago to escape Jason, had little on it to prove what he was up to. He was always cryptic in texts, and although I met his clients and understood generally what they were up to, it was never discussed in front of me. There are no documents. There isn't a paper trail. I have nothing hard and real that I could use to force Jason to stay away from me.

His phone is set to facial recognition, and so I tiptoe closer to him. His head has lolled to one side. If I can get access to his emails, maybe I can find something to blackmail him. I don't want money. I just want a guarantee that he'll stay away from me and my family. That he'll let us live in peace.

Gently, I hold the screen up to his face, but nothing happens. I try again, and again, and then realize his eyes need to be open. He's set the security to the highest setting. I shake him, holding his chin in place.

"Jason?" I whisper.

He doesn't even groan. I try lifting his eyelids. His irises are rolled back. I swallow hard, wondering what to do.

And then I hear the knock.

51.

SARAH ELLIS
Six months earlier

I haven't written in here in a while because there hasn't been much to report.

I'm still in Windermere. Tommy and I are still over. Sometimes I'm totally fine, and I convince myself it's for the best, and then other times it hits me like a truck, and I find myself crawling into my mother's bed, sobbing like an idiot and feeling so stupid I actually think I might die.

Journey calls a lot to check in on me. She's concerned about the number of guys I have on the go, but I just remind her that I support her years-long obsession with Felix, who still acts like a fourteen-year-old half the time, so she has to get on board with my decisions, too.

I haven't seen much of the old crew since Tommy and I broke up, because whenever I do see him I embarrass myself.

Andrea and I are both taking a few of the same premed courses, and yesterday we got partnered in our biology lab. I felt kind of shitty for having avoided her all term, but I think she felt bad, too, because after we finished the lab she invited me to go for coffee. It was kind of nice at first. We chatted about school and Daddy, too, because Andrea's dead set on being a cardiologist and he's invited her to shadow him sometime, but then Nathan happened to walk in and ruined everything.

The table was only designed for two, but Nathan found a free chair and wiggled his way in. I zoned out of the conversation for a while because they started talking about the lack of hot water in their coed residence bathrooms, but my ears perked up when Andrea mentioned Tommy.

"What did you say?" I sat upright in the chair, staring at her. "What did you say about Tommy?"

Andrea stammered, her cheeks flushing. "Nothing."

"She said Tommy's going to Cancun for spring break." Nathan met my gaze as I felt his knee brush against mine beneath the cramped table. I looked down, shaking from the news, and then I felt him press it against me again.

"Who's he going with?" I whispered.

Nathan shrugged, looking at Andrea.

"Who is it?" I panted. "A girl?"

"I don't know," Andrea said. "Some are girls. I think it's a group of people. From his res . . ."

The room spun away from me as I thought of Tommy getting drunk on the beach, fucking around with some girl who wasn't me.

"He doesn't deserve you, Ellis," I heard Nathan say.

"He's right, Ellis. You need to move on . . ."

My throat was closing in. My eyes were getting wet. I was on the verge of crying in public. And when all I wanted to do was run, throw myself either into Tommy's arms or, I don't know, off some bridge, I felt Nathan's grubby fucking hand on my knee.

"Stop touching me, Nathan!"

I didn't realize I'd stood up, but I found myself picking up the chair I'd knocked over. I was embarrassing myself again. I was making a scene. But most of all, I was *angry*.

I was angry at Nathan for being such a creep, at Andrea for how good she was at microbiology, at Felix for only ever calling me when he wanted to party, at Journey for getting into her dream college, at Tommy for having a new life, at everyone except the one person who was the fucking problem.

Me.

"You didn't have to do that," Andrea said to me, after Nathan had left following my outburst.

"Do what?"

"Be mean. Nathan's trying to comfort you, Ellis. He's nothing but nice to you . . ."

I scoffed. Andrea is so naive, and I was tempted to tell her that men *are* nothing but nice, and then they get what they want, and they leave you feeling like nothing at all.

Andrea didn't let up. I wanted to tell her that this wasn't the first time Nathan had touched me, but she was seriously upset and about to storm off, so I apologized for being dramatic and promised her I would say sorry to Nathan, too. After we finished our coffees, I asked her if she wanted to catch a movie on Main Street because I didn't want to be alone yet, but she said it was getting late and went back to her dorm. I went to the theater anyway, and I was deciding whether or not it would be super depressing to go inside by myself when this older guy started talking to me, and, well . . .

I'm home now, safe. I was sober tonight, so I can't even use that as an excuse. Like I said before, men are nothing but nice. But later, after it's over and you have nowhere to go but home, you remember that they leave you feeling like nothing at all.

52.

"Who is it?" I ask. I'm standing halfway between the bed and the door, in the short corridor by the bathroom. No one answers, so I take another step forward.

"Hello?" I say again, a little louder. "Who is it?"

"It's Carl."

I furrow my brows, and a beat later it comes to me. It's Carl from the concierge desk.

"Oh, *hello*," I say sweetly. "Can I help you with something?"

"Would you mind opening the door?"

"It's rather late—"

"How is Mr. Knox tonight?"

I race to the door and look through the peephole. Carl is standing next to a security guard.

I hold my breath, resting my forehead against the door.

Someone must have seen us enter on the hotel's security camera and summoned Carl. It would be risky to unlock the door, but it would be more dangerous not to. They might suspect foul play, or think I'm holding him up here against his will, which I am, and call the police. I'm tempted to let them. I want Jason to burn up in flames, but if there's a way not to get dragged down with him, I want to find it.

"Excuse me—"

"Yes, yes," I say, impatiently. "Just one minute, please."

I strip off my dress and kick it out of view, and I pull on one of the terrycloth robes hanging in the closet. Before I go back to the door, I look down the length of the hall. The armchair I've pulled to the edge of the bed is visible, but that's it. Jason's limp body is out of sight.

"Sorry." I yawn as I open the door, throw Carl my most wholesome smile. "I was just getting ready for bed. It's late!"

"How is Mr. Knox feeling tonight?"

"You saw us enter, didn't you?" I shake my head. "Then you know as well as I do, Carl, he's not feeling well at all."

"That's unfortunate." Carl nods. "I'd be happy to check on him. See if there's anything I can do—"

"It's nearly midnight." I try to close the door, but he stops it with his foot. "*Mr. Knox* is fine, thanks. He's had too much to drink—"

"I really don't mind, Ms. Bhaduri."

I bet he doesn't. Carl's words are kind and his tone cheerful, but his hand is now on the door. He's applying enough pressure that I have to lean against it to keep it from swinging open.

"I also thought Mr. Knox wasn't much of a drinker." Carl blinks. "I must be misremembering."

My heart is beating hard against my rib cage. I bite my lip to keep it steady, and then, when I'm ready, I open the door wide.

"You're not misremembering, Carl," I say. "Jason stays here all the time. You know he doesn't drink that much. You also know he's a lawyer, likes to stay here whenever he has business downtown." I pause. "You know he's *rich*."

Carl opens his mouth to speak but doesn't. I take a step forward, blocking their entry.

"But did you know Lacey found out about me, Carl? Or that Jason is being sued for malpractice, for some bullshit mistake his *assistant* made?" I laugh, softly. "Do you know his little Jillian has ADHD and got kicked out of school on Tuesday—"

"Ms. Bhaduri . . ." Carl's face is beet red, but when he tries to speak again, I wave him off.

"Or that all this stress has caused Jason to"—I lower my voice—"lose his erection?"

I shift my gaze to the security guard, who is unsuccessfully trying to hide a smile, and then turn my eyes back to Carl.

"Viagra, three beers, and a few lines of coke *really* knocked him out tonight, Carl. But of course, you and Mr. Knox are so close, I'm sure you already knew all that." I shrug, standing back from the door. "Now let's go check on him—"

"I'm terribly sorry, Ms. Bhaduri." Carl is stammering, a bead of sweat on the side of his forehead. "Truly. I've disturbed you long enough—"

"Yes, you have."

"I apologize. I was just—"

"You were just concerned about the safety of an esteemed guest," I say briskly. "Now, if you don't mind."

"Can we do anything? Anything at all?" Carl looks at the

security guard, as if for inspiration. "Breakfast. *Yes.* I'll bring up a breakfast tray personally in the morning. All of Mr. Knox's favorites." He nods at me, wanting approval. "Nine a.m.?"

"That'll do."

"And if there's anything else I can do. Anything. Anything at all—"

"No, there's . . ."

I pause, wheeling around to look down the hall. There's not much in there to work with. I do need Carl's help, after all.

"Jason lost his phone at dinner," I say. "The restaurant can't find it. He has to get some work done in the morning, and he'll need—"

"Of course." Carl smiles, nodding. "I'll have one sent up first thing."

"No," I say. "I'd like it sent up now."

53.

Saturday, October 8

I have a plan. I think.

Carl returned twenty-two minutes later with a brand-new iPhone, still in its packaging, and left it outside the door. It's now in my hand, which is trembling so hard I can barely hang on to it. I glance at the alarm clock on the bedside table. It's nearly 1 a.m. And Jason won't wake up.

I've tried poking him, shoving him, slapping him, but he just groans or ever so briefly writhes on the bed before settling back into his stupor. I go down the hall and fill the ice bucket from the machine, mix in some water and then dump it on his face.

That does the trick.

I pull the chair closer to him, but still out of arm's reach in case he should get free from his bindings. He's blinking, moaning and speaking incoherently. I wait a minute for him to come to.

"Where am I . . ."

He's mumbling now, starting to make more sense. Quickly, I lean forward and slap him on the cheek.

"Who are . . ." Jason's rolling his head back and forth on the bed. He opens his eyes as if they were being pulled open. He's still staring at the ceiling when I start to speak.

"You're on Ambien," I say. "That's what Rachel put in your drink."

His face falls to the side, toward me.

"But don't blame her. I told her it was molly."

His eyes bulge. He can hear me. He's starting to understand. He tries to move, but the binding stops him. He looks all the way up, and then down. Then he glances back at me.

"If you try to attack me again, if you so much as move a muscle . . ." My voice is wavering. I take a deep breath. "I'll kill you."

He laughs, feebly. "How—"

"With this knife."

I flash him the tongs from the ice bucket, and a beat later put them back next to me. He's loopy enough to buy it, I think. He doesn't say anything further, and I keep going.

"Now, let's get down to business. Shall we?"

Jason swallows hard. "Water?"

"No." I stand up. "You don't get shit from me. You're going to shut up and listen."

"I'm listening," he says, although he's not. His tongue is slipping out of his mouth. His eyes are starting to droop. I slap him on the face again.

"Jason!" I scream, a bit too loud. He's staring up at me, dazed.

"If you don't want me to slit Jillian's throat," I say forcefully, "you better pay attention."

I step back, and Jason's eyes follow me. I open the new iPhone and show him a picture of his daughter.

"If only other parents were as security-conscious as you and Lacey." I hold the phone closer so he can look at his daughter, who is smiling widely next to a little blonde girl. "Jillian Knox isn't a common name."

"How did you . . ." He trails off. He's struggling to stay awake.

"This little one here is Quinn. And Quinn's *mommy* updates Facebook on her movements about fifteen times a day."

Jason snarls. He tries to lift his arms, but the binding catches him.

"I wouldn't move if I were you," I say. "And if you ever want to see your daughter again, then you'll leave me alone. You'll let me go—"

"You're going to kill Jilly?" he asks evenly.

"I'm going to slit her throat—"

Jason cuts me off, laughing. Howling. My face flushes and I yell at him to shut up.

"You don't have it in you."

"Yes—"

"No." His eyelids flutter to a close. "You don't."

I open my mouth to protest, but he's right. Of course Jason doesn't believe me. Of course this won't work.

I'm used to having my way, to making people believe whatever I want them to. But that's because every lie, every maneuver—there was always a sliver of truth to it. A part of myself or reality I could draw on, or exaggerate.

But nothing inside me is a murderer. I could never kill a child. I don't think I could even kill a man like Jason Knox.

I sigh, exasperated, and start pacing at the foot of the bed. The alarm clock now reads 1:34 a.m., and I'm one hour closer to dawn, to the Ambien wearing off, and still have nothing to show for it.

My mind races. What do I know? What could I use against him? I . . .

"What's the next move, Sara?"

I stop dead in my tracks. Jason's eyes are still closed, but there's a smile plastered on his face. The same evil grin he surely had when he wrapped his large hands around Ellis's neck, thinking it was mine.

I wish I had the guts to kill him.

"You're going to pay for what you did," I say. My voice is shaking, but I don't care.

"And what's that?" he slurs.

"Everything," I spit. "You are disgusting. *Evil . . .*"

I never cry. I can control my emotions. But right then I simply cannot, and it starts pouring out of me, uncontrolled and with a will of its own. It is every tear I've ever held back. Every tough pill or circumstance I've had to swallow. Every terrible decision I've ever made. It's out now. It's a roaring wave.

"You killed Ellis!" I scream. "And you and Ollie, that night—"

"What are you talking about?" Jason mumbles. His eyes open for only a moment.

"You help men like Ollie run the world, huh?" I wipe my

nose. I'm standing too close. "And at what cost? Knowing what he does to those innocent . . ."

I'm crying so hard I can't even speak. I sink to my knees, crumbling forward.

My head is on the ground as I sob. I'm on fire, and if there was ever a moment I could kill a human being, it wouldn't be Jillian, or Jason, or even Ollie.

It would be myself.

54.

That fateful night two months ago, I went to Jason's hotel room as instructed and found a paper bag in his safe containing at least thirty thousand dollars. I put the cash in my purse, got back in the car and asked the driver to take me to the address Jason had given me. I'd been expecting a restaurant or bar, maybe the penthouse of a condo building. Instead, he took me to a house in one of the richer suburbs, large and modern. There was a basketball hoop over the garage and the lights were out. It looked like no one was home, but when I walked up to the front door, I heard the faint sound of music playing on the other side.

I knocked twice but no one answered. Hesitantly, I rang the bell. Two minutes later, a man opened the door. He was older than Jason, white, ugly. He looked me up and down like

I was a piece of meat. He was grinding his jaw. He was high as a kite.

"What's your name?"

He slurred his words and I took a step backward, nearly tripping down the porch stairs.

"Who invited you?"

"No one." I cleared my throat. I hated the way he was looking at me. "I work for Jason Knox."

"Jason! Where is he—"

"I need to speak with Ollie," I interrupted. "Ollie Cullen. Is he here?"

"Ollie?" He stepped out onto the porch. "He's tied up. Do you want to come in?"

"I'll wait."

"We're having a little party—"

"I'll wait," I repeated firmly.

The guy stared at me as I sat down on the porch bench. I pretended to text on my phone, avoiding his gaze until he turned on his heels and went back inside. Twenty minutes later, I sent my driver home. Twenty minutes after that, I texted Jason and asked him when the hell he was getting here, but he brushed me off.

He told me to do my job and wait.

"You're still here."

I looked up, dehydrated and fuming. The ugly man from earlier had returned. I'd been waiting for over an hour.

"Where's Ollie?"

"He's *occupied.*" The guy smiled limply, set his hand on my shoulder. He looked slightly more sober than before. "But you need to go, or come in. All right?"

"I'll wait—"

"No, you won't." He squeezed my shoulder, firmly. "I can't have the neighbors seeing you."

I bit my lip to keep from biting this guy's head off. It was Jason I was angry with. I was tired, tired of always having to do what Jason told me, no questions asked. I was sick of these cloak-and-dagger routines, when I was never privy to the bigger picture. I was fed up with being Jason's fucking assistant.

I had worked for him for over a year, and I was about to start my final year of law school. Most of my classmates who would get jobs at top-tier firms already had their offers, and every time I reminded Jason about his promise to hire me for real, he shrugged me off.

Would he ever hire me?

I knew what value I added to his off-the-books business, being able to secure the trust required to manage his degenerate, money-hungry roster of clients. Here, he could control me. Here in the shadows, he didn't have to share.

"So, are you coming?" the man asked me.

Jason wanted to lock me out. But right then, more than anything, I wanted to finally be allowed *in*.

I followed the man through the door, toward the back of the house, where the music was playing. The hallway was lined with family photos in expensive frames. The man in the photos was him, the same man who was now leading me down the hall. He looked much less sadistic in them, next to his wife with her blonde bob, their two children. A boy and a girl, a different age in every photograph, stopping abruptly when they hit their teen years.

"Are they your kids?" I asked, gesturing at the last photo.

"No." The man stopped, dabbed out a line of coke onto the back of his hand. "They're paid actors."

"Ha," I said stiffly.

"You want some?" His eyes bugged out as he took the hit, the way Rachel's always did.

"No," I said.

"Suit yourself."

We rounded a corner, which led into a room with high ceilings and floor-to-sky windows. It was full of men like Jason Knox. From a single glance, I could tell every woman in the room was being paid to be there.

The man disappeared and left me to look for Ollie. Everyone looked drunk or high off their rocker, dancing, laughing and smoking. The music was loud and cringe-worthy, and after I scanned every face in the room and didn't see Ollie's, I started to really notice the people I was seeing. The bashful way one of the girls, short and rail-thin, was leading a man to a back room by the end of his tie. The way another girl kept obsessively tugging at the hem of her clingy satin dress, as if she had yet to grow the confidence to show off her body. The way some of the girls—most of them, now that I thought about it—looked much, much too young to be here.

A shiver ran down my spine.

Across the room, a door opened and Ollie appeared. His face and neck were slick with sweat, and his hair was wild. He was grinding his teeth. He had his hands all over a girl, frighteningly young, makeup covering her plump, youthful face. A handkerchief of a dress covering her half-developed body.

"Sara!"

It was Ollie's voice calling me, asking me why Jason hadn't

bothered to show up yet. Ollie's wet lips on my cheek, kissing me in thanks for making the delivery. Ollie's hands taking the cash from my purse, trying to cup my ass. I heard it. I felt it. But I couldn't stop staring at the girl. And after Ollie disappeared with the cash, I couldn't stop myself from going up to her.

"Hey," I said to her. She was standing at the bar, unscrewing the lid from a bottle of Grey Goose. "I'm Sara."

The girl gave me the side-eye. "Hi, Sara."

"What's your name?"

She didn't respond, holding my gaze as she poured herself a drink and then took a sip. She nearly choked on the liquid. She looked like she wasn't used to drinking.

"Have you been here before?"

"Do you want to fuck me or something?" she asked me, without looking up.

"No." I forced myself to giggle, although inside I felt like I was about to throw up. "Well, kind of. But I'm on the clock . . ."

She looked up, and I felt her staring at my black shift, so different from what the other girls here were wearing.

I tried again. "What did you say your name was?"

She blinked at me. "Isabella."

"Hi, Isabella."

I knew full well that she was lying. She said the name like it was a question.

"Have you been here before?" She didn't answer me, and I continued. "Well, I've been to this house before," I said casually. "Not at one of these parties, though."

"What are you talking about?" She sounded annoyed.

"Well," I said, moving closer to her, "the guy's daughter, you know?" I gestured at another family portrait. "I went to elementary school with her. Can you believe it? I was here once for her, like, tenth *birthday* party, or something."

The girl relaxed, smiling at me. "Really? That's so weird."

"It's a small world." I paused. "I haven't seen her since we both went to different high schools, so that's like, what? Four years ago now?"

Isabella balked, studying me again. I didn't look eighteen. But I didn't look twenty-eight, either.

"How old are you?" I asked her.

"I shouldn't say."

"Come on, tell me——"

"Twenty-four," she mumbled, and just then Ollie's laugh echoed across the room. The girl jumped. A huge pit formed in my stomach.

"That guy you were with," I whispered. "Is he nice to you?"

"Define nice."

"What's his name again?" I tried. "Ollie?"

"Is that his name?" Isabella laughed, stiffly. "He told me to call him Daddy."

Bile rose in my throat. I wanted to vomit. I wanted to take this girl home and give her a bath, coddle her, protect her from these monsters. I sucked air, slowing my heartbeat.

Finally, I wanted the truth.

"How old are you really?" I asked again. I placed my hand firmly on hers. "Seriously. Just tell me."

"Leave it alone. Would you?"

"Tell me, please. How old are you?"

Isabella held my gaze, blinking.

"I'm eighteen next week," I said. "I don't care. You can tell me——"

"Fine." She laughed, lowered her voice. "*Fine*. I'm fifteen, OK? But if anyone asks, I'm . . ."

Isabella kept talking and the room started to spin. I saw spots. I saw my very life, and this young girl's, flashing before my eyes.

I glanced around the room, to each girl, their clothes and their jobs masking the truth. How old were the rest of them? And what was I doing here, helping men like Ollie and Jason exploit them like chattel?

I caught Ollie staring, and I forced myself to smile and wave. He was the client. I had to play nice. But what was the point? What would I ever be able to achieve in this life, anyway? To work for a man like Jason who traded in secrets and power and abuse. A man who had led me here with the promise of a job, one that I now realized he would never offer me.

Jason was never going to hire me. I wasn't a man. I wasn't well-bred. I wasn't worthy of ascending to his place in the world. Just like these young girls, I was on a man's payroll. I provided a service. I was a button he could click like a pizza delivery, or a blowjob.

I was just a different kind of call girl.

Sweat sticking to my skin, I told Isabella that I needed to go, and asked her to come with me. I clutched her wrist, and I begged, but she said she couldn't leave.

She said they would find her.

55.

Saturday, October 8

Jason sleeps while I sob. I'm a ball on the ground, knees to chest. The hotel lights are too bright. The floor is too soft.

That night, I left the house and walked until I found a main road, a pay phone. I waited until a half hour had passed and I thought Jason might finally have arrived at the party. And then I called the police.

For weeks afterward, I patrolled docket court listings, looking for proof that I had made things right. That Ollie, Jason and those other men had been arrested and prosecuted. I'd given the police everything: an address, names, the fact that one of the girls had admitted to me she was underage. But I couldn't find anything. Every single one of them seemed to have gotten away.

Jason didn't show up in time, so he wasn't there when the

police raided the house. He must have bailed Ollie out the following morning, likely the other men at the party, too. With their thick wallets, the most they would ever have to pay for their actions is money. Wiping my cheeks, I wonder what happened to Isabella.

I wonder if there was anything more I could have done to save her.

I don't know how much time passes, but eventually I know I have to get up. I wash my face in the bathroom and then return to Jason's bedside. He's still falling in and out of consciousness, mumbling, smiling. Jason is not afraid, because I don't have any proof of his actions. I don't have any way to hurt him.

Not yet anyway.

I pick up the phone and turn on the camera.

I would have liked my final fuck you to be more elegant than what I'm about to do. I don't want to stoop to his level. But sometimes, you don't have a choice.

Sometimes, the only answer is the most obvious one.

56.

It's morning and I pull back the curtains. Sunlight pours into the room, and I turn around to find Jason stirring on the bed. He's wearing a terrycloth robe. He's no longer tied down.

"Good morning," I say brightly, taking the armchair at the foot of the bed. He sits up, squinting. I wait a minute for him to come to.

"How are you feeling?"

Rubbing his temples, Jason throws his right leg over the side of the bed. I don't know how awake he is, or what he remembers. I stand up quickly and backpedal to the other side of the room.

"Stay there."

"You've untied me," he says blandly. He throws his other leg over the side, pressing his hands into the mattress on either side of him. "Are you planning—"

"Do not fucking move, Jason."

He looks at me for the first time, his gaze narrowing.

"Check your phone."

He hesitates, spotting his phone where I've placed it on the bedside table. He opens it.

"Any new texts?" I ask, waving my new phone at him.

He widens his mouth to say something, but then doesn't, and I see the flash of horror on his face as he realizes what I've done. The photos are incriminating for me, too, but I don't have a reputation to protect. I'm just the good Indian law student who got seduced by the big bad wolf.

"Our story is so *original,* isn't it?" I say breezily. "An affair with a law student?"

Jason sets down his phone, and his eyes twitch as he gazes over at me.

"I do like it rough, Jason. It turns out, we both do."

Jason stands up in one swift motion. He's halfway across the room before I can blink.

"Stay where you are," I spit, taking a step backward. I show him my phone. Several of the photos are attached to a draft email. I've already typed out Lacey's work address, which I found online, as the recipient. "I'll send them to her right now. I swear to god I will."

"What did you do to me last night?"

I smirk. "Nothing you didn't want."

"You're sick."

"*I'm* sick?" I laugh. "All I did was tie you up, take off your clothes, and make it look—"

"Like you raped me?" he interrupts.

"I didn't rape you," I said blandly. "And even if I did, Jason, who the fuck is going to believe *you*?"

Jason squeezes his hands together, pulsing. I can tell he wants to rip my throat out. He's not used to losing, and I wonder if I miscalculated. I have no proof of who he truly is, and I can't go to the police, but I can go to his precious Lacey.

The man before me has many layers, and he plays many roles, but at the end of the day, Jason Knox is a family man. And I'm betting my life on the fact that he'll do anything to protect that.

"I know what you're thinking, Jason. You'll retaliate later, right?" I'm shaking, but I do everything in my power to keep my voice steady. "Don't think for a *second* that I don't have other copies of these photos. In fact, I retained a lawyer just this morning to hold on to them for me."

I swipe out of the email app and open my voice mail, play the one I received just thirty minutes earlier.

"Hi, is this Sara? This is Lacey Knox calling you back."

I smile, almost giddy as I watch Jason's face turn white.

"My office said it was urgent. It's no trouble contacting me on a weekend . . .

"I've received the files you sent me," she continues. "We have them saved in a digitally secure location, and you can be assured no one will look at them without your say-so. And of course, if we learn something has happened to you, then we'll follow your instructions and forward them on as you've outlined . . ."

The voice mail pauses then, as Lacey breathes heavily into the phone. She sounds like a lovely person. I wonder what the hell she was thinking marrying Jason.

"To be honest with you, Sara, I am concerned about your request. Should we be talking to the authorities? Are you in need of any help? Please come down first thing Monday morning. We'll need to get a few more details . . ."

I end the message, meeting Jason's eyes. His face is bright red. Right now, I'm more terrified of him than I've ever been.

"Lacey will leave you if she finds out about me," I say. "You grew up without a mother, Jason. Do you want your little Jillian growing up without a fa—"

"What do you want?" Jason snarls. "A job? Fine. You win."

"You're going to leave me alone," I insist. "You're going to leave Tina and my family alone."

I wait for him to interrupt me again, but when he doesn't, I continue.

"You don't need me anymore, Jason. Ollie is not under investigation. You're in the clear." I click to the phone's messages app. "See?"

I hold the phone out so Jason can read the string of texts between Rachel and me, sent earlier this morning. Thank god I had memorized her phone number.

I watch Jason's face as he reads through the thread, which is mostly Rachel rambling an apology about how sorry she and Ollie are for standing us up at the Chelsea, that they had a bad reaction to the molly and ended up sleeping it off. That, to make it up, Ollie is going to take the four of us to St. Barts.

"Rachel said there's no evidence against Ollie. Look at the way she texts me." I pull the phone back. "Everything between you and Ollie is fine. They want to take us on vacation, for Christ's sake."

Jason nods, shifting his weight between his heels. A beat later, he asks, "You don't want to go to St. Barts, Sara?"

I can't tell if he's being genuine or mocking me. Before I

decide how to answer, there's a knock at the door. Carl's voice is on the other side.

It's 9 a.m. He's right on time.

"Come in," I call sweetly, and a beat later, Carl uses his master key to enter the room. He's pushing a cart teeming with fruit, coffee, milk and croissants. Two silver domes cover what I suspect is shakshuka, Jason's favorite.

"Smells delicious," I say. "Leave it just over there, Carl. That'll be fine."

"I hope you're feeling better, Mr. Knox." Carl nods. "And that your new phone is up to your standard—"

"It's perfect," I interrupt. "Isn't it, sweetie?"

I smile primly at Jason. His jaw is set. There's nothing left for him to do.

"Yes, Carl," Jason says gruffly. "It's all perfect."

57.

What did you give me last night?" Jason asks after Carl leaves. We're sitting in chairs several feet apart, plates of shakshuka untouched beside us.

"Ambien," I say finally. "I stole it from my professor's medicine cabinet."

"And Ollie and Rachel?"

I tell Jason how I drugged them, too, about every single move I made. In a sick way, I still want to impress him.

"Well done," he says afterward, the sarcasm dripping. "But do you really think you're going to be happy after this? You won't be able to get a good job, Sara. Your grades are shit and you have no contacts. You'll waste your potential lawyering at some mom-and-pop firm in an industrial park. Is that what you want? Defending the little guy who can't even pay your bill?

Arguing people's parking tickets? Because without me, that's as far as you're going to get."

My nostrils flare.

"That is, if you even graduate law school." He pauses. "How are your grades this term?"

"You're not allowed to ask questions. *I* ask the questions." I take a deep breath. My insides are twisting. I am ready to walk away, on the verge of leaving this twisted chapter behind me, but I can't. Not yet. Not without knowing the truth.

"Did you kill her?" I ask.

"Who?"

"*Her.* Sarah. Sarah *Ellis.*"

"The girl from the news?" Jason squints. "She was a student at Windermere."

"And you killed her—"

"Are you kidding me right now? Is this a trick or something?"

"Don't lie to me. It's over, Jason. Just tell me the truth—"

"I am telling you the truth—"

"You're lying!" I scream, standing up. "She was outside my house. She had the same jacket. She *looks* like me."

Jason starts eating, looking up at me like I'm shrill and crazy. I sit back down. I can't breathe. I'm hyperventilating, for real this time, and feel like I might pass out.

"She died last week, if I'm remembering the news article correctly," Jason says finally. "I was in Toronto. Ask your new lawyer." He pauses. "Lacey's mother had a heart attack. We were up there the whole week."

"I don't believe you." I look him dead in the eyes, but it's like looking into a black hole. "You tried to kill *me* because you found out I called the cops that night—"

"That was you?" Jason smirks. He raises his hand just an inch off the armrest, but then sets it back down. "I suppose it doesn't matter now."

"You didn't know?"

"I did not."

I'm struggling to breathe. "Of . . . of course you knew it was me," I stammer. "Why did you think I disappeared? That I stopped taking your calls?"

"The last thing you said to me that night on the phone was that you wanted a job. You were pissed off I hadn't hired you at the firm yet," Jason says matter-of-factly. "I thought—"

"No." I shake my head. "Ollie must have told you. I saw *everything*."

"Ollie was arrested, Sara. His mind was elsewhere." Jason pauses. "You went inside? *You* called the police? Sara, I had no idea until you told me just now."

My mind is racing, my heart beating like a hummingbird. I don't want to believe him, but deep down, I think I do. I can see it on his face.

But . . . but he must have known. Otherwise, it doesn't make sense. If Jason didn't kill Ellis, then who did?

"Jesus," Jason spits.

I bring my hands to my face. I'm crying again, tears streaming down my cheeks. Snot bubbling in my nose. I wipe my face with my sleeve just as Jason tosses me his napkin.

"I thought you had thicker skin, Sara. I really did."

"That girl Ollie was with was fifteen, do you know that?" I whisper. "How old are yours?"

"Unlike Ollie, I don't pay for sex," he says dismissively. "I know you don't think very highly of me, but I don't go around fucking little girls. All right? I don't go to Ollie's parties. I never do."

"That night, you were on your way—"

"I told them I was on my way," Jason says. "I had gone home. I was watching *Desperate Housewives* with Lacey. Ask her when you see her. She loves that show. We've watched the whole thing twice."

My chest is pounding and I'm trying not to cry, trying to make sense of his words and his world.

"So that's Ollie's business, then," I say. "I thought it was drugs. But it's girls, isn't it? He traffics—"

"Those girls chose to be there," Jason snaps. "They knew what they were getting—"

"They're little *girls*, Jason." I'm screaming. I don't care who else can hear me. "And Ollie is *selling* them. You're helping him get away with it—"

"Actually, Sara," Jason says icily, staring me down, "we have both been helping them get away with it."

I am a ball of knots. My mind sticks on one word.

Them.

"How do you think Ollie finds them, huh?" Jason reaches for his breakfast, brings a mouthful of shakshuka to his lips. "Your best friend Rachel isn't as big an idiot as you think."

My face goes white. *No.*

Rachel is behind this? How could she do that to other women, to those *girls*? How could she betray all of us?

I clench my damp palms together as I stand up, ready to leave. I am free of Jason, finally, but nothing is solved. Nothing is OK.

Ollie and Rachel will get away with trafficking girls, and

Jason will help them. He will find some other assistant to do his bidding. The world will keep turning, unchanged, trampling anyone who tries to put things right.

And what about Ellis? What about her justice?

She is still dead. Her murderer is still out there.

58.

SARAH ELLIS
Four months earlier

I flunked biology, so guess who's stuck in summer school retaking the course.

It's not all bad. There's this group of girls in my class who I've started hanging out with, and I'm so glad I met them, because honestly, I needed some new friends. Tommy's out of the picture, and Journey and Andrea don't like to party anymore, and then there's Nathan, who calls and texts me all the time and wants to hang out, pretend that everything is like it was when we were in high school, even though it clearly isn't.

Ever since Andrea told me off, I've tried to be nicer to Nathan. He brings me coffee sometimes, and we shoot the shit or go for a walk around town. But then yesterday I showed him my Bumble profile and the picture of the guy I was meeting up with later, and he got all pissy and protective and I realized

Nathan maybe has a crush on me. Maybe he always has. Maybe that's why he can be a little creepy with me, and maybe I shouldn't be such a bitch about it.

Anyway, the friend who *really* pissed me off today was Felix. He called while I was out partying with the girls from biology, wanting to hang out, and I tried to blow him off, but he could totally hear the background noise and wouldn't take no for an answer.

Felix didn't do too well at Harvard. I used to play tennis with this classmate of his who told me that everyone thought he was immature, completely full of shit, and even though I kind of already knew that, I didn't really *get* it until that evening. He showed up in a Ride already drunk, and then he spent the next hour hitting on all my friends, making crude, sexist jokes and remarks, trying to pretend he was much cooler and hotter than he actually is. I guess when you know someone your whole life, sometimes you can't see what's right in front of you.

"What do you think you're doing?" I asked him after I dragged him outside, on the pretext that I wanted a cigarette. "Why are you being such a dick to everyone?"

He pretended he didn't know what I was talking about, so I listed off everything he'd done to embarrass himself (and me) over the last few hours.

"Do you understand what I'm saying?" I said.

"Precisely. Duly noted." Felix grinned. He was slurring. "Won't happen again."

"Jesus, Felix. You're . . ."

I trailed off. I was a little high, and my reflexes were slow, so I didn't notice Felix was trying to kiss me until his lips were already slobbering against my skin.

"What the fuck!" I pushed him off, and he was so drunk, he stumbled backward and nearly fell on his ass. "What the *fuck*, Felix?"

I used the sleeve of my new denim jacket to wipe his drool off me while Felix composed himself and stammered a dozen apologies.

"Sorry." Felix patted my shoulder, but I pushed his hand away. "I don't know what that was. Fuck, Ellis, you're like my sister. I'm so sorry. It was stupid."

"It was the stupidest thing you've ever done," I spat. "And you've done a lot of stupid shit."

Felix's bottom lip trembled, got so wobbly I almost felt bad for him.

"You do know that Journey, my *best* friend, is in love with you, right?"

Felix stared at his shoes, shifting his weight.

"You have feelings for her, too, don't you?" I scoffed. "But you kiss me. God. You're—"

"Stupid. I know." Felix cleared his throat. "Are you going to tell her about this?"

"Yes."

Felix sat down on a bench, sighing. "I'm not a bad guy, Ellis."

I looked down, studying one of my oldest friends. I want to see the best in him, but it's becoming impossible to ignore how he leads Journey on and is super inappropriate with girls, even *me*, and keeps doing all these things over and over again that are, objectively, *bad*.

But does doing bad things make us bad people?

Tomorrow morning, I'm going to bike over to Journey's first

thing and tell her what happened. I need to do it in person. We'll probably fight. She'll accuse me of betrayal, and I'll say she's too good for him and shouldn't make the same mistakes I did, and then she'll tell me I'm just projecting, and we won't talk for a few days, but honestly, I think I'm rooting for them now. I want Felix and Journey to get together. I want them to fall in love, because then, inevitably, he's going to break her heart.

It feels like shit, but maybe it's the only chance any of us have of eventually moving on.

59.

can't stay. I have lost control, and before I lose any more pieces of myself that Jason can destroy, I storm out of the hotel room. I don't look back.

I find myself on the same bus I used to take home from undergrad. I sit at the back with my legs up on the seat ahead of me, not watching the city but the people up front. I haven't been on public transport since before I met Jason, back when I didn't have the cash to pay for a taxi or a Ride. It's fitting that this is the final send-off back into my old life. One where I will have to struggle to pay rent and climb the ladder and find a job, any job, let alone at a top firm. I have sacrificed my grades and my soul for the chance to rise above, but that's over now.

I got out. I wonder if Isabella ever did, too.

I stumble off the bus as the fatigue starts to hit me. I should feel more relieved than I do. I'm leaving Jason in the past, and even though I don't trust him, I do believe him. He didn't kill her. I am not responsible for her death. Does that mean I have to leave Ellis behind, too?

I walk the last few blocks to our grocery store. This part of town is always gray, even when the sun is shining, like it is now. The neighborhood hasn't changed at all since I left. The same old men are still smoking on their stoop. Teenagers are loitering outside of Mrs. Hossain's convenience store. A dead squirrel is wasting away in a rain gutter.

When I arrive at our store, I linger outside, stalling. The sign is tacky, with flashing red lights, and the "l" has run out of juice, so it now reads "Bhaduri's Deights." The building is old, though well maintained by my parents, who keep it scrubbed and dusted and apply a lick of fresh paint every other year.

It still looks like a piece of shit.

After a few minutes, I work up the courage to push open the door. Tina is behind the counter, hunched forward and typing on her phone. She looks up when the security bell chimes.

"Hey . . ."

She scowls at me as I approach, and I try to remember the last time I came home. The last time I was in here, the humble pride and joy of my family. But it's been so long, I can't even remember.

"Are you still mad at me?" I ask.

"Yeah."

There's a sheet of bulletproof plexiglass separating us. When I reach my hand through the opening where we take payment from customers, she swats it away.

The last thing Tina said to me when we fought was that I

didn't love her. I've wondered more than once if I'm incapable of love, if I feel feelings differently than everyone else. I don't want to believe it's true. I want to believe I belong here.

"I love you, Tina," I say. "I'm sorry."

"I know you are." She crosses her arms, inspecting me head to toe. "I know you were just being overprotective and didn't want me around Windermere. That's why I texted you yesterday."

"You did?"

Tina scoffs. "Yeah, I did. And you didn't even answer—"

"I left my phone at home, sorry. It's been a crazy few days—"

"Uh-huh."

"Tina, I'm sorry. OK?"

My voice is desperate. I hate groveling, and I want her to forgive me, which I know she will. But she is going to make me pay first.

A flood of customers come into the store, and so instead of talking, I help her. I bag the groceries while she scans every item, bantering with the customers as if she remembers them from another visit. I wish Tina and I didn't have to do this. I wish neither of us had to spend our youth helping our parents keep this dump afloat.

But then I remember Isabella, and I think maybe Tina and I don't have it so bad, after all.

The bell rings an hour later, but it's not another customer. It's Mom and Dad. Their faces light up at the sight of me.

"Guess who's home," Tina says, cocking her hip against mine. I smile. She's nearly forgiven me, and I wrap my arm around her shoulder.

"What are you doing here?" Mom gasps.

I shrug. "Thought I'd stop by and give Tina a hand."

Mom hugs me and won't let go, while Dad grabs a banana from the basket near the till. He thrusts it into my hand and tells me that I look gray, that I need to eat more fruit. They make such a fuss I start to feel overwhelmed, and when a customer tries to maneuver around the commotion my parents are making, Tina shoos the three of us into the storeroom.

Mom ushers me into one of the plastic seats at the table, where the four of us used to eat dinner most nights. Dad sets the kettle to boil, and they prattle away in a mix of English and Bengali, battering me with questions without waiting for the answer. How is school. Why am I here. Am I eating enough. Do I have enough money. Do I remember to take *haldi*.

"I'm fine," I say, to every question. I'm used to the fact that they express their love by badgering me, but I forgot how intense it is in person. "I'm good. I'm fine. And you guys?"

"We are well," Mom says. She's sitting in the chair opposite and still holding on to me, her palms massaging my wrist. As if I'll disappear as soon as she lets go. "We have been so worried about you—"

Dad nods. "And you didn't call yesterday. We were so alarmed—"

"Sorry . . ."

"You should have called—"

"I forgot to call you one day, guys." I pull my arm away, gently, as Dad hands me a cup of hot water with a lemon tea bag floating on top. "It's been crazy—"

"Yes, but of all days to forget." Dad slips into a chair, sighing. "Why didn't you tell us, Sara? Why didn't you tell us a girl at your university was *murdered*?"

I shrug, unsure of what to say. I suppose they were bound to find out. I look over at Mom. Her fingers have found the prayer beads she hides under her blouse, and I watch her thumb and forefinger rapidly flick over each bulb of sandalwood.

"How long have you known?" I ask.

"Your Sunil Uncle stopped by two days back. He *told* us. He saw it on the news only."

"*Beti*," Mom says, "how could you not tell us?"

"I didn't want you to worry," I say, which is half the truth.

"Telling your parents not to worry? That is like telling a plant not to breathe. The ocean not to *swim*."

I hide my smile at Dad's shaky metaphor, waiting for him to continue.

"But anyway. It is over now." He smiles. "At least we no longer have to worry."

I watch him pat my mother's back gently, noting the glance that passes between them.

"What?" I say suddenly. "What do you mean it's over now? That you don't—"

"Well, they found the man who did it, *nah*?"

I break out into a cold sweat as Mom grabs the string of my tea bag, dunks it in and out of the water.

"Oh?" I say casually. My heartbeat quickens. "Where did you hear that?"

"The news. Your Sunil Uncle knew we were so worried. He telephoned us this morning . . ."

I tune out the chatter and grab the new phone from my pocket, go to the news app. I type in Ellis's name and open the first article that appears, dated two hours earlier.

Arrest made in Windermere student homicide

Darren Peters, 43, was taken into custody late Friday night in connection with the murder of 20-year-old Sarah Ellis, who was found dead 10 days ago in the Hillmont neighborhood of Windermere, Massachusetts.

Detective Mark Kelly, who has been leading the investigation, said in a short statement to the press that Peters was seen in the area just minutes before Ellis was murdered. He refused to comment further on the case, except to note that prosecutors will be formally pressing charges in the coming days.

Peters, a local to Windermere, is a resident of the Hillmont Road Halfway House. A source close to the investigation says they suspect this is a case of a "mugging gone wrong," and that Peters is "well known" to both Windermere residents and area police. Peters has a lengthy criminal record and has spent more than half of his adult life in prison for charges related to drug possession, vandalism, assault. . . .

I flip the phone over. I can't read any more.

A source close to the case said it was a "mugging gone wrong," which were the exact words Detective Kelly said to me that first morning, speculating on who might have killed Ellis.

This doesn't feel right. This feels like Ellis's parents have ramped up the political pressure, and with Detective Kelly's reputation on the line, he has given up on finding the real killer. He is chopping down the lowest-hanging fruit.

"Did you know the girl, *beti*?" Mom asks, sipping from my cup of tea.

"I don't think so," I say, clearing my throat. "She was younger than me."

"Twenty. *Hah*." Dad shakes his head. "This is such a tragedy. That man should rot in prison."

That man.

Darren Peters, who lived at the halfway house on my street. I don't know him, but in the two years I've lived in Windermere, in all likelihood I walked past him all the time. There's a very good chance that, at some point, he asked me for money, and if I didn't have change in my pockets, which I usually didn't, that I averted my eyes and pretended I hadn't heard him.

Was it really him? Could it be that simple?

"Will you stay the weekend, *beti*?" Mom asks.

I look up and meet her tender gaze. I don't want to stay, but *yes*, I will. Now that Jason has been dealt with, I am safe. Unlike Ellis, I am alive and free, and I can do whatever I like.

"Have you eaten?" Dad asks me again. He retrieves a moldy orange sitting on the microwave, presses it into my stiff palm.

I don't want to be here. I don't want to eat this fucking orange. I don't want to let Ellis go, either, but maybe it's time. Maybe I have to force myself to do this, too.

60.

Monday, October 10

Being home, it finally hits me that I will never work in a high-end law firm like Jason's. I will never have the cash to buy myself another Saint Laurent dress, or my family a holiday house in Nantucket, or a luxury vacation to St. Barts. But thanks to Jason, my tuition has been paid, and I will graduate from law school. I will find myself a husband and some job, and I will eventually get us out of debt. We will live a modest, middle-class life only slightly less sad than the one we live now.

It's more than enough for my family. I hope it is enough for me, too.

Dad drives me to the bus depot first thing Monday morning. I've noticed that while Tina and Mom have gotten new phones in the last few years, Dad still uses the iPhone 4 he bought secondhand, too many years ago to count. Before I get out of the car, I wipe the new phone clean and leave it in the drink holder between us. When he starts to protest, I cut him off.

"It's yours. I insist."

"You can't afford it."

"I decide what I can afford," I say. "You raised me to be independent, and this is what you get."

Dad takes the phone. He's starting to tear up. I quickly kiss him on the cheek and leave before he does. It would embarrass him to cry in front of me.

There's no traffic leaving Boston, and I'm back in Windermere by 8 a.m. I speed-walk home, grab my phone, laptop and backpack, and am on my way to the university a half hour later, in time for my morning classes.

Ajay is in the front row of the lecture hall, waiting for me. It feels like a million years since I've seen him, but it was only Thursday night when Tina was in town and we played DDR and ate pizza at his condo. Over the weekend, I logged into my email on my parents' computer to check in, tell him I went home for a few days and that I would see him in class today. I don't want to be a mystery anymore. I don't want the people who care about me to worry.

"Did you have a good time?" he asks me as I slide into my seat. "You look refreshed."

"Tina's forgiven me for sending her home," I say. "She wouldn't stop pestering me about you."

"Oh yeah?"

I avoid his gaze. "So how was your weekend?"

"The usual," he says. "Studying. I started watching *Deadwood*."

"Is it good? I've never seen it."

"I just started, but yeah." Ajay smiles as he fishes his textbook out of his backpack. "I think you'd like it."

He catches me staring and our eyes lock.

Ajay really is handsome. And good to me. He's the kind of guy I should be with. He's the kind of guy who would keep me on the right track.

"Maybe we can watch it together," I say.

"Yeah." He shrugs, looking down at his textbook. "Maybe."

I know I have led Ajay around in circles. I have given him hope and then taken it away, but he is too good for games. *I* am too good for them.

"Will you go on a date with me?" I ask him.

He looks over, startled.

"You invited me over for dinner last week," I say. "I'm free tonight."

"Do you mean it?"

I want to mean it, and so I nod.

"Except . . ." Ajay hesitates. "I'm the one who's supposed to do the asking, Sara."

"Says who?" I laugh. "OK, fine. Then ask me."

He beams at me, and I step out of the shadow and into his warm, dewy light. Ajay asks me, officially, to go out on a date, and when I say yes, he grabs my hand. I'm afraid. I hope he never lets it go.

The class empties and Ajay and I stay at our desks, talking. I feel natural around him when I let myself. Eager and sensitive, and *smart*. I feel like a better version of myself. Someone who I could have been if I'd never met Jason. Someone I still hope to be.

Eventually we go grab a coffee, and then we return to the

Commons. Although the sun is out, it's only just warm enough to be outside and most of the tables are empty. Ajay sits down on one of the benches, and instead of taking a seat across from him, I sit right next to him. I'm chilly, and when the breeze picks up, I squirm closer.

"Do you want to go inside?" he asks when he feels me shivering. I shake my head. We still have fifteen minutes until our next class starts, and pretty soon it'll snow and we'll wish we could stand to be outdoors.

"Let's stay out here."

Ajay sips his coffee, and then tentatively moves his arm and places it around my back. When it's secure around me, I lean into him.

"This is nice," I say quietly. I want to say more. I want to apologize for making him suffer, but if I'm going to leave the past in the past, I can't. I'm turning over a new leaf.

"What should we order for dinner tonight?" he asks me. "I don't cook. You know that, right?"

I laugh. "I didn't, but that's fine."

"Sushi?"

"Sure," I say.

"Perfect. Come straight over after babysitting. I'll chill a bottle of wine for us, and we'll eat sushi and watch *Deadwood*. We'll take the night off studying."

I like that he's being bold, that he says what he wants. If this is going to work, I need him to stand up to me.

"Sounds perfect."

"And this weekend . . ." Ajay leans in, whispering, "we're going on a *real* date."

"Is that so . . ." I tease.

Ajay debates with himself on whether to take me to one of the nicer restaurants in town or on a drive through the country, maybe to Amherst. While he's talking, I look across the Commons. I see someone watching us.

It's Tommy.

I haven't seen him since Friday morning, when I left his dorm and arrived home to find Jason waiting for me. I chew my lip, extracting myself from Ajay's arm. I need to get rid of Tommy.

"Can you give me one minute?" I say to Ajay. "I'll meet you in class, OK?"

I'm speaking hurriedly. I don't want Tommy to come over here. I glance over my shoulder to see if he's moved, and Ajay follows my gaze. He must have seen me with Tommy last week when we were walking around campus, because a flash of recognition crosses Ajay's face.

"Who is that?" he asks, standing up to join me. His mouth is tense, jealous. "Are you two . . ."

"No," I say. "He's no one. He's just a friend."

"Right. The way I'm just your friend?"

His comment stings but it's fair. I have led both of them on, Ajay for much longer. Tommy is just a puppy. A boy. Intrigued by the older woman. But Ajay needs me. In a way, I think we need each other.

Ajay is my path to redemption.

"You're not just my friend," I say.

Ajay looks at me like he doesn't believe me, so I kiss him. After I pull away, he smiles, but it only lasts a moment.

"What does he want?" He looks over at Tommy again. "Should I go talk to him?"

"I can handle it, Ajay." I'm trying not to sound irritated. "Can you go inside, please?"

Eventually Ajay goes inside, although I suspect he's watching me from the lobby window. I make my way to Tommy, walking slowly.

"So there's another guy," he spits as I approach him. "Is he your boyfriend?"

I stop short a good ten feet away from Tommy, my hands in my pockets. His voice is both bland and pissed, almost pubescent. I look at him now and don't understand what spell came over me, why I was so drawn to him. He's a twenty-one-year-old child, and I used him to feel closer to Ellis, to make sense of something that has no answer. I should feel bad, but Tommy is just a kid. He'll be fine.

"I tried texting you," he says angrily. "I tried calling. I even drove down your street to see if you were OK—"

"I was visiting my parents," I interrupt. "I left my phone at home."

"Right."

"Really," I urge. I'm annoyed and wish I didn't have to deal with this. "I'm sorry. OK? But this was never going to work."

Tommy looks pained. I wonder if he's done all the rejecting in his life and has never been on the other side. Maybe I'm helping him. This is a lesson all of us need to learn.

"I'm seven years older than you."

"Age doesn't matter."

"It matters when you're about to get a real job, and want to get married and start thinking about a family."

Tommy looks at me like he doesn't believe my reasons. I take a step closer to him.

"They found Ellis's killer," I say. "Did you see that?"

Tommy nods, looking at the ground. His eyes are red and almost dripping with anger. I don't know how much of that is meant for me.

"We both need to move on. We need to get over her." I pause. "And that means we can't—"

"I won't let you." Tommy looks up, in a rage of panic. "No, Sara. We belong together. We do—"

"Tommy, don't be ridiculous," I snap.

"This isn't over," he says, moving toward me, but when he tries to take my hands, I shrug him away.

"This *is* over," I say, edging backward. "Now leave me the hell alone."

61.

Wednesday, October 12

We take a study break to watch the press conference on Ajay's giant smart TV. He's making us another Nespresso and I'm horizontal on the couch as Detective Kelly flashes a smile on-screen and announces that Darren Peters has been charged with second-degree murder.

Ellis's parents are standing just off to the side. Her dad steps up to the mic and makes a speech about justice and community and family. He thanks the Massachusetts State Police and prosecutors for their "tireless efforts." He announces a scholarship they've started in his daughter's name.

And then it's . . . over.

"How do you feel?" I hear Ajay ask. I sit up. His condo is open-plan, and from where he's standing at the kitchen counter, he can see both me and the television. "Do you feel any sense of closure?"

I don't answer as he rounds the counter and joins me on the couch. I pull my legs up as he passes me a mug.

Closure.

Last night, when CBS News broke the story that Ellis was at Gavin's the night she died and that there was no CCTV footage of the evening, I didn't so much feel closure as satisfaction. I smiled so hard my cheeks hurt, thankful that Cassidy had finally tipped them off. Now Gavin will have reporters crawling up his ass, and if he isn't already in trouble with the law, maybe the spotlight will pressure the government to take away his liquor license and shut him down. Or at least slap a hefty fine on his desk.

I don't want Gavin to pay because what he did was illegal. I want *justice*; I want him to pay because he is an asshole and the way he treats people is wrong.

But now, watching Detective Kelly wrap up his big murder investigation in a neat and tidy bow? Telling us all that he's delivered us justice for Ellis?

I don't feel closure. I feel wildly unsettled.

"It's over now, Sara." Ajay kisses the inside of my wrist. "You can put this behind you."

I smile. "You think so?"

Ajay moves closer to me on the couch, waits for me to speak.

"I want it to be over, Ajay, but something feels off." I pause, wondering if I should tell him about the political pressure Detective Kelly was under. "What if Peters didn't do it?"

"Well, then at trial—"

I laugh, cutting Ajay off. "This won't get to trial."

"No?"

"Come on, Ajay." I sip my coffee. "You read the case law. You watch the news. Peters has a record. And we both know that means his public defender will advise him to plead guilty so he has a chance of parole before he's an old man. It doesn't matter if he did it or not."

Ajay shakes his head, smiling. "You have that little faith in the system?"

Yes, I want to say, but instead I say, "I have that little faith in people."

"So, you don't think Peters did it?" Ajay asks. "You think that girl's murderer is still out there?"

I bite my tongue, wondering if it really matters what I think. Maybe I'm too close to it. Maybe Peters *did* kill Ellis. But then why does this whole thing feel off? And if Ellis's murder wasn't a "mugging gone wrong," then what was it?

62.

SARAH ELLIS
Six weeks earlier

Daddy wants me to transfer out of Windermere.

He told me this morning. I was just stumbling in and we crossed paths in the foyer, because he was headed out for a run. He made us both coffees and sat me down in the living room, his face pained when he suggested I could do with a change of scenery.

I wasn't totally surprised to hear it. Things were actually OK earlier this summer. I even got an A retaking biology. But after the class was over, I had a lot of free time on my hands, and I ended up hanging with those girls from class a lot more. They don't have summer jobs, either, and we kind of just . . . I don't know what we did, but I lost track of time, of myself, of . . . everything. And I have no idea whether my parents do or don't know what I've been up to. Although I'm fairly sure that by now someone at the country club has told them about me and the golf pro.

"What do you think?" Daddy asked, when he suggested I switch to another university.

"Classes start in a couple weeks," I said, trying not to slur my words. "It's too late."

"Didn't Andrea transfer?"

He doesn't remember Journey's and Felix's names half the time, even though he's basically known them since we were in diapers, but Andrea wants to be a doctor, so he remembers hers.

"Tufts, is it?"

I hesitated. Daddy must have overheard me yesterday on the phone with Journey when I called to spill the tea that Andrea got a scholarship even bigger than the one she's on now, and is up and leaving me, too.

"Yeah," I said.

"It's a good school."

I was still off my rocker and not sure what he wanted from me, but then he asked me if I actually wanted to be a doctor, and then he ended up telling me about the mistakes he'd made when he was younger, and talking to me about life, like *real* life, the way he always did with Adam.

We talked so long Daddy had to skip his run and go straight to work, but before he left, he said he'd support me if I wanted to take a semester off, go traveling and bum around Australia or wherever. He even offered to give me the money.

Yep. Someone definitely told him about the golf pro.

Anyway, it's a good offer, and I'm not sure why I haven't thought about it before. I don't know what's even keeping me here anymore. The girls from my bio class are fun, but a little too much sometimes. They are the definition of self-destructive behavior. The truth is, they make me feel like shit when all I want is to feel better, to feel something—

My mother's awake. She says she heard everything. She says I can barely take care of myself living at home, and there's no fucking way I'm going to Australia.

63.

Saturday, October 15

Ajay and I leave town with nothing but a vague sense of where we're going, an old-fashioned paper map and Ella Fitzgerald playing on the sound system in his Mazda. We go apple picking and then stop at a craft brewery before making our way through a farmers market in a small town we stumble on. Later, over dinner at a hole-in-the-wall seafood restaurant near the coast, we talk about how we never did things like this with our families. We talk about *us*, Ajay and Sara, as if we are already a couple.

I try to focus on the here and now, but every time I see a flash of dark hair, I turn my head and expect to see Ellis. Every time the conversation lulls, however briefly, my mind wanders back to the press conference. To Darren Peters. To Detective Kelly.

I don't want to obsess anymore, so I have three glasses of wine at dinner and it blurs the edges for me. Afterward, I feel calmer, and when we leave the restaurant, I even tell Ajay we should take a selfie together, because it's the sort of thing girl-friends are supposed to do. It's late and the puddles on the road have started to freeze. Our breath is frosty as we smile for the camera, and I nuzzle into Ajay's neck. He takes a few pictures, kissing my cheek in one, and then playing with the pompom on my beanie in the next. We stand there after, looking through the photos. He asks me if it's OK if he sends one to his parents. I tell him that it is.

"Are you going to tell your family?" he asks.

Even though it's been less than a week, I nod. I've already told Tina, and she won't be able to keep the secret from our parents much longer.

"Will they like me?"

I roll my eyes. "Don't fish. You know they will."

Ajay grins.

"Will your parents like me?"

"They'll love you."

Ajay stops me on the sidewalk and kisses me again. He keeps doing this. He's not afraid of public displays of affection. I hope it's not because he wants to show me off.

"Let's stay the night," he says, pulling away. We both look around the street, dead quiet and cold. I can't even remember the name of the town we're in, but its Main Street looks like a carbon copy of Windermere's.

"Where?" I ask him. "We're not that far from home——"

Ajay cuts me off. "It's not that. I just . . ." He kisses me again. "I just want you right now."

I wrap my arms around him. We haven't slept together yet. I suppose tonight, after our first real date, will be the night. I can't afford to contribute anything to our dates, to pay for dinners or apples or jam or a bed and breakfast in some romantic New England town.

"I'm going to take care of you, Sara," he murmurs into my ear, as if he's read my mind. "I'm going to take care of everything."

I don't like the way he's phrased this, but I let it go. I understand the intent.

"I'm . . ." Ajay trails off, and I feel his head turn. I wait a moment, and then pull away to see what he's looking at.

"What is it?"

Ajay's staring behind me at the street. There are a few cars parked back there, next to a bar, a liquor store, an ice cream parlor and a few other businesses whose signs I can't read.

"What is it?" I ask again. I turn around to face Ajay. He looks cross, even alarmed, and I'm about to start panicking when his face relaxes and he turns his eyes back to me.

"Nothing. Sorry." He smiles brightly. "Just thought I saw someone."

My face goes white. I whip around to see what he was staring at, but he pulls me back around. He squeezes my hands, grounding me.

"Don't worry, Sara." Ajay kisses me again. "It was nothing. It was a mistake."

64.

A week passes, and then a few more. The leaves turn brown, the weather gets cold, and Ajay and I move into full-on relationship territory. It's new for both of us. Ajay has never had a serious girlfriend, and I have never been someone's serious girlfriend. I have been a daughter, sister, friend, lover, assistant, mistress. I have starred in a million different roles, but never as this.

Since our journey out of town, I have stayed over at Ajay's condo every night, going home only to pick up more clothes, my phone charger and toiletries. We make love, as Ajay calls it, most evenings, and afterward I fall asleep tangled with him in the high-thread-count sheets he admitted his mother picked out for him. We joke about the fact that I have basically moved in, that at this rate, our parents will be throwing us a big fat *shaadi* by Christmas.

I sleep well at first, wrapped in Ajay's arms, but as time goes on, I feel the anchor slipping away. My nights of good rest get farther and farther apart, until I have no choice but to drink too much wine at dinner or take Ambien to fall asleep. I swipe pill after pill from Professor Miles's medicine cabinet. I wait for her to notice, but she hasn't. Not yet.

On the nights I'm sober, I've stopped sleeping. I toss and turn after Ajay's eyes close, catching only an hour, or two if I'm lucky, before Ajay shakes me awake so we can go to class. I miss my basement suite in Zo's house. I miss the comfort of my own bed and space, my independence. But Ajay tells me he wants me here with him, and even though it's against my nature, I agree. I tell myself it's not because I'm scared to be alone. I remind myself that Jason didn't know I called the police and had no reason to hurt me, that I've shaken loose from Ollie and Rachel, that Darren Peters *must* have been the murderer. That I need to leave Ellis in the past.

I remind myself that Sara Bhaduri no longer has a reason to be afraid.

It's nearing the end of November and I'm at the kitchen table, sitting across from Benji. He's doing his math homework, and until five minutes ago, I was studying, too. Ellis's parents held a press conference this afternoon and I'm reading the online coverage. Although there have been no updates on the prosecution of Darren Peters, Drs. Ryan and Beverly Ellis have just announced that they're suing Gavin's Brew Pub Incorporated for negligence in the civil courts. They allege that the campus bar failed in its duty

of care to its customer, Sarah Ellis, by allowing her on the prem-
ises, serving her alcohol and failing to provide adequate security.
They allege that the actions of its owner, Gavin Kaczynski, led
directly to the death of their daughter.

I have not been able to stop myself from following the "Ellis
story," because it hasn't gone away. Newspapers and broadcast-
ers up and down the East Coast have been relentless in their
coverage, even though there is rarely any new information to
report. Two weeks ago, a source, who I suspect is Ellis's mother,
told reporters that she was not on Hillmont to buy drugs; that
Ellis had accidentally taken the wrong Ride home. I am thankful that my name has not yet been leaked to the press. I'm
already afraid of being called as a witness if the case against
Peters goes to trial, and unlike Detective Kelly, I have no desire
to step into the limelight.

I can't turn on the TV or open my news app without seeing
the detective's smug face as he shakes hands with the governor,
or without reading a pull quote from the small-town copper
who put the pieces together and saved the day. Among others,
he has been interviewed by WNBC, PBS, CBS Boston and all
the major Massachusetts newspapers. Often they show Ellis's
parents, too. They are holding up OK, or so they say. They're
waiting for Darren Peters to confess. They're waiting for con-
firmation that their daughter's murderer will rot behind bars.

"What smells so good?"

I look up from my computer and see Professor Miles peeling
off her coat. I didn't notice her come in.

"Chai," I say, as Benji races over to greet her. "Would you
like some?"

"Did Benji have any?"

"Yes, but it's decaf."

She nods approvingly. Lately, she's having trouble finding ways to criticize me, here at home or in the classroom. I've done every single reading for her last three seminars and handed in an essay ahead of schedule. If I do well this term, I'm going to ask her to take me on as a research assistant. I have started hunting for jobs in Boston for after graduation, and I'm going to need more than a babysitting reference from her to get one.

"Have you practiced piano yet, Benji?" she asks him.

"I'm still doing my homework—"

"Why don't you go practice now, and I'll help you finish that later."

Benji muffles a sigh and disappears from the room. Professor Miles joins me at the table, runs a hand through her hair. "What a day," she proclaims. "But how are *you* doing, Sara?"

I smile. "Oh, fine."

She's also been chatty when she gets home these days, although usually she just wants to speculate on the prosecution against Peters. She's told me twice about her friend who works for the district attorney who is "frustratingly tight-lipped about the case."

"Do you want me to start dinner before I leave?" I ask.

"No need. I thought we'd have takeout tonight." She looks at me. "You've been such a help this year, Sara. Really. And after the semester you've had!"

I shrug.

"I'm glad to see things are looking up for you."

I don't know what she means by that. I wonder if she's read my essay and if it impressed her, but then she continues.

"I heard through the grapevine that you and Ajay Shah . . ."

She raises one eyebrow at me. "Have been spending more time together than usual?"

Ah. So she's heard. Ajay is a popular guy, and the fact that he chose to date the mysterious Sara Bhaduri has been the talk of the law school. To be honest, I'm surprised it has taken this long for Professor Miles to figure it out.

"You did well," she says. "Sorry if it's none of my business—"

"It's fine," I say, even though I resent her comment. "And . . . guilty as charged."

"He's a lovely guy. Good head on his shoulders, too."

"He's what I need," I say truthfully.

"Well, I'm so glad for you two. Really *glad.*" She pauses. "Has Ajay told you about the little get-together I'm having tomorrow night?"

Ajay has told me about it, although I've known about Professor Miles's famous autumn soiree since I arrived at Windermere. Every year, the day before Thanksgiving, she brings in a catering company from Boston and populates her house with uppity Windermere professors and her colleagues at the law school, as well as the student editors of the Law Review.

"The invite does *not* include a plus-one," she says, speaking slowly to make sure I realize how generous she's being. "*But.* Ajay can bring you, if he'd like. He should get some perks as the editor-in-chief."

"Well," I say, "that's very kind."

"My daughter is coming home from Brown for the holidays. Have you met Brooklynn?"

I shake my head.

"Well, introduce yourself at the party. She's wonderful. She makes the house *lively* again."

Professor Miles has never talked about her personal life with me, but today she does. She tells me about how she met her husband at Harvard Law, that they lived in dreamlike happiness only for him to die of cancer.

"You must think I'm a cold-hearted bitch," she says afterward, teary. "I don't have any pictures of him in the house."

I remember the family photos in her bedroom, which I see every time I snoop around and steal the Ambien, but I don't say anything.

"His face upsets Benji. I had to put them away." She sighs. Hearing about me and Ajay together is making her think of her husband. It's strange to see her so vulnerable.

"What was your husband like?"

She smiles brightly, standing up, and tells me to follow her.

I pretend I'm not familiar with the upstairs of her house, and praise the decor in the hallway and her bedroom, the dimming evening sunshine that floods in from the west-facing window.

She points at the central photo in the gallery wall above her bed. Benji is just a toddler, Brooklynn eleven or twelve, and Professor Miles and her husband are holding them and each other like they've won the lottery.

"It's my favorite photo of us."

"It's lovely, Madison."

I glance over to find her studying my face. I know that she wants to see herself in me. When I was performing poorly in her class and flailing through life, she was a condescending bitch. But now I'm pulling myself together. I'm dating a fellow law student. Every day my marks, and my prospects, are improving. Now she's inviting me into her life.

"Your husband was very handsome," I say, because I know she wants to hear it. "What's his name?"

"Benjamin." She laughs. "It's very old-fashioned to name one's son after his father, but now I'm glad we did it."

"He looks just like him."

"Would you like to see some more pictures?"

It's getting late. I know Ajay is anxious for me to get back to the condo tonight because he wants us to drive out of town to the large suburban grocery store that stocks Asian groceries. He doesn't know how to cook, and I'm a little tired of doing it myself or eating takeout, so to delay the chore, I agree to look at photos. Professor Miles grabs a scrapbook from beneath her bed. We sit down side by side. It reminds me eerily of sitting with Dr. Ellis.

The photos are in no particular order, as if they lived in a shoebox at one point and were stuffed randomly into the plastic sleeves. She shows me pictures of Brooklynn as a baby, the three of them on holiday in Cape Cod or Manhattan. The happy couple, as young lawyers, in front of their old apartment in Kenmore Square.

"*Here* we are getting married near Martha's Vineyard," she says, flipping to the next page. "It was a small wedding. Fifty people or so. We were both in debt up to our eyeballs after law school." She laughs. "You think Windermere is expensive? Just think how much it cost us to go to Harvard."

I grit my teeth, smiling. "Uh-huh."

"And this," she exclaims, turning the page again, "I think this is the first picture we ever took together."

She points at a blurry group photo, taken in someone's living room. Professor Miles and her husband are wedged in the middle of a brown leather couch, snuggled up close, as their friends squeeze into the frame.

"We weren't even together then," she says. "I don't think. Or maybe we were."

"You were friends first," I say to be kind. "Like Ajay and me."

"Exactly." She smiles. "And this was our crew."

Professor Miles and her husband are the only people of color in the photo. The ten or so other law students are all white, with white tennis shoes and sparkling white teeth. I glance over them, and I'm just about to move on to the next photograph when one of the faces gives me pause.

He has brown hair, not gray, but as I focus in, there's no doubt about it.

One of the faces belongs to Jason Knox.

"You look like you've seen a ghost," I hear the professor say. I look up, panicked, and force a smile back on my face.

"I didn't eat much today."

She looks back at the photo, running her fingers over the plastic sheeting. My heart is racing. Professor Miles was friends with Jason Knox?

"Are you still in touch with these people?" I ask casually. I'm having a hard time keeping my voice level, but she doesn't seem to notice.

"Not really. These days we just see each other at the odd party or conference." She laughs. "We all got jobs and had families. It's unfortunate, but it's how it goes, I suppose."

"What about him?" I point at Jason. Sweat is sticking to my shirt, beading down the back of my neck. "He looks familiar . . ."

"Oh, yes. That's Jason Knox." She turns to me. "Didn't he—"

"Oh, of course." I smile, pausing. "I thought I recognized him. He judged my moot court in first year."

"Yes, yes, that's right. I remember him telling me he was very impressed by you." She pauses. "You're brilliant, Sara. When you apply yourself."

Professor Miles flips the page and starts telling me about the next photo, in which she and Benjamin Senior are out for a celebratory dinner after sitting the Massachusetts bar exam.

My head spins as I zone out from the chatter, thinking about the photograph on the previous page. Thinking about Jason.

Boston is a small world, and the Ivy League–educated legal community is even more tight-knit. It is not that big a coincidence for my professor to have a connection to my enemy, to a man I have only just escaped. It means nothing.

And after I convince myself that is the case, I bid Professor Miles good night, and I leave.

65.

I call Ajay and tell him I have to babysit late, that we have to delay the shopping trip. I am not ready to go to his place. Whenever Ajay thinks I'm upset, or sad, or anything but perfect, he badgers me about what's wrong until I have to make up a problem for him to solve, and right now there is nothing to fix.

I switch my phone to silent, stick it in the bottom of my backpack and hit the pavement. I don't understand why I'm so unsettled. Rationally, I know that the fact that Professor Miles and Jason are friends has no bearing on me. Yet it's a piece of information I didn't possess until today, and it's reminding me of all the things that I don't know. Perhaps that I haven't wanted to know.

I walk around campus twice. I consider going to my own

apartment, although I don't, and eventually I find myself down the street from Gavin's.

The police and state prosecutors say that the Ellis case has been solved, that all the clues fit together like a puzzle. They say the well-known neighborhood criminal is responsible, but in my gut I know he isn't. There's a piece missing, and when it's found, the picture will be different. Have I been afraid to find it?

I can't keep popping Ambien or drinking too much wine forever. I can't keep letting myself avoid the truth. Eventually, it will find me. I feel it. I know I need to find it first.

I wrap my scarf high around my face before I approach Gavin's. Usually it's busy by this time of night, but right now it's practically dead. There are only three tables occupied and no line at the bar, behind which Gavin is alone and looking at his phone. I am glad to see the media coverage has hurt business.

I walk around the block until I'm on the residential street out back, where I last saw Ellis alive. The kitchen exit is shut, and even though I know how to jimmy open the door, I suspect that with all the bad press Gavin has finally hooked up the bar's CCTV. I stand twenty feet away, near a parked car, and I don't know what I'm searching for, but I don't have to wait long. A few minutes later, the door opens and one of the kitchen guys comes out. I remember his name as soon as I see his face. Abdul. The organic chemistry student from Bangladesh.

"Hey," I say, stepping out of the shadows. "How are you?"

Abdul looks up, momentarily startled. When he recognizes me, he smiles. "Sara?" He places a cigarette on his bottom lip.

"You still haven't quit smoking, I see."

"Not quite." He lights the thing, takes a puff and then tucks his lighter back into his apron pocket. "What are you doing here? I was sorry to hear Gavin fired you."

"Do you know why?"

"Cassidy told me. She told everyone. Gavin found out that she'd tipped off the press and fired her, too."

"He can't keep getting away with stuff like this." I pause. "Maybe he won't. It looks pretty dead in there."

"Business is down. He let all the bartenders go. John and Li, too."

"Shit. Now it's just you in the kitchen?"

"And only because I agreed to a reduced wage. I need this job. I don't have time for the commute."

I vaguely remember something else Abdul told me during my first shift months back, the only other time we spoke, and my cheeks flush with embarrassment. Abdul said he used to work at a packaging plant forty-five minutes out of town. Despite his lovely personality and perfect grades, his perfect English, nobody else in little ol' Windermere would hire him.

"Anyway," he says, stomping on his cigarette and lighting another, "I just need this place to stay open a few more months. I graduate in the spring. You too, right?"

I nod, composing myself. "And then we can get the fuck out."

He laughs.

"Abdul," I say quietly, "can I ask you something?"

"Shoot."

"Cassidy said that Gavin told you guys not to talk to the police about what happened that night. Is that true?"

Abdul studies me. Uncomfortable, I wrap my coat more tightly around myself.

"Yeah," he says, after a while. "He didn't want any more

heat on the place than there already was. He told us he'd fire us if we didn't keep our mouths shut, so that's what we did. We said we didn't see anything out of the ordinary. We said we didn't remember seeing the girl."

"Did Cassidy tell the reporters that Gavin blackmailed you?"

Abdul shakes his head. "She wanted to screw Gavin over, not us. She didn't want us to get in trouble for lying."

"And did you lie?"

"I don't know about the other guys . . ."

I'm holding my breath. Abdul shifts his weight between his heels, smoking. Finally, he looks up.

"Abdul, did you see something?"

"It's probably nothing, Sara. But, *yeah*. I did see you take that girl out back. I'm sorry, I should have helped you take care of her, but she seemed all right, and Gavin always wants the grill cleaned by—"

"It's not your fault," I interrupt. "Tell me what you saw."

"You had your arms around each other and were laughing about something. It was cute."

I smile, thinking of Ellis. "Yeah?"

"Yeah, and . . ."

Abdul's face goes dark. I take a step forward.

"What is it?"

"Well . . ." He pauses. He won't look at me. He's staring at the ground again. "Right before you walked out the door, she turned around. She seemed a little scared, to be honest. She looked like she was checking to see if somebody was following her."

My hands start to shake. I stuff them into my pockets, trying to steady them. Was Ellis scared? I try to think back to us leaving. Why hadn't I noticed it?

"Say something, Sara. Shit." Abdul laughs, stiffly. "Don't judge me, OK? I know I should have told the police what I saw, but I can't afford to lose this job. I was thinking about coming forward, truly, but then I heard they found the guy who did it. So it was probably nothing."

My limbs are trembling. The night she died, Ellis was afraid of someone. Did she ask me to take her out through the kitchen on purpose?

Was someone following her?

"Sara," Abdul says abruptly. He catches my eye. "It was probably nothing. Right?"

"Right," I say, to make us both feel better. "It was nothing."

66.

SARAH ELLIS
Wednesday, September 28

My phone is blowing up.

The group chat with the old crew has been pretty quiet since Tommy and I broke up, but Journey's home from Georgetown for a few days for her gran's eightieth birthday party and she's trying to convince everyone to go out tonight. She wants the old gang back together.

Andrea said she had a "Tufts dinner thing" and it was too far to go for just drinks, although predictably Felix said he would make the drive, and Cambridge is even farther away. Nathan is in, too, of course, because what else would he do? The rest of us have all made new friends. I'm pretty sure he's the only one who hasn't.

Journey texted me privately to make sure I was coming, but I'm not sure I'll go, because Tommy hasn't replied to the thread.

I walked by him on campus today, so I know he's in town, but it won't be good for me to hang out with him. On the other hand, it's not like I have anything better to do. The girls from bio—I don't know why I still call them that in my head—are crashing some freshie event, but after the crazy shit we pulled over the weekend, I could kind of use a break.

I took a shower and now I have a voice mail from Journey telling me how dare I leave her messages on read, and that I didn't make enough time for her when she was home this summer, so I better get my tits out and show up at Gavin's tonight.

"Is Tommy going?" I asked when I called her back.

"He said probably."

"Probably?"

"I don't know why he wouldn't, so just assume the answer is yes." She paused expectantly. "It's been a year, Ellis."

"Eight months, actually. But yeah. I know." I knew I needed to get to a place where I could see Tommy, be in the same room as him, and stay in one piece.

"I'm ready," I said finally.

"Are you sure?"

"Are *you* sure you're ready to see Felix?"

Journey and Felix haven't seen each other in person since I told her he tried to kiss me, which she was rightfully pretty pissed about, even though I explained to her he was just being a drunk idiot and he really did have feelings for her. I wonder if that's why she's angling for a big group outing, a buffer, rather than having to talk to him face-to-face.

Journey paused a minute before answering.

"Who knows, Ellis. But what the hell. What's the worst that could happen, right?"

I don't know why, but I started giggling, and then Journey started laughing, and pretty soon we were in stitches and my mother was banging on my door, checking if I was OK.

"It's just Journey," I told her, wiping away the tears.

My mother cocked her hip to the side, shaking her head.

"But you're crying."

"I'm laughing."

She looked so surprised. Like, her jaw literally dropped. It was as if she couldn't remember what my laugh sounded like or something.

67.

I can't sleep.

It's annoying how peaceful Ajay looks when he's lying there next to me in his dreamless, happy slumber. I go into the living room and curl up on the couch until the first hint of dawn appears, and then I start the coffee and go wake him up.

I should have noticed Ellis was afraid. She must have suggested the kitchen exit, and I should have refused. Was it a guy from the bar who wouldn't leave her alone? One of her friends? Or maybe it really was Tommy. Maybe the police got it wrong. Could he have come back to Windermere after the hockey game without anyone noticing?

I should have done something to help her that night. I should do something *now*, but I don't know what. Detective

Kelly would find the evidence of Ellis's fear circumstantial at best, and might not even believe Abdul. He might not understand the job insecurity so many immigrants feel, and might question why Abdul did not come forward before. He might accuse him of wanting his turn in the limelight.

I'm distracted this morning, but Ajay doesn't notice. He's packing a duffel bag and keeps going on about how nervous he is about the upcoming holiday. Tonight is Professor Miles's party, but we don't plan on staying late. First thing in the morning, Ajay is driving us both back to Boston so we can spend the holiday with our families. He'll meet my parents, and they'll feed him breakfast—Mom and Dad have been fretting about what to serve for days—and the following afternoon I'll go to Ajay's family's house in the suburbs for lunch. It's moving fast, but that's OK.

It's harder to jump off a speeding train.

Ajay and I go to class, and then I go back to my apartment. Professor Miles has a dress code, and I don't have anything at the condo I can wear.

The place is dusty, and it smells like I haven't taken the garbage out in weeks, but I ignore it and start packing a bag. A wool skirt and blouse for tonight. Stockings and heeled shoes. I pack quickly, and I'm about to put my coat back on and leave when I hear a knock. Before I can think about who it might be, I hear Zo's voice calling out to me.

"Zo?" I say, running for the door. It's cold outside and the pavement is icy. "What are you doing here?"

"Saying hello, dear. Is that all right?"

I smile, opening the door and ushering her in from the cold.

She's wearing a parka so long I'm worried she'll trip, and an oatmeal-colored scarf wrapped up over her chin. I get a whiff of mildew when I lean down and hug her.

"Packing?"

"I'm going home for Thanksgiving."

"I'm off as well, soon. My son is swinging by to pick me up. He won't let me host." She unwraps herself from the scarf. "I've been relieved of my duties as head of the family. Now all they'll let me do is mind the new baby—but I think they had the baby to mind *me*."

I laugh, listening to her talk about her family. She takes the desk chair and I sit on the foot of the bed across from her. I offer her some tea, but she declines, which is good, because I don't have any.

"You've been well, then, Sara?"

Zo seems alert today. She knows my name and her eyes are bright, switched on. I'm pleased she didn't call me Rita.

"I have, thanks. I'm sorry I haven't come to visit you again—"

"No apologies in this house, dear. I don't want you up there dying of old age with me. I want you in class. I want you studying."

She's so warm it's like sitting by a fireplace. I lean in closer, smiling.

"You haven't been home much, though, have you? New boyfriend?"

"You could say that, Zo."

"That lucky dog. Don't let him derail your own life, though, like mine did. You'll keep this place, won't you?"

Ajay has suggested I give it up, but I don't tell Zo this. I tell her I won't.

"Good! Well, when I heard you down here just a moment ago, I thought I'd better jump on the chance and check."

"Oh." My cheeks burn hot. "I'm so sorry. Was I making too much noise?"

"Not at all. Before you ran off with your fella, I liked hearing you move about." She reaches for my hand, squeezes. "I was so worried that night that poor girl died."

My eyes lock with Zo's.

"The police wouldn't let me out of the house. Until I heard you rumbling around downstairs, I thought something might have happened to *you* . . ."

Zo's chattering fades away into white noise. My ears are hot, humming, and I can feel my heart pounding in my chest.

I close my eyes, summoning the memory. I'm walking on Hillmont. It's dark and quiet and I can feel someone up ahead before I see him. Officer Reynolds is standing there, a hand up high, the other one protectively on his holster. He tells me to stay back, but I refuse. I keep going, and when I see Ellis, I collapse. I wake up, drowsy, in the back of a police car, drifting into and out of reality.

And then I go to the station.

I open my eyes. I can't conceal my panic from Zo, and I gasp as it hits me. I didn't go inside my apartment that night, so Zo couldn't have heard me.

She heard someone else.

68.

"Oh, don't look so alarmed, dear. I don't spy on you!" Zo exclaims. "It's nice to know someone isn't too far away. It's like having my boys in the house again."

I smile for her, although I can't manage any words yet.

"And I'm especially glad I heard you that night. Otherwise, I would have worried myself sick."

"Well." I clear my throat. "Here I am."

"Here you are." She nods. "But you'd better run, hadn't you? Your boyfriend will be waiting."

I insist on walking Zo back up to her door. I don't want her to slip. Then I grab my tote bag and make my way to Ajay's. It's dusk and I'm getting paranoid again. I feel like I'm being followed.

And I don't know what to believe.

Zo may be misremembering what she heard the night Ellis died, but if what she said is true, someone was in my apartment. Was it Jason? I believed so readily that he wasn't involved, but maybe I shouldn't have. Maybe he did kill Ellis. Maybe I am still trapped in his game.

But how does that even make sense? Abdul said Ellis was afraid when she left the bar; someone, perhaps even Tommy, might have been following *her.*

There is something I don't know. It's lurking in the shadows, and I can't live like this. No matter what the cost, I can't live without knowing the truth.

I scroll though my phone and find the number from which, months ago, Detective Kelly contacted me. I call the number, and when it goes straight to voice mail, I speed-walk back into town. I pass a Starbucks and order a venti mocha, and then I go to the police station. Just my luck, Sally the receptionist is at the front desk.

"It's *you,*" she says brightly as I enter. "The girl without a phone. Are you here for Detective Kelly again?"

"I am." I set down the drink on the counter. "And I thought you might need a pick-me-up."

She glances at the cup skeptically, and then back at me.

"You mentioned last time that Detective Kelly had yet to bring you your venti mocha—"

"Don't you have a good memory!" She cuts me off, beaming. "Well, thank you, darling. It's a nice gesture. But I'm afraid he isn't in right now. Duty calls."

"Do you know where he is?"

I am being transparent, crass. Sally knows that I'm trying

to bribe her with the Starbucks, but I don't care. I need to talk to him.

"He's busy—"

"Sally, it's urgent. It's . . ."

I trail off as her eyes widen. I don't know if the information I have is important, but in the wrong mouth, it could be stretched into something worse than gossip.

The kitchen guy thought the victim looked a little scared.

The old lady may have heard some noises.

What I know is nothing on the surface, but scratch beneath it, something is there. At whatever cost, Detective Kelly needs to know, too.

"Is it about a case?" Sally asks me. Her face is serious now, business. She takes the lid off the mocha and blows on the surface.

"Yes."

"And do you have his cell?"

I read the phone number I have out to her, and she nods.

"He's not answering," I say.

"Well, keep trying," Sally says, lowering her voice. "He's on his way to New York *City*. And if you turn on CNN at around 9:05 p.m., you'll see why."

69.

Outside the station, I leave Detective Kelly a voice mail telling him I have new information about Ellis's murder and that he should call me back as soon as possible. I send him a text saying the same thing, then I go to Ajay's.

He's annoyed that I took so long, and by the time I change, we're fifteen minutes late to the party. Professor Miles has filled her house with fancy food and fancy people, jazz music and amuse-bouches. Ajay is in heaven. I wish I hadn't agreed to come.

I keep checking my phone, willing Detective Kelly to call me back. Will he believe me? I wonder if Darren Peters has finally confessed, if the police will even investigate the murder further. They should bring in Abdul for questioning, John and Li, too, and find out if they can corroborate Abdul's story or know if anyone followed Ellis and me out the kitchen exit. And what about Gavin? He was the one who found Ellis passed out in the bathroom, or at least one of the customers told him she was there. Maybe Gavin remembers more than he admits.

I stay by Ajay's side for the next hour, half listening to his conversations with other editors on the law review and various professors and faculty members. I'm glad Ajay is good at parties, because I don't have the bandwidth to be articulate tonight. My head is lost in time and space, floating across town to Gavin's, back to my basement apartment. If someone was in my house that night, even though nearly two months have passed, the police might still find fingerprints. Whose would they find? Over the past two years, only a handful of people have been inside. Ajay, Zo, Jason . . .

I shudder, thinking about him, half expecting him to walk through the front door any minute. I wonder if Professor Miles invited him.

"Expecting a call?" Ajay asks me. I'm checking my phone for the thousandth time tonight, and I look up sheepishly. We're at the bar and he's pouring himself another glass of wine.

"No," I say, "just tired."

"And a little bored?" He offers me the bottle, but I press my hand over my glass and shake my head.

"A little, maybe."

"Me too." He laughs. "But . . ."

"Yes?"

He looks at me disapprovingly. "You need to put your phone away."

My "serious boyfriend" has just given me an order. I am

speechless. I would be immeasurably furious if I weren't so distracted, but in that moment I decide to go along with it. Detective Kelly isn't going on the air for another thirty minutes. According to CNN online, he'll appear just after the hour alongside one of our House representatives, and they will be interviewed on the Ellis case and the current state of the criminal justice system. He will not be looking at his phone right now; the makeup team will be powdering his face and getting his microphone working. I send him one last text telling him where I am, and then slip my phone back into my purse.

The minutes pass by more slowly now. Ajay introduces me to his first-year tort law professor, who doesn't say much but won't let us leave the conversation, either. At 8:45, Professor Miles turns down the music and summons the student editors of the law review for a photograph in the library. Ajay kisses my cheek before disappearing, and just when I'm starting to worry that I'll be stuck conversing with this boring professor forever, I feel a tap on my shoulder.

"Are you Sara?" a girl asks me after I excuse myself and turn around. She is the spitting image of Professor Miles, her hair natural and cropped short, a maroon sweater dress hugging her perfect figure. "I'm Brooklynn."

"Hey." I extend my hand, and she shakes it firmly. "It's nice to finally meet you."

"You, too." She steps closer. "Have you been to one of these before?"

"No. You?"

She shakes her head. "First time Mom's invited me. She's shocked I got into Brown. She wants to show me off."

I smile. "How long are you home?"

"I'm here for a week, but I'm ready to go back already, if you know what I mean."

I don't know what to say to that, and so I sip the dregs of my wine. Professor Miles isn't an easy woman, but if she gave me a free ride to the college of my choice and a house like this to come home to, I wouldn't be bad-mouthing her to a stranger.

"So, I *heard* that Ellis took your Ride the night she died," Brooklynn says suddenly. "Is that true?"

My chest tightens.

"Sorry, I know Mom promised you she wouldn't tell anyone, but she can't help herself. You know her." Brooklynn sips her drink and starts chewing on an ice cube. "I'm surprised that part of the story isn't in the papers. Do the police know? Do the prosecutors?"

I hesitate. "They do, yeah."

"Why haven't you gone to the papers to tell them it was your Ride? I bet you could get yourself in the *New York Times*."

"Well," I say, shifting my weight between my feet. Brooklynn is annoying me. "I suppose I don't want to color the investigation—"

"Do you *know*," she interrupts, "a lot of people don't believe it? They think the Ride-switch story is a cover. They still think she was on Hillmont buying drugs."

"Which people?" I pause, and then I understand. "Oh. Right. You went to Ellis's school, Bishop Bailey, right? Were you friends?"

"We knew each other." She shrugs. "But I was a year behind her, so not really."

"Do you have her on Instagram?"

Brooklynn stops chewing, eyeing me.

"Or maybe her family deleted her account already . . ."

"No, they haven't." Brooklynn is staring at me, suspicious. "It's still up."

"Would it be totally weird if you showed me?" I wait a beat, and then push on. Suddenly, I'm desperate. "Her profile is private, and I don't know, I'm just curious . . ."

"I get that." Brooklynn pulls out her phone. "Sure."

She doesn't hand me her phone but just holds it out while I scroll through Ellis's account, slowly. These are not the pictures Dr. Ellis had in her scrapbook. These are of Ellis in the weeks and months leading up to her death, where she's out partying, or posing in front of a wall of graffiti with her hip cocked to the side, or taking a picture of herself in the mirror.

She is a gorgeous girl, there is no doubt about that, and as I scroll from photo to photo, I see how much I still don't know. How much I'll never know about this mysterious girl who might have died in my place.

I keep scrolling. I don't know what I'm looking for, but I keep going even after Brooklynn gets bored of the charade and starts to sigh. Eventually, I stop at a photo dated fifteen months ago. It's a selfie of her and a boy at the beach. They are lying on their stomachs, their chins propped up on elbows, sand and ocean sparkling in the background. He has blondish-brown hair and his jaw is covered in scruff. His eyes are off to the side, aloof. Ellis is staring over at him hungrily.

"Who is that?" I ask out loud, tapping my thumb. The location is set to Cape Cod, but the boy is not tagged in the post.

"Her ex-boyfriend," Brooklynn says impatiently. "You done yet?"

"I didn't realize she had another boyfriend."

"She's only ever had the one."

My heart pounds in my ears. I open my mouth to speak. My tongue is dry. I try to swallow.

"What's his name?" I ask, looking back at the photo. At the boy I have never met before in my life.

"Tommy," she answers. "Tommy Eagle."

70.

SARAH ELLIS
Thursday, September 29

This cute girl with the same name as me rescued me tonight at Gavin's.

I got *super* drunk, even though I meant to stay sober. I knew I would have to see Tommy, and I wanted to keep my wits about me—you know, act like the mature ex-girlfriend I most certainly, definitely am. Anyway, Journey and I got to the bar early enough to score a booth, and I drank a Diet Coke while she, Felix and Nathan shared a pitcher of piss-warm beer, and I was feeling super stable and prepared when Journey leaned over and showed me a text from Tommy. His dad got tickets to a Bruins game. He wasn't going to make it.

It felt like a swift kick in the coochie, if I'm being totally honest, and Journey gave me a look that said, "I love you and I know you were kind of looking forward to seeing him," and

I just shrugged, and then she went to the bar and ordered a million shots of tequila, most of which I drank, and let's just say the rest was history.

I remember drinking games . . . I remember yelling at someone at some point for some reason that made sense at the time . . . but I definitely don't remember most of the night.

I sort of "woke up" when I heard someone shouting "Last call," and I realized it was just me and Nathan left in the booth. I looked around, searching for Felix and Journey. A grin spread across my lips when I found them. They were pulling their coats on by the door, and they had their tongues down each other's throats.

"Wow, check them out!"

Nathan didn't hear me. He was droning on about something I couldn't have cared less about.

"Huh?" I interrupted.

"Do you know what I mean, though?" he continued. "The Republicans can't afford to lose his supporters. If they want to unite the party—"

"Wow," I said drily, "hot take."

Nathan's cheeks reddened as I sat up straighter in my seat, and just as a wave of nausea rocked me to my core, I noticed that Nathan had his arm all the way around me. And his other hand was stroking my leg pretty close to my crotch.

"Don't touch me," I slurred.

"It's OK, Ellis," Nathan coaxed. "Just relax."

I literally couldn't believe what he was doing, and I felt like I was about to throw up, right there, all over us. I pressed my hand against my cheek.

"I'm going to be sick."

Nathan squeezed my inner thigh, hard enough that it hurt. I clenched my legs together and tried to stand up, but when I moved, he grabbed me by the elbow and pulled me back down.

"Back off," I managed, swaying. "What the f—"

"Come *on*, Ellis." He cupped the top of my ass. "I know you want— "

I pushed him away and stood up, and there was a flash of anger in his eyes that I didn't expect.

"We belong together, Ellis."

My body convulsed. I tasted vomit in my mouth.

"Don't laugh at me."

"Then don't be a fucking *creep*, Nathan."

His face went white. It made him look like a ghost.

He tried to follow me to the bathroom but stopped when I started making a scene, pushing his hands away. I vomited as soon as I got to the toilet, and the next thing I knew, I was on the floor of the bathroom stall and this girl Sara was helping me stand up. I must have passed out. I don't really remember.

She's so cool, Sara. We didn't talk for very long, but she's such a good listener and I feel like she gets me. I'm pretty sure we're going to be friends. Do you ever have a feeling about someone? I was going to ask her to come over and hang out and watch a movie or something, but I spotted Nathan sitting in his parked car with the lights out like a pervert, and I got spooked and left.

I don't know what to do. Nathan has crossed the line one too many times, and I'm going to block his number tomorrow and kick him out of the group chat. I don't care if Tommy thinks I'm just being dramatic, and Andrea calls me rude, and Felix says I'm being a hypocrite because I forgive *him* whenever he acts like a pig.

But, I don't know, I think something changed for me tonight. Like, I can't keep ignoring this stuff anymore and just hoping it'll stop, convincing myself that *I* am the problem. I can't go on pretending I don't notice how guys treat me, or use me, because I do.

And it's not right.

I'm feeling a lot better than earlier, but I need a glass of water *urgently*. I don't think the driver is too pleased about it, but I'm horizontal on the back seat of the car. The window is open and the breeze feels good on my face, and my clothes feel good on my skin, and I just feel really kind of good, you know? I know that's strange after a night like this, but I do. The weed has put my head right, and after talking to Sara, everything seems clearer, brighter—

Wait, where *am* I?

It feels like I've been back here for an eternity, and I should have been home by now.

My mother won't be happy, but in the morning I'm going to tell Daddy I want to go to Australia. I'll promise not to party too much, and to spend their money on something wholesome and active or . . . something. Maybe I'll do a yoga retreat or learn how to scuba dive. Maybe I'll get a job picking oranges.

Maybe, when I'm ready, I'll move back to Windermere and go to law school like Sara.

I know I keep saying it, but I really want to do better. I want to be good. And, this time, I really want to mean it.

71.

Wednesday, November 23

The room spins away from me as I storm away from Brooklynn, speechless. I don't bother with my coat as I slip out the front door, sit down on the front stoop. Blood is rushing to my brain, so I dunk my head between my legs, shaking. I can't breathe, and I clutch my chest, trying to slow down my panting. Trying to understand what the fuck is going on.

Tommy Eagle is not Tommy Eagle. But then, who is he? Who is the boy I first saw at the funeral, who seemed to know Ellis like he loved her? The guy who *fucked* me?

He looks familiar, but I don't know him. He is not Tommy Eagle.

Tears are leaking from my eyes as I sit up straight, calming myself. I check the time on my phone. Detective Kelly's segment on CNN should be over by now. Any minute, he'll call me back, and I'm about to dial his number again when I sense something moving in the shadows.

I stand up slowly, the phone clutched in my palm. I'm shivering, although I can barely feel the cold. The wind is brisk, and dead leaves dance across the sidewalk, beneath the wheels of parked cars. I blink, and when I see a shadow quiver behind a tree, I know that I'm not being paranoid. I *am* being followed.

I can see the truth emerging.

"I know you're there," I say forcefully. When no one immediately appears, I walk down the path winding through Professor Miles's rock garden.

"Hello?"

"Hello."

Even though I summoned him, his voice is unexpected. A shiver runs down my spine when he appears from behind a parked car.

It's him.

The boy who isn't Tommy Eagle.

"Don't come any closer," I say.

"Sara?" He laughs. "What a coincidence. I'm—"

"I know you're not Tommy."

He stops. There's just enough light to see his face tense up, his nostrils flare.

"Who *are* you?" I whisper.

He doesn't respond, and my head spins as I remember him watching me at the funeral. Seeing *his* photograph at Ellis's house, and in the detective's photo album. He did know Ellis. I had noticed the way he was staring at her in their class photo and incorrectly assumed he was Tommy.

"Did you kill her?" I ask him.

My voice is hoarse, wavering. Those few nights we spent together, I'd been in a dream, walking and thrashing around, afraid of Jason, when the true demon was right next to me.

"It was you, wasn't it?"

I take a step backward, studying him.

"You were obsessed with her. You followed her that night, and you killed her. Didn't you?"

"Sara—"

"You killed her and then—" I gasp, pressing a hand to my mouth. Zo called the cops, and he must have thought he couldn't get away in time.

"I left the window open that night," I say. "You broke into my apartment to hide. Zo heard *you*."

My face is burning, and I take another step back, nearly tripping on the rocks. I want to scream. I grip my phone. I need to get away from him, and I'm about to call for help, but then he speaks.

"Sara, there's no reason to be alarmed, OK?" He smiles brightly, but I can see through it. He wants to hurt me. "Let's get out of here. Let's talk, just the two of us—"

"I'm not going anywhere with you."

"I can explain."

"Explain what, you sick fuck? Why you killed her? Why—"

"I just wanted to talk to her, Sara. I just want to talk to *you*." His voice makes my skin crawl. I don't recognize him anymore. "She wanted me to take her home. She *did*. She flirted with me all night. She kept looking at me. She touched my arm—"

"You're disgusting—"

"She's disgusting," he barks. "That slut would sleep with anyone but me."

"So you followed her that night. You followed her Ride, and then you strangled her."

"I thought she was going to hook up with some other guy, after spending all night with *me*—"

"And that gave you the right to *kill* her?"

"She screamed. She made me do it. She wouldn't shut up. I—I *had* to."

Tears are streaming down my face. Ellis is dead. This boy *killed* her. He stole her future, and nobody can ever give it back.

"You're a mess, Sara. Look at you. Just like her." He smiles, takes a small step forward. "You need me."

"I said, stay where you are—"

"You and Ellis are so similar." The boy's lips curl upward. "You both pretend to be the Virgin Mary, but you are complete disasters. You know that?"

I'm shaking, standing there in the dark, freezing cold.

"I held her textbooks. I bought her coffee. I saved her seats. I was her fucking toy poodle, Sara." He clenches his fist, stares up at the sky. "Finally, *finally*, Tommy ended things and I thought—I *thought* maybe she'd grow up. She'd come to her senses—"

"But she didn't," I finish.

The boy's face is blank. Soulless. "She barely even knew I was alive."

"She saw you for what you are," I fire at him. "Scum. *Nothing*. A fucking murderer—"

"I didn't mean to kill her," he spits. "She ruined the last three years of my life, and I wasn't going to let her ruin the rest of it. I needed to know that I wasn't going to get caught. I was in your house. I needed to know you didn't suspect—"

"So you followed me," I say. I think about that first night, walking home from Professor Miles's house. Checking out a book from the basement of the library. The look on Ajay's face when we were on our date a few towns over and he looked like he'd seen a ghost. "You still are. You were following me that night we met in the cafeteria—"

"You were the one who said hello."

"I thought you were Tommy."

"Fuck Tommy. Ellis was wrong to pick him—"

"What exactly was your endgame here?" I spew. I'm not in control. I need to get away from him. I need to call the police. Cautiously, I take a step back toward the house. "How long did you think I was going to believe you were someone else?"

His eyes twitch.

"You think you love me, don't you? Ellis is gone. You killed her. And you needed a new obsession—"

"Shut up."

"Do I remind you of her?" I spit. My thumb is on the home button on my screen, and I glance down quickly as it moves toward the number nine. "Did you picture her when you fucked me? You're pathetic."

"I'm warning you—"

"You think you can take whatever you want, huh? That it's your birthright?" I press down on the number nine and then move my thumb up to one. "Well, guess what? You can't. You're nothing. You're a *creep*—"

He lunges for me, and I don't have time to get out of the way, to complete the 911 call. My body hits the rock garden as he tackles me to the ground. I'm winded, crushed beneath his weight.

He's too big, too heavy. He wraps his hands around my neck, and I can't push him off. I see my mother's face as I lie there struggling to breathe, thrashing. I see my father, too, and Tina, wiping the sweat off my face with the back of her hand. They tell me that they love me. They tell me that this is the end.

I will be strangled on someone else's doorstep, just like Ellis. No one is coming outdoors during a party. No one is outside tonight, in this deathly cold. I am alone in the world. I am not going to be rescued. But as I choke on the last bit of air in my lungs, I decide to survive.

I look into his eyes as he looms over me, forces his strength against my windpipe. My legs and arms kick aimlessly as the pain starts to dull, and I can sense it's almost over. I'm seeing spots. I'm seeing red. But then my right hand scrapes against a rock, and I find the strength to grab it.

He is tiring, too. His face is wet. He is panting. The exertion of murdering a woman takes it out of weak, sniveling little boys. His grip eases, just for a moment, but it's enough. I tense my body, my hand gripping the rock like an amulet. Then, with every ounce of strength I can muster, I smash it against his head.

72.

Six Months Later

S araswati Bhaduri."
    The dean pronounces my name correctly. I beam, my shoulders back as I walk across the stage. He is waiting for me on the other side, Madison Miles and my other professors applauding just behind him. The dean hands me my degree and shakes my hand, and then we turn to face the photographer so she can capture the moment. My wide smile, and flowing black gown, and cap with gold trim.

My graduation day.

The dean moves on to the next student, and I continue across the stage. At the far corner, I stop again as instructed, posing for the secondary photographers, the well-wishers in the auditorium with their iPhone cameras.

The first few rows are a sea of black, my fellow classmates.

Just behind them are my parents and Tina, who arrived two hours early to reserve seats near the front. My mother is crying, my father is cheering like he's at a cricket game and Tina is taking photos with one hand and waving at me with the other. I grin and do a little twirl, which causes them to cheer harder. When I see the student behind me approach, my time in the spotlight is up. I wave at my family one last time, and then I return to my seat with the other graduates.

"Congratulations," someone says to me.

I look over. It's Fiona, or Fifi, as she likes to be called. She is one of the many classmates who have been treating me like a friend since I returned to school with Ajay's arm around my shoulder and bruising on my neck.

"Thanks," I whisper. "Congratulations to you, too!"

I hate the minor celebrity-like status I've achieved ever since the story came out, but that will be over tomorrow when I am able to leave Windermere for good. When I can go back to a place where everyone has already forgotten what happened.

I was still in the hospital recovering from a ruptured trachea when a red-faced Detective Kelly went on television and told the world they'd arrested the wrong man. He explained how they'd searched Nathan Price's car and dorm room, finding Ellis's high-school copy of *Macbeth*, a pair of her underwear and a bathing suit, as well as her purse, wallet, and phone. He also mentioned that her phone contained a journal entry that documented how Nathan Price had sexually harassed and stalked her the night she was killed.

"We ruled him out based on the information we held at the time," Detective Kelly said vaguely, only to be skewered by reporters about the fact that it had taken the near-murder of yet another student for him to figure out the truth.

Shortly after that, several of Ellis's friends, as well as a former teacher at Bishop Bailey Hall, told the press that there was always something off about Nathan Price. In hindsight, they said, he did seem rather obsessed with her. Even the police, upon a further review of Ellis's phone records, noticed the disturbingly persistent way Nathan seemed to communicate with Ellis, sending her texts and emails that often went unanswered or rebuked.

Funny how, for men, whatever they do is right until there's indisputable evidence that forces us to say they are wrong. Funny. If Nathan Price hadn't started stalking me, he would have gotten away with murder.

In the aftermath, Sally spoke to the reporters, too. She told them about how I'd come down to the station just hours before Nathan Price tried to kill me, that Detective Kelly had never bothered getting back to "the poor girl who could have been next."

The detective has since left Windermere. Everyone blames him, but I don't. He's no worse than any of us, just a cog in a machine that doesn't care about him, a scapegoat to make us all feel better about the world. Rumor has it he transferred somewhere more rural. I wish him well. I wonder if he's gone home.

The graduates continue their parade across the stage, and without thinking, I reach up and finger my neck. The bruises have finally faded, and my windpipe has made a full recovery, but sometimes I can still feel his fingers around me like a vise. The boy who isn't Tommy Eagle.

I didn't kill him. The rock gave him a mild concussion, and he was conscious by the time I managed to crawl to the front door for help, and Professor Miles's autumn soiree became even more famous.

Now, Nathan Price is in prison. He pled guilty to second-degree murder and attempted murder, and will have little to no chance of ever getting parole. I've tried not to think about him in the six months that have passed, and I try not to think about Ellis, either, but on a day like today, I can't help it.

She will never graduate from university. Her parents will never sit in this auditorium and tell her how smart she is, and capable, and beautiful, the way my family did before the ceremony started. Because of Nathan Price, Ellis doesn't have a future. She lives only in the past of the people who loved her, in the memories that they shared.

I press my hand against my chest, my heartbeat slowing and a sense of calm washing over me. I don't know how, but she lives on in me, too.

Ajay is this year's gold medalist and delivers the valedictorian address, somber and hopeful and at times even funny. I laugh at his jokes, along with the others, and after the ceremony and our official class photo, I seek him out at the bottom of the stage as we return our caps and gowns.

"Congratulations," I say, approaching. "Great speech."

He looks up, frowning at the sight of me. "You think?"

"You spoke really well."

"I was nervous."

"Well, I couldn't tell at all."

The auditorium is starting to empty. We are supposed to go outside. Student administration has erected a large white tent on the lawn, where there are appetizers and orange juice and white wine waiting for us.

"I saw your family at the front," he says. "They cheered for me, too."

"Of course they did." I smile. "Although I doubt your parents did the same for me."

"At least they didn't throw garbage."

I laugh, and even Ajay's face splits into a grin. This is the third time we've had a civil conversation since the breakup, and the very first time one of us has cracked a joke about it.

Ajay took care of me after I got out of the hospital. He packed up all my things from Zo's basement and moved me into his condo, folding my clothes and organizing them into his closet as I watched him from the bed and managed sips of ginger ale through a straw.

He took notes for me during the week of school I missed, and called my parents every day on my behalf when it was still too difficult for me to speak. He hired a housekeeper to cook and clean, and he catered to my every whim, and for those first few months, briefly, I felt . . . I felt like I could move forward with him. I felt like I could let go of my past and accept a future by his side, content and average.

I was very wrong.

I thought my family would be devastated. It's why I put off ending things with Ajay for so long. But my mother told me there were plenty of other fish in the sea, and my father said he'd never warmed to Ajay to begin with, that he didn't like how Ajay tried to control me. My parents may run an ethnic grocery store, but they are not stereotypes. They raised Tina and me to take charge of our own lives, to go for what we truly want.

And that's exactly what I'm going to do.

"What's next for you?" Ajay asks me. Walking in stride, we leave the auditorium and go outside. "When do you sit the bar?"

"The last week of July. You?"

"Same." He pauses. "And what happens after?"

We're outside now, at the top of the grand staircase that leads down to the lawn. The sun is high in the sky, and there is a buzz of freshness and excitement among the students, a collective sigh of relief. A rose-tinted outlook toward the future.

"I got a job," I say, scanning the crowd for my family. "I . . ."

I trail off when I spot them. They are not alone.

"That's fantastic," I hear Ajay say. "Where—"

"Huh?" I whip around, back to Ajay. My pulse is racing. "Pardon?"

"I said that's fantastic you got a job," Ajay says. "Where are you going to be working?"

"In Boston."

"Really?"

He looks hopeful. He'll be back in Boston, too. He's still not over the breakup and is like a dying dog in need of a shotgun.

"Ajay, I'll see you around. OK?" I force a smile. "I have to go."

I jog down the stairs, my heels clacking against the stone. Down on ground level, I can't see my family anymore. I cut through the crowd, in the direction of where I saw them. I wonder if they're still there.

I wonder if I was imagining who I saw standing right next to them.

My breath is shallow as I worm my way through the crowd. I'm waylaid several times by well-wishers, fellow students who want a selfie or to introduce Sara Bhaduri, the girl from that news story six months ago, to their parents and partners. I smile through gritted teeth, offering them the bare minimum before excusing myself.

I need to find my family. I need to . . .

I duck around a large party, and just then, I see him. He looks the same as ever, a chiseled jaw and gray hair and a smile he thinks can light up a room. I slow down, watching him. He is holding a glass of wine, and his other hand is on my father's shoulder. Dad is laughing, and they're speaking in animated voices about something, but I'm too far away to hear what it is. My mother is nodding proudly, and Tina is smiling, her black maxi dress swishing against the lawn, a hip cocked to the side.

"Look who it is!"

Mom catches sight of me, and a beat later they all turn to look. Wide-eyed, I approach them and protectively wrap my arm around Tina's waist.

"You were wonderful, *beti*," Dad says proudly. "My camera roll is full."

Mom blubbers. "We are so proud of you—"

"Good job, sis," Tina says, squeezing me back. "You clean up well."

I swallow hard, smiling at each of them. And then I look at Jason.

"Surprise," he says. The skin around his eyes crinkles as he smiles at me.

The air is tense, and silent. My chest is tight, and I'm wondering what I'm going to say, when Tina speaks for me.

"Sara doesn't like surprises. Look at her. Even good ones."

"This is a good surprise." Jason grabs a glass of wine from the tray of a passing waiter, presses it into my hand. "Isn't it, Sara?"

I take a sip, holding his gaze.

"Of *course* this is a good surprise," Mom says, embarrassed. "Sara. It's your graduation day. Are you not happy to see your new *boss*?"

If I had a friend, if I trusted anyone enough to confide in them, they would look at me right now and ask: What the hell is wrong with you, Sara? Why did you let a good guy like Ajay slip through your fingers? After everything that's happened, why are you going back to *Jason Knox*?

I catch sight of Madison Miles across the lawn, schmoozing, and I offer her a small wave of gratitude. It was her that I thought of when I arrived home at the condo one evening to find Ajay studying at the kitchen table, having waited for me to organize his dinner, and the idea of having to be his little Indian wife made me sick to my stomach. The thought of spending my life smaller, nicer, weaker, for *him*?

Kill. Me. Now.

I could be Madison Miles, easily. I could be a strong woman of color who follows the rules and breaks down barriers in the conventional way. The sort of woman who is a decent lawyer and half-decent mother, who likes to believe she is exceptional in her ability to have it all.

The thing is, I don't particularly like children, or when a man tells me what to do, and Madison Miles may be a role model but she's not my role model. I had a taste of something special, a glimpse of how the other half lives, and I want more than what society has told me is acceptable. I want to pay down my family's debts and buy them the life they deserve. I want to pay Tina's way at the college of her choice.

But most of all, I want to be rich.

I glance around the lawn at my gleaming fellow graduates. They are so proud of themselves, crowding into self-congratulatory huddles, thinking they've done something worthy and this happy moment is their prerogative.

Only one in ten of them, or even one in twenty, will go on to do any good in this world. Many will get bored by the law, or burned out, and the rest will continue to prop up a system that doesn't work. They will buy organic food, and retweet articles about greenhouse gases and Black Lives Matter, but they will never once go to a protest. They will never lift one of their perfect, manicured fingers to benefit anyone's life but their own.

I don't judge them. They can't help themselves. Life was handed to them on their grandmother's bone-white china, and it would have been rude not to take it, not to accept what is theirs. To send it back to the kitchen and ask the chef to divide it into smaller pieces so everyone can have a bite.

Law school has been an education. I have learned about the common-law backbone of our country, and our constitutional rights, and the fact that no one gets what they deserve.

They get what they have the courage to take.

"Nice dress," Jason says to me, when we have a moment alone. "Did I buy that one for you?"

"You can't do that in the office," I say.

"Do what?"

"Act familiar." I take a step closer. "I don't want any rumors. I'm your new associate and we barely know each other. Understood?"

Jason holds my gaze, challenging me, but I won't back down. He is tiresome and predictable, but he is my first-class ticket out of here, and until I arrive at my destination, I suppose I'll need to keep him around.

We have come to an arrangement, Jason and I, a carefully negotiated cease-fire that will benefit us both. He's hired me officially at the law firm, and in return, I will continue working for him off the books. I will manipulate and gain the trust of our clients, but I will no longer be the assistant, or play the pretend mistress. I will get a seat at the table where the real business is conducted. I will help vet new clients, which we will not take on if they exploit women or children.

I will get my hands dirty and, of course, my half of the profits.

I sip my wine and Jason tells me about a client across the lawn, who he helped buy a Montauk property with cash the family had been keeping offshore for generations. The Connecticut lawmaker at the juice bar, a different classmate's father who was nearly removed from office before Jason balanced his books and disguised the embezzled funds.

Corrupt, incorrigible men will always exist. They will always need a little bit of "legal advice."

It might as well be from us.

I have deleted all the photos of Jason and me and instructed Lacey to do the same, told her I no longer required her services. Jason watched me do it. He even had his private investigator go through everything I owned to make sure every copy was permanently deleted.

It was a big ask, but I made sure he returned the favor. Have you read the papers recently? Ollie and Rachel Cullen have been arrested for child sex trafficking. It's all over the news. Even my parents heard the story.

Rachel didn't just find girls in clubs and on the street. Her associates groomed them online, and someone (Jason) tipped off the FBI about where to find them.

The digital paper trail is damning, and more than a dozen people are going to jail, although Jason tells me that Ollie and Rachel's new lawyer will probably get them out in a few years. It's not nearly enough—they deserve to die in there—but maybe it's enough time to change a young girl's life and give her a chance. Wherever she is, maybe it will give Isabella a chance.

"Do you want to get out of here?" I say to Jason.

My family has returned with strays, other proud mummies and daddies, and my parents are bragging to them about Tina's early acceptance to Yale.

"Racy," Jason whispers. "Now who's starting rumors?"

I dig my heel into the top of his foot, my face neutral.

"You scuffed my shoes."

"Let's go shopping," I say. "I'll buy you a new pair."

Jason barks out a laugh, and the whole group turns to us, asks us what is so funny.

They're good people and will never be in on the joke. But neither will Jason. He thinks he's my boss, but now that I've pushed my way into the room where the real business is done, *I* am in charge.

Jason hasn't realized it yet, but I will be the one calling the shots.

In five years, I want you to go online and stalk me. Comb through my social media, and my LinkedIn profile, and look for the bread crumbs. Go to Boston, where I'll own a big house with a pool I don't use. A gallery wall above the bed showcasing nothing but my degrees, myself and me. Survey the neighbors. The boisterous couple next door. The oil family across the street. Call my colleagues. My clients. Talk to everyone I've ever known. All the people who thought I was on their side.

Mention my name, and a smile will appear on their lips. Ask them what I'm like, and they will tell you I am the best goddamn lawyer they ever saw. That I can talk circles around opposing counsel, and make the law apply how and where I want it to, and that, without even trying, I surpassed the infamous Jason Knox.

It's never easy to play a role you aren't born into, but by now you know that I'm a good actor.

You know that I am capable of—nearly—anything.

Acknowledgments

I am so thankful to my family, particularly my parents, Anita Chakravarti and Parm Lalli, for your love and support and for believing in me when I said I wanted to be a writer. Thank you to my husband, Simon Collinson, who lifts me up every day, and to my wonderfully supportive friends. A special shout-out to Annie MacDonald, who was the first person to read an early draft of *Are You Sara?* and gave it a glowing review.

Huge thanks to my agent, Martha Webb, for being my champion and giving me the push I needed to try writing a thriller, as well as for working with me tirelessly on those first few drafts. And a big thank-you to the dream team at Cooke-McDermid and Cooke International, especially Ron Eckel, Hana El Niwairi and Paige Sisley.

I want to thank Jenn Lambert and Asanté Simons, my editors extraordinaire, for believing in this book and pushing me to become a better writer. It's been pure joy working with you both to bring Sara's story to life. And I am hugely appreciative of everyone at HarperCollins Canada and William Morrow for bringing *Are You Sara?* into the world, including Cindy Ma, Neil Wadhwa, Kelly Cronin, Sam Glatt, Yeon Kim, Natalie

Meditsky, Rita Madrigal, Jess Shulman, Stephanie Vallejo, and Sue Sumeraj. A big thanks as well to Stephanie Caruso at Paste Creative.

Finally, thank you to my great-grandmother Saraswati Mukerji, to whom I dedicated this book although we never had the chance to meet. Thank you for teaching the women in our family strength and resilience, and that we can be anything and anyone we want.